A MILLION TO ONE

A

MILLION

TO

ONE

ADIBA JAIGIRDAR

An Imprint of HarperCollinsPublishers

CONTENT WARNING:

This book contains mentions of parental neglect, parental abandonment, parental death, and abuse. It also contains instances of death (specifically death by drowning).

HarperTeen is an imprint of HarperCollins Publishers.

A Million to One

ISBN 978-0-06-291632-7

Typography by Corina Lupp
22 23 24 25 26 PC/LSCH 10 9 8 7 6 5 4 3 2 1

First Edition

To everyone who lost a loved one during this pandemic,
and to all the loved ones we lost

ONE

JOSEFA

"SHE WENT AROUND the corner!"

Josefa stiffened at the gravelly voice right behind her. She had somehow managed to make it all the way to the quays from the bottom of Sackville Street. She thought she had lost the guard at the last turn, but clearly not.

"Are you sure?" came the voice of the second guard. Closer now.

One more minute and she would be caught red-handed. On one side of her was the Liffey in all its leafy-green glory. She wasn't sure if a swim in it would get her arrested or save her. She did know that it would destroy the very thing she had put herself at risk for, so she shrugged off that idea as soon as it came to her.

On the other side of her were buildings, each a few stories high, with windows getting smaller and smaller with each floor.

Josefa's only chance.

1

The climb to the first windowsill was little more than a leap. Inside, she could see a bed pushed up against the wall and a stack of worn books on the floor. She pressed on the glass, hoping it had been left unlocked, but no luck. Who would leave their second-floor window unlatched by the quays anyhow?

The second windowsill was a little trickier. She had to balance herself precariously on the narrow wooden beam, reach up to the next window, and pull herself up.

"She's not here." The gruff voice of one of the guards came from below. Josefa took a stilted breath at the sound. She was sure if either of them glanced up, they would catch sight of her immediately. The windowsill was so narrow that it barely hid her from view, but it didn't expose her either.

"Are you sure she came this way?" The second guard glanced to the corner of Sackville Street, which led the way down the other side of the Liffey. From her lofted position, Josefa could easily make out the flash of his bright red beard, caught in the glint of the dipping sunlight.

The first guard grunted something quietly—gruffly—so Josefa couldn't make it out. She flattened herself against the window instead, wishing the sun would descend a little faster, willing the guards to turn away and give up their hopes of finding her. She was, after all, just one petty thief in a city that was filled with them.

She didn't chance another glance down. Instead, she reached below her—barely managing to balance herself on the windowsill—and pulled the window open. She couldn't help but grin at the success. But that lasted for only a moment before she tumbled inside, nearly crashing into the half-naked woman by her bed.

"Oh, so sorry," Josefa mumbled, trying to keep the blood from rushing to her face and hoping that she hadn't made enough of a ruckus for the guards outside to hear. "I'm—uh—a little lost. My bedroom must be right beside yours. I thought this was mine."

The woman, with her dress clutched in front of her now, was looking at her with wide eyes. "If you're here to rob me—"

"N-no," Josefa said, holding up her hands to show the woman that she meant no harm. "Just . . . next bedroom." She gave the woman what she hoped was a charming smile before swinging open the door to the hallway and slipping outside.

She breathed a sigh of relief and then her heartbeat quickened. Because there, right in her line of view, were the two guards. Officer Redbeard, tall and lanky, looking awkward and out of place, and beside him, the guard who was obviously determined to catch Josefa. His face was contorted into a violent anger as he explained himself to the matron of the place.

Josefa didn't risk watching them for too long. She sucked in her breath and wove down the hallway, trying to figure out how she could get out of this without the guards catching sight of her. She could keep climbing up—but that might just get her trapped further. She could try to sneak past—but that had an even higher risk of her getting caught.

Josefa cursed herself. She had been a little too eager today, leading her to make rash decisions. Still, there was no denying the fact that the adrenaline pulsing through her was giving her a head rush.

If Violet were here, she would know what to do. She made it her business to be able to talk herself out of every situation. Josefa, on the other hand, was better at getting herself into trouble than getting herself out of it.

Now the confused matron and angry-looking guards were making their way quickly down the corridor. They must have seen Josefa tumble in through the window, because—as she slid into the dark recess of the hallway, hiding herself away in the unlit shadows, the matron knocked on the very door she had just stumbled out of.

The woman from before, now fully dressed, swung the door open.

"There is nobody here but me, as you can see," she said, stepping aside with a flourish and giving the guards a full view of her bedroom. Disheveled—but empty.

"Thank you, Ms. Petit," the matron said, her smile as cold as the guards'. "We would, of course, be immediately alerted if there was any sort of a break-in at our boardinghouse."

The way she said it made it seem like their boarding-house was something special. From the plush carpet that Josefa stood on, she knew that it was. The boardinghouse where Josefa stayed had no carpets at all. They were lucky just to have proper mattresses on their beds, and curtains to draw over their windows to give them a bit of privacy. She knew of plenty of boardinghouses that didn't have even those basic things.

Josefa had no idea why Ms. Petit hadn't told on her, but she thanked her lucky stars. Especially as she watched the guards leave through the window, disappointment smeared across their faces. Josefa grinned, slipping past the matron at her desk when she had her head bowed low, and stepping out the door soundlessly.

She glanced up at the glow of lamplight in the window she had climbed through. The woman—or Ms. Petit, as she had learned—gave her a grim wave. Josefa wasn't sure what to make of it, but she returned it thankfully before turning away.

She plucked out the wallet she had nicked from one of the men outside the pub. Inside, there were a few scattered coins that clinked as she dug through the pockets. There was a picture of a woman who Josefa could only assume was his wife. She had short blond locks and a smile that showed all her crooked teeth. Finally, she found what she was looking for. Pushed to the very bottom of the wallet.

She pulled the pieces of paper out between her thumb and forefinger. The chase had definitely been worth it, because there in front of her was her ticket onto the *Titanic*.

TWO

VIOLET

> *Ljubi te,*
> *V*

A DROP OF black ink from her pen dripped onto the paper, and Violet cursed under her breath. She had stained the end of her letter, the tips of her fingers, and even part of the desk. Exactly what she needed.

Shaking out her hand, as if the ink would simply slide off, Violet sighed. She tucked the letter inside the book she had been reading and buried her head in her hands.

With every letter that Marko sent, Violet felt more and more helpless. Her little brother was only twelve, and he was left to fend for himself in their tiny town in Croatia. He was barely making ends meet, but Violet was barely able to afford her own lodgings.

She pulled out his last letter from the bottom of the desk, feeling a tug of sadness at the sight of her brother's familiar scrawl. It came with the usual description of the orphanage where their mother had abandoned Marko a year ago. A dilap-idated and worn-down place with not enough beds or food for all the children who needed them. Marko never spoke ill of it, though. Violet had to read between the lines to understand what Marko was really dealing with—a place where he had no family, no friends . . . nothing, really.

But it was this last letter that had really pained Violet to read. The letter where Marko had finally told Violet that it would be only a few weeks until he was forced to leave the four walls of the orphanage behind to survive in a world where he had no one. Or rather, the only person he had—Violet—was oceans away, in no position to help.

The orphanage was horrible; that much Violet knew. But anything was better than Marko being left to figure out how to live in the streets. Violet couldn't let Marko lead that life.

But she also didn't know how to prevent it. She didn't know how to reply to Marko's letter detailing his problems, when Violet was unable to do anything. The pen had flooded ink from the desperation of trying to find the right words. But what were the right words to say that you were failing as an older sister? Violet certainly hadn't been able to find them.

A knocking sound from her right finally made Violet pick her head up from her hands. She glanced toward the window, expecting a bird, perhaps. Instead, she caught sight of Josefa's dark brown hair. Turned away from the window, as if she were looking down at the street below her. All the same, her knuck-les were against Violet's window, tapping out a steady rhythm.

"What did you do now?" Violet asked, flinging the window open. Josefa nearly toppled onto the floor of her room, catching herself at the last moment and dropping to the ground with a graceful flourish.

"Good evening to you too," Josefa said with a little bow. Like this was an act that she had been perfecting.

Violet crossed her arms over her chest, trying to cover up the fact that she had been on the verge of tears when Josefa knocked on her window.

"Is someone following you?"

"I would never be that careless," Josefa gasped, like the idea that she would do something like that was absolutely preposterous. But Violet wouldn't put it past her.

Josefa was clever. Clever enough to get away with basically anything, but there was something about almost not getting away that she seemed to enjoy. To practically thrive on. It was part of the reason why Violet was used to Josefa crawling in through her window at all hours of the day and night. Like breaking the perfectly valid curfew set up by the matron of the building was something she relished. Not because Josefa had somewhere to be, or something to do. But because she could.

Now Josefa flung herself onto Violet's bed, the previous grace gone from her body. She cast a curious glance at the letter peeking out of the book on her desk and the ink stains on the wood. Matron O'Neill would not be happy about that.

Violet lurched forward, tucking Marko's letter away and taking her seat by the desk again. "So? Where were you?"

Josefa shrugged, but there was a smile tugging at her lips. Violet knew that look far too well. It was the game that Josefa liked to play, holding a secret over Violet's head to get her interested. It was how Violet got sucked in to far too many of Josefa's dangerous schemes. Breaking into homes they had no business being in, and conning people who had enough money to have their guard up but were far too easy to take from. That—and desperation.

But Josefa had been teasing her with this piece of information for weeks now. She said it was going to be her best plan yet. Violet wasn't holding her breath; Josefa said that about every single plan she concocted. But this was the longest Josefa had dangled a secret in front of her.

Still, Violet did not have the time to entertain her friend's games today. "If you don't want to tell me, then don't." She hated the way an uncontrolled anger seeped into her voice, clipping her words with the accent she had tried so hard to rid herself of. Still, it slipped in there, unbeknownst to her. Whether she liked it or not, it was a part of her.

Josefa leaned back on the bed, a grin on her lips. Violet forgot how much she enjoyed this.

"I have been planning this for months. I've just snagged the last necessary piece. The least you can do is let me enjoy taking my time telling you about it," Josefa said. Violet sighed, glancing at the pocket watch left by her book.

It was the only thing she had kept of her father when she had decided to leave two years ago. She had taken it because it was of value. A clunky object rimmed with gold. Her father had kept it on him at all times. Taking it had been as much about how much the thing could make her if she sold it as how much her father would miss it. Probably even more than he missed her.

But in the end, she had decided to keep it. A relic of a life she used to have. A person she used to be. A reminder of why she needed to do the things she did.

She picked it up and ran her hand over the inscription on the back, feeling the ticking of the watch in her hands. Almost like a heartbeat. *Doći će i naše vrijeme*, the inscription read. It was something her father always said: *Our time will come.* Violet's father's time had not come yet, and she was still waiting for her own time. For her own hopes and dreams to be realized, even if most days it seemed near impossible.

"Have you heard of something called the *Titanic*?" Josefa asked, her voice a little too ecstatic.

Violet turned to her with a raised eyebrow. "The ship?"

"The ship." Now Josefa's excitement was palpable. Violet could feel it as readily as the watch ticking under her fingers.

"You want to . . . steal the *Titanic*?"

Josefa sighed, glancing at Violet, as if to see if she had any other guesses. She could think of a million. People were paying good money to board the *Titanic*. If they targeted those passengers while they were in Ireland, they were sure to get more than enough to cover their monthly expenses, and for

Violet to have enough to send back to Marko to tide him over for at least a little while. Or perhaps tickets? The *Titanic* had been nicknamed the Millionaire's Special. It was the unsinkable ship. A voyage across the Atlantic with some of the wealthiest clientele to set foot in this nation. Tickets were not easy to come by—even third-class or second-class tickets, never mind first class. Violet was sure anyone would pay good money if they managed to get their hands on a spare.

But when she voiced her guesses aloud to Josefa, she simply sighed again, like their conversation was a disappointment for her.

"Think a little bigger." Josefa leaned closer. "Have you heard of something called the *Rubaiyat*?"

"The Ruby what?"

"The *Rubaiyat*!" The rise in the pitch of Josefa's voice indicated that she had had about enough of this conversation. Violet bit back a smile. Josefa might delight in keeping things from her, but Violet was quite qualified in goading information out of anyone.

Violet's expression was perfectly formed. One raised eyebrow and a steady stare at Josefa.

"It's a book. A collection of poems, actually," Josefa finally breathed out with all the eagerness of a child. "Very famous. Very old. Very . . . exotic. By a Persian poet. You know. It's the kind of thing that rich people adore."

"Right . . ."

"Well. There's a special edition of the *Rubaiyat* that's going to be on the *Titanic*. Laden with jewels."

"Rich people love that even more."

Josefa leaned back on the bed, a smirk taking hold of her lips. "We're going to steal the *Rubaiyat*."

Violet's shock was not feigned this time. Her father's watch dropped with a heavy clunk on the ground beneath her.

"*K vrapcu.*" Mumbling the curse under her breath, Violet picked the watch up, the ticking of it a comfort against the sudden spike of her own heartbeat.

"Josefa . . . I'm not sure we're ready for that." She and Josefa had some experience with thievery, but they were petty crimes. Enough for Violet to get by. Enough to keep Josefa content. They took the kind of things nobody missed. Trinkets from the homes of the rich that you could sell on the streets of Dublin without drawing any eyes. And whatever they could lift from people's pockets without anybody being any the wiser.

"Ready or not, this is an amazing opportunity. We can't let it pass us by," Josefa said. Violet could tell she was enjoying watching the expression on her face. She shifted in her chair, the book with the ink-stained end of her letter to Marko catching her eye.

A jewel-encrusted collection of Persian poetry. Incredibly rare, Violet would assume. She couldn't even imagine how much that would be worth. Definitely enough to tide her and Marko over. Enough for her to return home. Enough for them to finally be a family once again.

Doći će i naše vrijeme. The words reverberated around in her head.

When Violet looked up and caught Josefa's eye, she was smiling wider. Like Josefa already knew Violet's decision.

"Exactly how would we go about it?"

THREE

MR. BLACKWELL'S CIRCUS ANOMALY 9:05 P.M.

HINNAH

HINNAH LOOKED BELOW at all the people gathered to watch her. At all the lights that illuminated her form. She took a deep breath and closed her eyes. She didn't want adrenaline to carry her through this—that always went wrong.

Hinnah balanced the pole in her hands and took a step forward. The tightrope wobbled under her feet, but she was undeterred. She knew that if she made a mistake, she would plunge to her death. Or at least to a very serious injury.

This was the first time Hinnah had done this act without a net underneath her. This was the first time Hinnah had decided to put her life at risk for her act.

She steadied her breath and took another step. With each step forward, she could feel the unsteadiness of the rope beneath her feet. Like the world was going to give out from under her any minute now. She could almost feel the audience watching her at the edge of their seats.

Hinnah bit down a smile. She didn't do this for the glory—

14

there wasn't much of that in the circus anyway. But she wouldn't lie and say she didn't enjoy these moments.

One more step. And another.

And—the rope shook dangerously below her. The pole in her hands giving way to the left. She gripped on to it tightly, trying to balance it. But that only made things worse.

She had put too much weight on one side, and she swayed to the right.

Hinnah was going to lose her grip.

She was going to fall. And there was nothing below to catch her.

She chanced a glance down. Not at the audience or the lights, but at the ground. The empty space where she would fall.

Somehow it spurred her on. Hinnah took a shaky breath, and instead of teetering on the edge of the tightrope, she stepped forward—fast. There was no grace in it, she knew that. It wasn't the way the act was supposed to go. All circus acts were a performance meant to dazzle. Hinnah wasn't doing that—she was just trying to survive.

The rest of the tightrope walk was simpler. Faster. Blood pumped loudly in Hinnah's ears the entire time.

When she stepped safely onto the platform, the audience clapped and cheered. But Hinnah didn't feel that sensation of pride enveloping her. She'd had a close call. She had almost fallen.

That wasn't how it was supposed to go.

Even as she heard the ringmaster announcing the next act, she could tell he wasn't happy.

Hinnah climbed all the way down, feeling deflated. But when she glanced at the audience, some of that dissipated. There were familiar faces to the front. She *never* saw familiar faces in the crowd.

Josefa and Violet didn't *quite* look like they fit into the group of onlookers. But they didn't completely look out of place either. Violet, with her grim expression, didn't seem like she was enjoying this performance, while Josefa's eyes were alight. Her gaze was glued to the next performers. The Great Quinn Sisters and their amazing trapeze act.

"What was that?" The voice of Mr. Blackwell, the ringmaster, cut through Hinnah's thoughts. She turned to meet his glare and almost instinctively stepped back into the shadows.

"I'm sorry," she mumbled, though she wasn't quite sure what she was sorry for. She had messed up; she knew that. But it could have been so much worse. She could have fallen. She could have—

"You said you wanted to try something more dangerous," the ringmaster snapped at her. "You said you were ready. But *that*, that was a disgrace."

Hinnah wasn't sure what to say. In reality, she hadn't really wanted to walk the tightrope at all. Trapeze was her talent. Bending her body to impossible shapes. This was what she had mastered ever since she decided to join the circus, on a desperate whim. But back then, she had a partner: Eliza. They weren't partners anymore. They hadn't been ever since they arrived in Dublin and Hinnah decided to stay while the rest of the performers continued on their journey.

"If you let me try my trapeze act, you'd see that—"

But it was fruitless. The ringmaster blew out a frustrated breath of air and turned away. "One more slipup, and you're out," he called as he stomped away to introduce the next act.

Hinnah sighed and left the circus tent. In the back, there was one small trailer where all the performers had space to change and get ready. It was barely big enough to hold two people at once. But it was all they had.

The circus performance was still going. They always left the best for last. So Hinnah had the place to herself as she slipped off her formfitting clothes and into the simple top and skirt she had worn out of the boardinghouse this afternoon. She was about to step outside when a series of knocks sounded against the door.

None of the other performers knocked. This was their shared space.

"Yes?" Hinnah called out hesitantly.

"Hinnah?" The voices on the other side sounded familiar. She swung the door open. Violet and Josefa stood there, shoulder to shoulder, eyes casting around them. As if they were afraid someone would catch them in something they weren't supposed to be doing.

"Hello." Hinnah couldn't help the note of confusion that slipped into her voice. She was not a stranger to Josefa and

Violet, but they had never come to visit her at a show before. Their relationship was confined to the boardinghouse the three of them shared.

"Hinnah." Josefa nodded.

"Can we come in?" Violet asked.

"I don't know if . . ." Hinnah trailed off, glancing at the trailer around her. This wasn't really her space, and nobody other than her fellow performers had ever been in here before.

"We'll be quick," Josefa said, and the two of them pushed past Hinnah.

Josefa took in the room with curious eyes for a moment, and Hinnah couldn't tell if she was impressed or not by everything that this small, cluttered trailer held. She closed the door with a satisfactory click and turned to the two girls with what she hoped was cool disdain.

"Is everything okay?" Hinnah cringed at how nervous she sounded.

"You were spectacular!" Josefa exclaimed, the grin on her face so bright Hinnah wondered if it hurt.

She felt the rush of blood to her cheeks and glanced away, trying not to meet either of their eyes. Hinnah had never performed in front of people she knew before. And even though she had worked with Violet and Josefa enough for them to know some of what she could do, she couldn't help but feel embarrassed. That *this* was the performance they had seen.

"I was . . . I could have been . . . I should have been better."

18

"You were like fifty feet in the air!" Josefa said.

"Well, probably not *that* high," Violet corrected her, but there was the hint of a smile on her lips too. "You were quite good, though."

"Even when you slipped up, you pulled it off like no problem," Josefa said. "That's what we want!"

Hinnah looked at the two of them with a raised eyebrow. "What do you mean? Why . . . are you here?"

"Have you heard of the *Titanic*?" Violet asked.

Of course Hinnah had heard of the *Titanic*. *Everyone* had heard of it. Their boardinghouse had been buzzing with the news of it ever since the launch at Belfast last year.

Nothing quite this exciting ever happened in Ireland. Hinnah was just sad that it wasn't happening here, that she couldn't bid the ship goodbye from Dublin port. Sadder still, she couldn't board it herself and travel across the Atlantic on a grand old voyage, instead of being stuck in her boxed room in this unwelcoming country.

"Who hasn't heard of the *Titanic*?" Hinnah asked.

Josefa and Violet exchanged a glance. Then Josefa turned to Hinnah with a twinkle in her eyes. "Hinnah, we have a proposition for you."

Usually, when Josefa and Violet approached Hinnah, it was because they needed a third person for a job. Hinnah was the person who helped them break into places. She would climb through windows, up roofs. Crawl into those tight spaces

Violet and Josefa had no hopes of getting into. Once she had even climbed all the way down a chimney to help Violet and Josefa break into some lord's house. Everything she had learned at the circus meant she was skilled at getting into and out of places, and she liked the extra money it brought in for her. Most important, Hinnah didn't ask many questions.

But Hinnah wasn't sure how the *Titanic* could factor into any of her skill sets.

She glanced between Josefa and Violet, unsure of what it was she was about to get herself into. "Okay . . ." She couldn't deny her own curiosity.

"We have a plan to board the *Titanic* and steal a rare, expensive—"

"Jewel-encrusted," Violet interrupted with a curt nod.

"Jewel-encrusted poetry collection that we know is on board the ship. We want you to join us."

This had to be some kind of a joke. It seemed like too big a task, too big a risk. Hinnah didn't have the skills to help with something like this. And how were the two planning to board the *Titanic* anyway? The ship was due to set off in just four days, and she was sure the tickets were beyond anything they could afford.

"Why would you need me?" she asked.

For a moment, Josefa only blinked at Hinnah. Like the question was surprising—not what she was expecting to hear today. "Well, obviously because neither Violet nor I can do what you can. Just look at what you pulled off today. Even in the

face of failure, you pushed forward. You're very determined."
The admiration in Josefa's voice wasn't something Hinnah was accustomed to.

She couldn't help the blush that crept up her neck at the compliment. Nobody had ever called her determined before. Where the ringmaster had seen only Hinnah's faults, it seemed that Josefa had seen only her talents.

"What about the tickets?" She knew that even a third-class ticket was more than she made in months.

"Don't worry about that," Josefa said, like money was of no consequence. Hinnah couldn't imagine living like that. Though maybe if she joined Violet and Josefa, she wouldn't have to imagine it.

Taking a deep breath, Hinnah asked, "What would I have to do?"

FOUR

EMILIE

THE RIVER LIFFEY stretched out in front of Emilie like a long mirror. Lights and colors danced along the water, as if putting on a show for Emilie's benefit. Or maybe it was mocking her, Emilie thought.

She stepped closer to the river, trying to memorize the way colors reflected off the water. She tried to think back to the painting on the wall in her room at the boardinghouse, and how everything about it had looked so completely wrong. It was the Liffey; there was no mistaking it. But something about the way she had painted it didn't feel quite *right*. It didn't capture the essence of the river that was in front of her now. And no matter how much time Emilie spent trying to understand what was off, she couldn't put her finger on it.

For the past year, this was how things had been with everything Emilie did. Like everything was missing a spark, and no matter what she did, Emilie couldn't find it again.

Maybe it had died along with her father.

Emilie heaved a sigh, wishing that she could dive into the depths of this river. At least there, she could forget about her problems for a little while.

She and her father had spoken at length about the Liffey. Though he had never been to Dublin—not even to Ireland—he had loved the paintings of Dublin by Samuel Frederick Brocas. One of his favorite Irish painters. The two of them had spoken about visiting Dublin, all the places that he had captured so beautifully with paint and a paintbrush.

Emilie thought that coming here, visiting those places, would help her remember those times with her father. Help her capture not just Dublin, but the crux of their relationship.

She had been wrong.

Emilie walked farther up the street, toward O'Connell Bridge, so lost in her thoughts that she barely noticed the familiar face approaching until they were close enough to touch.

"Emilie!" Josefa's grin was wide, but there was some kind of anxiety hidden behind it. Emilie tried to ignore the flutter in her stomach at the sight of her, with her dark brown hair blowing in the breeze and her hooded eyes intense.

"Josefa," she murmured, stepping back to put distance between the two of them. This was the closest they had ever been to each other, and from the way Josefa's gaze settled on Emilie, she knew that Josefa had sought her out. Emilie would almost feel pleased at the attention if she hadn't heard the stories about Josefa.

"What are you doing here?" Emilie asked. She really wanted

to ask how Josefa had found her, and *why*, after months of passing by each other at O'Neill's boardinghouse but never approaching one another.

"I have something important to discuss with you," Josefa said.

Emilie frowned. She knew the kinds of things Josefa got up to—and she also knew *she* had no business helping Josefa. Though she admired Josefa's talent and wit, and found herself intrigued by her life, Emilie couldn't get away with the things Josefa did. Unlike her, Emilie was visibly different, almost everywhere she went. She was closer to her father's pale complexion than her mother's darker one. But her brown skin still stood out starkly here, among the Irish, who bruised too easily and became red from the sun even on a cloudy day.

"Something important?" Emilie asked, crossing her hands over her chest. Josefa didn't seem put off by Emilie's hesitance. In fact, her grin widened at Emilie's stance. Almost like she had expected her to put up some kind of resistance.

Josefa stood tall, squaring her shoulders in a way that made her look like a child playing at being an adult. "Just listen."

She drew the two of them to one side, away from passersby and so close to the water that just one step would lead them right into the river.

Josefa threaded her fingers together nervously. Emilie hadn't known Josefa was capable of being nervous—definitely not from the confident facade she put up.

"I'm going on the *Titanic*," she said in a rush.

"Oh." Emilie wasn't sure how to respond. Of all the things she could have expected, this was definitely not it. She knew that Josefa was not the type of person who would waste away her life in their boardinghouse, in this city, in this country. But such a sudden decision. To travel to a place so far. America seemed like an impossibly long distance away. And to go on the *Titanic* no less, the ship that everyone was both curious about and envious of.

"Well. We are," Josefa added after a moment. "Have you heard of something called the *Rubaiyat*?"

Emilie's head was spinning. "The book by Omar Khayyam?" It was one of Emilie's favorite books, because it had been one of her father's favorites. They used to read it together, and Emilie had fond memories of how her father's voice brought so much life to Khayyam's words.

Josefa nodded. "There's going to be a jewel-encrusted copy of the *Rubaiyat* on the *Titanic*. We're going to steal it."

"And who is we?"

She glanced up at Emilie with a slight smile. "Violet, Hinnah, me . . . and, I was hoping, you."

Emilie didn't know why those words made her breath hitch, but she tried to ignore that. This didn't seem like a situation where she should let her heart dictate her actions.

"You were hoping I would board the *Titanic* with you to go to America, and steal a priceless artistic artifact?"

Josefa shrugged. "Nothing is priceless. It's worth . . . enough for . . . all of us to live our lives how we want to."

Emilie turned away from Josefa and toward the Liffey. She had visited this place countless times during her short stay in Dublin. In the hopes that it would give her . . . something. Some thread of connection. Some inspiration. Motivation. Some way to go back to the person she had been before her father's passing. But all she had to show for it was an incomplete painting she couldn't even bear to look at anymore.

"I'm sorry." Emilie shook her head. She couldn't imagine any of it. How could she be of help to Josefa anyway? And what a strange group of people to put together. She had spoken to Violet once or twice, and the girl had always been cold and unpleasant. Hinnah, on the other hand, had an edge of insecurity about her that was masked with a kind of confidence that was deeply off-putting. And Josefa . . . Emilie didn't know how to describe her. Their paths had crossed during their short stay living in the same building, but this was the first time they had really spoken. To make a request like this, so out of the blue. To ask her to cross the Atlantic to another place altogether.

"I'm just not sure if I'm the person you should be asking," Emilie offered as a way of explanation. "I just mean . . ."

"I'm sure there's something you want," Josefa said. When Emilie turned back to her, Josefa was looking at the river too. Almost like she knew what Emilie had been struggling with. Like she knew all the things that Emilie wanted but couldn't figure out how to achieve.

"How did you know I would be here?" Emilie pressed.

Josefa's face brightened. "You're always here," she said. "When you're not in your room, with your paintings."

Josefa held her gaze for a little too long, and Emilie wasn't sure why, but in that moment, it seemed like Josefa could see more than just Emilie as she presented herself here. Like she was seeing down to some depths that Emilie herself hadn't quite figured out yet.

"Look . . . ," Josefa said, breaking their eye contact with a shake of her head. "You're the only person I want . . . on this mission. We need your unique talents."

"My unique talents?" Emilie wasn't sure what those were.

"I've seen what you can do. And we're going to need an artist. Someone who can forge, help us create new identities."

Emilie wasn't sure how she felt about the idea of forging new identities. But she would be lying if she pretended her interest wasn't piqued.

"I've also heard the *Rubaiyat* is beautiful," Josefa offered.

Emilie imagined it was. She wondered what her father would say. Not about the opportunity to steal it, because she didn't think that was something he would ever even consider. But the opportunity to see it. Hold it. Touch it.

The only one of its kind.

Would he think she was foolish to let that opportunity pass her by?

"Okay," she breathed. "I'm listening."

FIVE

JOSEFA

JOSEFA HAD NEVER called a meeting like this before. In front of her sat the three people she knew were absolutely essential for the mission she had been planning. Hinnah and Emilie sat side by side on her bed, the little distance between them marking the strangeness of them being there at all. And Violet, as always, sat on the wooden chair facing away from the window. There was a sharpness to Violet's gaze as she took in the other two.

Josefa wasn't sure if it was nervousness or excitement that was making her pulse race. Perhaps it was a mixture of both of those things. She could hardly believe that months of planning were finally going to come to fruition.

"You all know why we're here today," Josefa began, clapping her hands together. Everybody's eyes were on her as she stood at the front of the room. She could feel their gazes boring into her, but instead of feeding into her nerves, it was electrifying. Josefa had never been a part of something so grand before. She reveled in this attention.

"The *Rubaiyat*," she said slowly, "is a rare prize. And if we can pull this off, it will be in our hands in a matter of days." Josefa imagined the feel of the heavy book, the roughness of the jewels that encased it on her fingers. A few months ago it had felt like a dream, but now it was almost a reality.

"That's easy to say." Violet interrupted Josefa's speech, leaning forward. "But how are we going to do it?"

"The *Titanic* leaves in three days," Hinnah added in a low voice. "How are we even going to board it?"

"And the *Rubaiyat* is not just a piece of jewelry you can pawn," Emilie said, meeting Josefa's gaze with her dark eyes. "How would we even sell it?"

Josefa heaved a sigh and cast a sweeping glance across the three girls. She had been waiting for this moment.

Ever since Josefa had begun to plan this mission, she had known it wasn't something she could pull off alone. She had begun to put together the perfect team for it months ago.

Violet had been an obvious addition. She was skilled, she had the right motivation, and most important of all, Violet was the only person Josefa really trusted. They had been friends since the two of them met at this very boardinghouse, and their kinship and trust had only built up from there.

Hinnah was a less obvious choice. She was talented—maybe more than anybody else in this group—and her talents weren't easy to come by. But Josefa had always kept at her arm's length. Telling her only the information that Hinnah needed to help them. Nothing less. Nothing more. That's why she realized

Hinnah was so perfect for this group of people. She had proved herself to be trustworthy time and again, even when Josefa had barely trusted her.

But it was Emilie who had been the last addition. She was still a virtual stranger to all of them. She sat uncomfortably at the edge of her seat, as if she were ready to leave at a moment's notice, her familiar blue hair clip glinting as it caught the light. Josefa's stomach fluttered with butterflies simply because Emilie was here, but she could see the distrust breeding in Violet's eyes. It was no secret that Emilie was not quite like the rest of them. She hailed from Paris, where she had lived a life of leisure, and none of them really understood why she had made her home in this crumbling boardinghouse.

But that was what drew Josefa to her. She couldn't explain it, but ever since Emilie showed up here, Josefa had found something fascinating about her. Not just her circumstance, but the way she composed herself. How she moved in this world—unlike anybody else Josefa had ever met. But Emilie didn't know any of this. Josefa could understand her distrust. She could understand all of their hesitation.

With a flourish, Josefa pulled out the very objects she had been on the run for yesterday. Four pieces of paper that seemed almost ordinary, but were anything but.

"Tickets," she said, "to the *Titanic*."

A hush fell over the room once more, and Josefa basked in the way the other three girls stared at the four tickets in her hands.

"How did you afford that?" Hinnah finally asked.

Josefa didn't get the chance to respond before Violet cut in with a sigh. "Hinnah, do you really think Josefa paid for those tickets?" Her voice was chiding, like Hinnah should know better. Hinnah probably *should*, considering their history. But Hinnah was young and naive, and she somehow always believed the best about people despite where life had led her. Josefa often wondered if this was the very reason why Violet had befriended the girl. She watched now as Violet turned her fond gaze away from Hinnah and looked scrutinizingly at Josefa.

"You didn't tell me you had these." If Josefa didn't know any better, she would think Violet was almost offended at not being told before the others.

"I was waiting for the right moment." Josefa shrugged. There was no point in showing your hand before the timing was right. Josefa had learned as much in her life.

"Just because you have the tickets doesn't mean that we're going," Emilie said. Her voice was somber, her lips pressed into a thin line as she cast her gaze from Josefa to Violet to Hinnah. "We've built a life here," she said. "We can't just . . . go. Just because Josefa planned . . . this."

Josefa tried not to let Emilie's words sting her, even if she did feel a bite of anger. She had expected questions, curiosity . . . not refusal. She should have prepared for this, she realized. As much as she had learned about Emilie from her observations over the past few months, she didn't really *know* Emilie.

For a moment, she doubted herself. Had she made the right

decision, asking these three on her mission? The most important one of her life?

"Look, I don't know about you," Josefa said slowly, tucking a sliver of hair behind her ear. "But I wasn't planning on spending the rest of my life . . . here." At the last word, she cast a glance around at the window that didn't shut all the way. At the walls with their chipped paint. The door almost coming off its hinges. This place had always been just a stop on Josefa's journey. To where, she hadn't known when she first arrived. But she had always known her time here would be short. She suspected the same for the other three. After all, girls here didn't stay for long before moving on with their lives. Sometimes, to better things. Often, to worse.

"Josefa's right. We don't have *lives* here." Violet sighed. "Look at everything the world's thrown at us. Everything it's taken from us. Maybe now it's our time to take something back."

Josefa grinned. She could always count on Violet to back her up.

"There's a reason why I asked all of you to do this with me," Josefa said. "I can't do this alone. You each have skills that I want—*need*—for us to succeed." She turned to Hinnah, shooting her the warmest smile she had to offer. Josefa knew that Hinnah leaned into praise. "Hinnah, I've never met anybody who can perform the tricks that you can. You can push your body past limits that I can't even imagine. I can hear you practicing at all hours of the day. I've seen what you can do at the circus. Nobody else can do what you do."

Hinnah hesitated for only a moment before giving a solemn nod of her head. Josefa knew this meant Hinnah was on board.

"And Violet is probably the greatest actress any of us have ever met," Josefa said. Though Violet was not one to betray emotion if she could help it, the trace of a smirk appeared on her face. "She has the enviable skill of being able to charm her way out of trouble, or into the best kinds of opportunities."

Violet's smile widened, like she was remembering the kinds of charming she had had to do during their friendship. There were small occasions, like Violet drawing someone into conversation while Josefa picked their pockets. But there had been bigger occasions too. Like the time Violet and Josefa had sneaked into a party at an estate belonging to the Williams family. Violet had been in charge of distracting the partygoers, while Josefa stole everything she could carry and get away with. There had been many unforgettable occasions like those, and that thought sparked more confidence in Josefa. She had left Emilie for last, because she knew Emilie would be the hardest to persuade.

"And . . . Emilie." Emilie sat up straighter at the mention of her name, raising one eyebrow at Josefa. "I've seen what you can do with a paintbrush. With your skills you can be the one to help us forge our way through this mission. I have never met anyone with your talents." Josefa grinned, but Emilie only held Josefa's gaze blankly for a long moment, before glancing away. Her face was so stoic that Josefa couldn't read what she was thinking.

"You haven't answered our questions," she finally said.

"Of course, I have a plan," she said. "I wouldn't have asked you all here if I didn't." Josefa paced back and forth for a moment, wondering how to divulge the information without revealing some things that she still had to keep close to her chest.

Josefa finally turned around. "Getting onto the *Titanic* will be the easy part," she began. Josefa could see Hinnah shifting in her seat at her words. "We have the tickets, and Emilie, if she's willing, will forge the travel documents we need. But it's when we get on board that the difficult parts begin."

"Forging travel documents seems like a big risk," Violet interrupted, casting a wary glance at Emilie sitting beside her. "I mean . . . if they aren't done just right . . ."

"Emilie can do it," Josefa said, turning her bright smile to Emilie. But Emilie's expression remained unchanged. "Once we're on board, we have to find information. Hinnah, I know you can get in and out of places. We'll need you to figure out the layout of the ship. It's going to be important for us to be able to get around the ship unnoticed."

"The *Titanic* is supposed to be massive," Hinnah mumbled, though she didn't seem put off by the task.

"And, Violet, you'll have to charm your way into finding out where the *Rubaiyat* is being kept. It's being transported to a buyer in America. There's a man named Clayton Lake . . . I have reason to believe he's in charge of making sure the *Rubaiyat* gets there safely."

"So, I get the easy task," Violet mused, though she didn't seem perturbed by the idea of this challenge.

"What about you?" Emilie asked, her eyes trained on Josefa once more. "What is your role going to be?"

Josefa had almost forgotten that Emilie had never done this before. That she had probably never done anything even close to what they were planning.

"Well, I'm the master strategist," Josefa said with a grin. "But . . . I'm also a great thief, if I do say so myself." Out of the corner of her eye, she could see Violet nodding along in agreement. "It's how I got the tickets for the *Titanic*, and it's how we're going to get the *Rubaiyat*. Once we *know* where it's kept, how it's protected, we'll have to get our hands on it . . . and we have to leave them with a replica, so at least we'll have some time before they become suspicious." Josefa glanced at Emilie, as did the others.

Emilie shifted in her seat, her eyebrows scrunching together. "You want me to *forge* the *Rubaiyat*? That means I would have to find a way to re-create its jewels, its bookbinding," she said. "I can't even . . . I don't think . . ."

"It just has to be passable," Josefa said. "Enough that nobody will suspect us until we get off the ship."

"So we'll have to wait until the last possible moment to get it, because I'm sure Emilie can make the *Rubaiyat look* passable, but I doubt she can make it *feel* passable," Violet interjected.

"We'll wait until the last possible moment," Josefa said with a nod. "The voyage is supposed to take seven days. That gives us

35

plenty of time to find information and set everything in motion, before we slip in and take the book."

"And what about after?" Emilie pressed. "When we have the *Rubaiyat*? What are we planning to do with it?"

"That's easy." Josefa shrugged. "We're going to strip it of its jewels. There is one jewel embedded in its binding that is worth more than we can imagine. Over a thousand pounds. That's what *really* makes this edition of the *Rubaiyat* something to marvel at."

Silence descended on the room for a moment before Violet caught her eye, her brows furrowed. "Won't they get suspicious of how we got hold of it?"

"And who will we even sell the jewels to?" Hinnah asked, teetering so far on the edge of the bed that Josefa worried she would fall right off.

"They won't be suspicious, because I know someone in New York who will help us make the sale," Josefa explained. "I have done this before. I have some connections."

"How do you know someone in New York?" It was Emilie who spoke then, her dark eyes boring into Josefa's. "Have you really been there before?"

"I don't have to have been there to know someone," Josefa said, waving her hand in what she hoped was a dismissive way. They didn't need to know that Josefa's connection in New York was an old friend she had met at boarding school. One who had made quite a name for herself among girls like her.

"What about all of the people on the *Titanic*?" Violet asked this time.

"What about them?"

"Some of the wealthiest people in the world are going to be on that ship. Millionaires, businessmen, famous artists. Why don't we simply take them for what they're worth and forget about the whole *Rubaiyat* business?" she asked. "What's some book compared to the diamonds that rich women wear around their necks?"

"We could rob the diamonds off some rich woman's neck," Josefa entertained. "If we wanted to get caught, tossed off the ship at best. Prison, at worst. And for what? Money that will tide us over for a few months? A few years, at most?"

Violet bristled at Josefa's questions.

"With the jewels from the *Rubaiyat*, none of us have to worry about money again. If we're going to take this risk," Josefa said slowly, casting her gaze around at all of them in turn, "I can assure you, the payoff will be worth it."

"If we succeed," Emilie added.

"No, not if. *When* we succeed," Josefa finished, holding her gaze.

SIX

EMILIE

EMILIE COULD TELL the others were on board when Josefa had pulled the three of them into her bedroom. Before she had even unveiled her plans. All the questions they asked seemed like a formality more than anything else. But Emilie still had her doubts.

That was why she found herself outside Josefa's room at the crack of dawn the next day, her knuckles playing out a steady rhythm against the wooden door.

Josefa's door swung open. She was as bright-eyed as ever, no trace of sleep in her sharp gaze.

"Emilie." Josefa seemed almost pleased to see her as she stepped aside, allowing her to enter the room once more. The solitary desk pressed against the wall was piled with papers that Emilie didn't remember being there yesterday. And a small leather-bound notebook that Emilie had spotted Josefa with before.

"You haven't slept, have you?"

Josefa dismissed the question with a wave of her hand, like sleep was of no importance. "I wanted to make sure that . . . we have everything we need."

"So, you're really going to do this?" Emilie didn't know why, but the thought of this boardinghouse without Josefa sent a pinprick of hurt through her. She was infamous among the girls here. There were whispers and rumors about what Josefa did in her spare time. Why she broke curfew so often. How she managed to dodge the wrath of Matron O'Neill. Some of them were tame enough, some more salacious than Emilie would ever find comfortable. The rumors covered everything from petty theft to conning people out of house and home. But none of that had ever stopped Josefa from pursuing what she wanted.

Emilie wondered if *anything* stopped Josefa from getting what she wanted.

"I have to," Josefa said now, like the idea of not boarding the *Titanic*, not stealing one of the rarest pieces of art in this world, was unthinkable.

"Have you even thought about what would happen if you fail?" Emilie asked. "Have any of you? Because maybe the *Rubaiyat* can mean a life away from places like this, but getting caught would mean places far worse. Are you really willing to spend the rest of your life in prison if you get caught?"

Josefa finally met Emilie's gaze. "I know," she said. "But it's worth the risk. This is the opportunity of a lifetime."

Emilie shook her head. "I can fully believe you stay up at night to dream of your next big heist," Emilie said. "But—"

"Not everybody wants an adventure," Josefa cut in before Emilie could finish voicing her reservations. "Not everyone has the same ambitions as me. Violet has a little brother to support. Hinnah probably just wants to get out of this awful place. And I'm finally going to have my freedom with my share. I won't be bound to some boardinghouse, or the rules my parents always set out for me. I can have a life of my own. Any life that I want. I can be whoever I want to be, dress however I like, go wherever I please. And you . . ." Josefa paused. "You could do anything, Emilie." There was a brightness in Josefa's eyes that drew Emilie in. This wild kind of belief that sparked in her eyes—belief in *her*, even though they barely knew each other.

"I'm sure there's something you want," Josefa said, still holding Emilie's gaze. "You could go back to France or Haiti; you could go to an art conservatory; you could own your own gallery; you could teach art like your father did."

Emilie's heart beat faster with every word that Josefa said. Everyone knew about her father, the art teacher of the Sorbonne. The one who had tragically passed. But nobody knew the reason she had left Paris: because she couldn't bear to be surrounded by memories of him when he wasn't there. Nobody knew why she came to Dublin: because they had dreamed of traveling here together, to learn more about his favorite Irish painters.

Emilie had hoped that by coming here on her own, she would finally be able to reconnect with her work. To be able to paint once more. But that hadn't happened. She was still stuck.

And now Josefa was laying all of Emilie's wildest fantasies at her feet, like it would take nothing to achieve. She couldn't imagine how Josefa knew all of Emilie's dreams.

"You could find somewhere to work on your paintings. Somewhere with endless inspiration. With the money from the *Rubaiyat*, you could really do anything you wanted."

There was such a strong thread of confidence in Josefa's voice that it was difficult to even try to refute it. The worst thing was Emilie knew what she would do if she had the kind of money the *Rubaiyat* promised. She would travel to Haiti and finally learn about her mother's family—her family. She could have gone after France, after her father's passing. But Emilie couldn't bring herself to then. Still reeling from her grief, going out in search of family she had never known felt like a betrayal. And now it was too late. She had gotten a taste of the world. One where no boardinghouse wanted a Black girl like her. Where finding a job to support herself seemed impossible. She had only enough to survive these days, not like when she'd had the safety of her father.

But she could rectify all that now.

"I could," Emilie admitted slowly. "I could do . . . any of those things."

And for the first time since the funeral, Emilie felt a flicker of hope in her chest.

SEVEN

VIOLET

DINNERTIME AT THE boardinghouse was always a raucous affair. But as Violet slid into her seat beside Josefa, she remembered that she almost enjoyed this time. This was, after all, where Josefa and she had first met.

"Are you ready?" Josefa asked, barely glancing at Violet. Her eyes were trained firmly on the matron.

"Of course," Violet said, pushing strands of hair out of her eyes. She knew that the key to a lie was maintaining absolute eye contact. It sounded easier to do than it was, but Violet thought she was quite good at it by now. "Are *you* ready?"

"I'm always ready." Josefa grinned.

Violet rolled her eyes, but as the matron passed by their table, she quickly leaped to a stand.

"Matron O'Neill," she called out, stepping closer to her.

"Ms. Jurić." Matron O'Neill greeted her with a grim nod. Even though she was speaking to Violet, her eyes swept over the rest of the girls as they dined, chatted, and laughed. She was

42

ever observant and had a keen eye for trouble.

"I was hoping that . . . Would you help me with something?" Violet asked. She cast her gaze down, brushing some of her blond hair out of her eyes, in what she hoped conveyed nervousness. When she looked up again, Matron O'Neill took her in with a frown.

"What is it?" Matron O'Neill asked.

"Could we talk privately?"

Matron O'Neill didn't seem happy about that, but after one last cursory glance around the dining hall, she indicated with a nod that Violet should follow behind her. It was all Violet could do to not glance at Josefa with a proud smirk as she shuffled outside the dining hall.

"What do you need?" Matron O'Neill asked.

"Well, I've met someone," Violet began, and Matron O'Neill made a sound in the back of her throat. Like she didn't quite believe her. Violet wasn't known for fraternizing with boys, unlike some of the other girls here, and the matron knew that.

"And he wants me to meet his parents," she finished off with a bashful glance. "It's maybe my one chance of . . . having a family again."

Matron O'Neill considered her for a moment that seemed to go on for too long. "What about your brother?" she asked finally.

When Violet had first come to this boardinghouse after leaving her entire life behind in Croatia, she had confided in the matron about her troubles, in a fit of desperation. Matron

43

O'Neill had taken kindly to her at that time. She offered Violet the chance to stay here without rent, if she helped her out with the running of the boardinghouse. Violet helped with the cleaning and the cooking, mostly. And often Matron O'Neill would task her with keeping an eye on boarders for breaking curfew or bringing contraband into the building, because they'd never suspect a fellow boarder would turn them in to the matron.

"This will help him," Violet said finally. "If . . . I have a family, then he does too." Violet had lied about a lot of things in her life, but this one actually hurt. She had to remind herself that she was doing this *for* Marko. Because she was his only family, and he was hers.

"So, if this works out, I guess you won't have any need for me or this boardinghouse anymore." To her surprise, Matron O'Neill was smiling. Like she was happy Violet was going out to find love and a new family.

If only she knew what Violet was really out to get.

She almost felt badly, until she remembered that the matron didn't treat everyone here as kindly as she did Violet. She wasn't sure if it was because of Violet's sheer desperation when she first got here, or maybe it was just because her lying and acting meant she could easily get into the matron's good graces. But she was all too aware that Hinnah had spent the better part of her time here worried about when the matron would kick her out into the streets.

"I guess so," Violet said. "But what I could use is a dress for the occasion. I don't have anything proper. They're from

Dublin, and a good family. I want to make a good impression."

"Well, I can lend you something," Matron O'Neill said. She slipped out the massive ring with all the keys to the boarding-house on it. They jangled heavily as the matron looked through them, trying to find the right one for the storage room where she kept all her fancy things. She didn't wear those dresses or the rare pieces of jewelry often, but everyone knew she had them. Just last week, they had seen her with a beautiful emerald necklace and matching earrings as she dashed out for an important dinner party.

Violet kept a sharp watch as the matron slipped the right key out of the ring.

"Come on, I've got a few odds and ends you can borrow," she said, and the two of them shuffled down the hallway toward the storage room. The matron unlocked the door and stepped inside, ushering Violet in after her.

Matron O'Neill had left the key in the doorknob. She had only a moment outside the door, and she knew she had to use it wisely.

Violet slipped her fingers into the pocket of her petticoat, where she had tucked away one of Emilie's paints. And as she entered the storage room, she made sure to leave just the tiniest imprint of red paint on the key.

The rest was up to Josefa.

Josefa knocked on her door just after midnight. It was her signature knock—two short taps followed by another longer one.

Quiet enough that nobody else would pay attention.

"Took you long enough!" Violet said as soon as she had flung the door open. "Did you get it?"

"Of course I got it." Josefa held up the key so Violet could see it in the light. The slight tint of paint Violet had left on it a few hours earlier had almost disappeared. "Come on."

The two of them crept through the hallway full of boarders, listening to the sound of girls' whispers and snores, and down the flight of stairs. Violet had never been on the ground floor in the dead of night before. This place was usually busy, full of girls catching up, avoiding the matron's eyes, dining, and laughing.

Now, though, it was dead quiet, and there was something almost eerie about it.

"It was down here," Violet whispered, leading Josefa away from the dining hall and toward the little room the matron had led her to just hours ago. Josefa slipped the key in the door while Violet kept an eye out. She knew that the matron was most likely asleep, but she had a habit of doing random checks in the middle of the night. To keep the girls safe, she always said. But Violet thought the matron enjoyed being in charge of so many young girls and having some semblance of control over them.

"It's not working," Josefa said as she jiggled the key in its lock.

Violet frowned. "Are you sure you got the right one?"

"You said the one marked with red paint," Josefa said.

"Move." Violet pushed Josefa to one side and took hold of

the key herself. The lock had seemed to open so easily for the matron, but the key was stuck in the doorknob. She twisted, but nothing happened.

"Try the other direction," Josefa suggested.

She twisted the key back, but it didn't open the door. Somewhere in the distance, a door creaked open. Or maybe it was just a window pushed open by the wind. Still, Violet couldn't help the rise in her anxiety. She glanced back at Josefa, but she was peering behind them. Like she expected the matron to approach at any moment now.

"Did you hear that?" Violet asked.

"It's nothing," Josefa said, though she didn't sound convinced.

"Just get the key to work and then—" Footsteps echoed down the hall now. A little too close for comfort. They all knew where the matron's room was and what her footsteps sounded like. They all listened for them as they sneaked in and out of their rooms at all hours of the day. *Especially* Josefa. Which was why the stricken look on her face when she turned to Violet meant all the more.

"Can't you just pick the lock?" Violet asked in a whisper.

Josefa shook her head. "It takes time . . . it'll take too long now. Just try it again." Her voice held steady, but Violet knew her friend well. They had done this too many times to count now, and Violet knew when Josefa was confident and when she was losing it. If the matron caught them, their plans would be put in jeopardy. The matron had power—she knew the local law enforcement, and she had never been very fond of Josefa.

They both knew that her strange fondness for Violet was why the matron had pretended to be ignorant of many of Josefa's activities. If she caught them trying to break into her things, Violet knew her fondness would dissipate. It didn't matter how sorry she felt for Violet and her situation with her brother.

So, Violet took a deep breath and gripped hold of the key tightly. She gave it one good twist, and to her surprise, the lock clicked.

"We're in," she whispered, pushing the door open and slipping inside. Josefa followed after her.

They waited breathlessly for a moment for the matron's footsteps to pass. Once they did, past the storage room and up the stairs, Violet let out a sigh.

"That was close," she said.

"This is why you don't shit where you eat," Josefa said, shaking her head. "It's a recipe for disaster."

"Well, that's why we waited until we're almost leaving to steal from Matron Merciless," Violet said. She stepped up to the rack of clothes the matron had shown her earlier today. She had let her borrow one of her nicer dresses, but there were things far more expensive here that the matron wouldn't even let Violet touch. Now, though, she let her fingers trace all the delicate patterns and lace linings as she took dresses off their racks.

"This looks about right for you." Josefa nodded at a cream-colored dress that wasn't to Violet's tastes in the slightest.

"Really?" she asked.

"Well, at least for the Violet who'll be on the *Titanic*," Josefa added as clarification.

Violet shrugged and tucked the dress away into a suitcase to take back with them, while Josefa pulled at the chest by the door that held some of the matron's jewelry.

"Matron O'Neill is certainly richer than she pretends to be," Josefa said, thumbing through a necklace that seemed to glint, even in the near darkness of this room. "These will come in handy." She pocketed the necklace with a grin, and Violet rolled her eyes. She wasn't sure if Josefa was really looking for things to help them look the part or simply swiping things for her own pleasure. Knowing Josefa, probably a little of both.

"It's strange, isn't it?" Violet said after a few moments. "This might be our last night here."

"Wonderful is more like it," said Josefa.

"Well, if it weren't for this place, we would have never met," she said.

"It wasn't an ideal meeting," Josefa pointed out. "If I remember correctly, you despised me on sight."

"Only because you're remembering incorrectly," Violet scoffed. "The only reason why I took a dislike to you was because you were waving around those pearls like they were your birthright."

"I was waving them around because they *weren't* my birthright, if you remember," Josefa pressed. "They were my win. I worked hard to get them. I wasn't going to stand around and take it when some stuck-up blonde questioned all that hard work."

"Because you have always been so humble," Violet pointed out.

"I managed to convince you of my good qualities in the end," Josefa said.

"All you managed to convince me of was that there was value in our partnership. And that . . . I supposed you did deserve to wave around those pearls and boast about your accomplishments. As annoying as it was." Violet rolled her eyes. Still, she couldn't help but think of that day they met and all their other memories here fondly.

"Do you think we've got everything we need?" Josefa asked, breaking Violet out of her memories.

She gave a quick nod of her head as she gathered up half a dozen dresses. She knew she couldn't get caught up in her sentimentality. She had come to Ireland to escape, just like Josefa. To escape Zagreb and her father. It had cost her Marko. She *had* to go back to him, even if she would miss Josefa and their many adventures together.

Josefa listened for a moment for the sound of the matron's footsteps, but there was only silence now. The two of them slipped out of the storage room and back upstairs to their rooms.

"The last night of our old life," Josefa whispered excitedly as she bid Violet goodbye at her bedroom door.

"And the first day of our new life starts tomorrow," Violet finished off.

EIGHT

HINNAH

AS HINNAH APPROACHED the circus that evening, she felt a strange sort of emptiness at the thought of leaving all these familiar things behind.

"You're not supposed to be working today," Mr. Blackwell said as soon as he spotted her. After her performance last night, Hinnah wasn't surprised at his prickliness, but it hurt all the same.

The circus had been her only real home for the past few years, after all. Ever since she'd left Karachi and stumbled upon the group of strangers who would change her life forever. The circus was where she had learned that her body was worth more than her family saw it for. That it could perform amazing feats, and that she could push it to limits that she didn't even know existed a few years ago.

But ever since she had decided to stay on in Dublin, in the hopes that putting down roots for a little while might give her family and friends in Karachi a chance to respond to all the letters she sent them detailing her life, things had changed. She didn't have any friends in the circus here. And while she and her friend Eliza O'Sullivan had worked on their acrobatic routine together, without Eliza, Hinnah was forced to find some other act. One that she wasn't quite as skilled at.

"I came to collect some of my things," Hinnah explained.

"Collect your things?" Mr. Blackwell eyed her with some disdain. "I said that if you made a mistake like last night again, you were gone. You haven't even done another performance."

"I know." Hinnah shifted her weight from one foot to the other, trying to figure out how to best explain her departure. "I've just . . . I decided I'm leaving. To . . . another country?"

Mr. Blackwell's frown deepened. Which Hinnah didn't even think was possible.

"Well, good for you," he said, in a tone that suggested it wasn't good at all. "But there's nothing for you to *collect* here."

Now it was Hinnah's turn to frown. Over the past few months, she had accumulated *some* things to help with her performance. Mostly it was the formfitting clothes that helped her with her tricks, since skirts and dresses weren't the optimal outfit.

"I've left some of my clothes in the dressing room," she explained. "The outfits I wear when I'm performing."

"That's the property of the circus, not yours," Mr. Blackwell said. With that, he turned around and began to march away from her. As if their conversation was over.

But it couldn't be.

Because those clothes belonged to Hinnah. She was the person who had paid for them. She was the one who wore them on the nights of her performances. Just because she left them for safekeeping in the shared dressing room didn't mean they weren't hers.

Still, Hinnah hesitated for a moment. Afraid of what Mr. Blackwell would say if she demanded that she be allowed to take the outfits. She almost wished she had asked Violet or Josefa to come along with her today, though they had never accompanied her to the circus before. But she knew the two of them wouldn't have let Mr. Blackwell march away like that without a word. They would have something to say.

Hinnah took a deep breath and gingerly strode forward, trying to rearrange her expression into one that nobody would mess with—she hoped.

"Mr. Blackwell." Hinnah willed her voice to be authoritative but almost winced at how weak it came out.

He turned around and rolled his eyes at Hinnah. Like he was tired of her. "There's nothing else I have to say to you. You screwed up your performance last night, and now you're leaving without any notice, and *still* you demand that we give you these outfits which are *only* performance clothes. You have no claim to them. The next tightrope walker we hire will make more use of them than you—and I'm sure she'll be far better at the job."

Hinnah tried to blink back the hot tears of anger that burned in the back of her eyelids. Mr. Blackwell had never been kind to her in her time here. But he had never spoken to her like this—as if she were worth nothing.

And the worst thing was, Hinnah had no reply to give. She *had* messed up last night, and she was leaving with no notice. But it wasn't like performing at the circus was a stable job. Hinnah knew all too well how people she worked with for months would disappear without a word overnight, never to come back for a performance again. This was just how things *were*.

But still, she almost wanted to apologize to Mr. Blackwell for inconveniencing him. Of course, he had already turned around and begun to speak to one of the other performers. One who didn't make mistakes or leave without any notice.

Hinnah considered for a moment rushing past Mr. Blackwell into the dressing room for her things, but she thought better of it. She knew that nobody here would support her if she got caught. She had no friends in this circus. Wasn't that why it was so easy for her to leave?

As she made her way back to the boardinghouse, she couldn't stop thinking about the fact that nobody had written to her in all her time in Dublin, either, though she had sent dozens of letters back home. Hoping—praying—that her family and friends hadn't forgotten all about her. Hadn't wiped her clean from their memories simply because of what had happened.

Did Hinnah have any friends in the world at all? she wondered.

* * *

Later that night, as Hinnah finished packing up the last of her sparse belongings, a knock sounded at her door. Josefa waited for her on the other side, looking ready for action. She leaned in almost as soon as Hinnah flung the door open, with a conspiratorial grin—though if Hinnah was being honest, that was the only kind of grin she ever really saw on Josefa.

"Violet and I just got some dresses for us," she whispered.

"Really?" Hinnah asked. After her utter failure at trying to get her outfits from Mr. Blackwell, she could use a win with Josefa and Violet.

"We could use your help with something, if you're up to it," Josefa said.

Hinnah squared up her shoulders, trying not to look too eager. "I'm up for it."

"We're getting the train tomorrow evening, and the ship will set sail the next afternoon. I think we would all be better off if we had a little spare spending money."

Hinnah wasn't sure what "spare" spending money even looked like, considering she had only just been scraping by to survive ever since she'd left Karachi.

"We're already taking the dresses from the matron, so we don't want to try our luck here again . . . ," Josefa mumbled.

The perfect idea came to Hinnah unprompted. "I know who might have a little spare spending money for us," Hinnah said with a small smile. "Mr. Blackwell."

55

* * *

Months and months of working at Mr. Blackwell's circus meant that Hinnah was familiar with the regular routine. That was how she knew that it was just before midnight that the circus troupe left the marquee, leaving Mr. Blackwell alone with all the night's earnings before he locked up the place.

She watched from the shadows as one by one the circus performers shuffled out and disappeared into the depths of the night, before stepping toward the familiar marquee that housed the circus.

Hinnah knew Mr. Blackwell's routine by heart. In her early days in his circus, Hinnah was tasked with the duty of helping him clean up—for a little bit of extra cash that she desperately needed.

She slipped in through the front entrance and ducked into the shadows. Mr. Blackwell was a stickler for his routine: First, he counted up all his cash in the trailer at the back. He locked the trailer, knowing that all the circus performers had gone home, and did a sweep of the marquee. He made sure that everything was in place, ready to go for the next day. He would tuck the trapeze swings out of the way and blow out all the lamps inside the tent.

It didn't take Mr. Blackwell longer than a few minutes, but Hinnah knew that was her moment to strike. Because right after, Mr. Blackwell went back to the trailer, where he put the cash into a lockbox to take home.

Hinnah made her way to the other side of the tent, toward

the back entrance, which led to their solitary trailer. It wasn't long before Mr. Blackwell came shuffling in, humming a soft tune to himself.

Hinnah waited for just a moment—long enough for Mr. Blackwell to make it all the way in before she silently dashed out the way he had come. She knew she had only a few minutes if she didn't want to get caught.

The trailer was locked—just as Hinnah had expected, and Mr. Blackwell was the only one with a key. But Hinnah had never been the kind of person who needed access to a front door.

She turned to the side of the trailer, toward the window that she knew everybody always cracked open. It was hot and stuffy in the trailer, and this was their only form of ventilation. Hinnah wasn't sure she had *ever* seen this window closed.

She hopped up and grabbed on to the window ledge with her hands. It wasn't too far up, even if the window was tiny. Hinnah used the strength of her arms to pull herself all the way up, squeezing through the small space.

She landed on the other side with a soft thump. Not as graceful as she had hoped she would be, but that was fine. It's not like Mr. Blackwell was here to judge her landing.

Hinnah grinned when she spotted the cash on the dressing table. It was the night's earnings, and there was more than enough here to satisfy Josefa and meet all their needs during their time on the *Titanic*. Or until they had the *Rubaiyat* in their hands, and their lives changed forever.

She pocketed the cash and turned back, but before she

could climb out something caught her eye.

The rack of circus outfits. Hinnah could see her own outfits peeking out—the ones that she had spent so much time saving up for. They were the most expensive things she had ever owned. They were the only things she had had to call her own ever since she left Karachi with only the clothes on her back.

Hinnah glanced at the door. There were no footsteps indicating that Mr. Blackwell was coming back. She still had time. She was sure Josefa wouldn't mind it. If it were her here instead of Hinnah, she wouldn't even think twice about it. She would take what she wanted and think about the consequences later.

So Hinnah began to pull her outfits off the rack, as quickly as she could. She hadn't brought anything to carry the outfits out, but that didn't matter.

Hinnah pushed the clothes through the window. They might get a little dirty, but Hinnah was willing to live with that.

She was about to climb out after them when the door handle twisted. She had somehow missed the sound of Mr. Blackwell's footsteps. She pulled herself up to the window once more, but she was too slow.

The door swung open behind her, but Hinnah clambered out before Mr. Blackwell could see any more than her backside. She gathered up the dresses while Mr. Blackwell came up to the window.

"Hey!" he cried out, but Hinnah was already sprinting. The outfits weighed her down, but Hinnah didn't care. She wasn't going to let Mr. Blackwell have them—not after everything.

"Stop!" Mr. Blackwell's cry came from behind her—a little too close. He was right on her heels as she stumbled into the marquee. The place was dark with all the lamps blown out. Hinnah knew that was an advantage for her. She sped up, her heart pounding against her chest, and her clothes heavy in her arms. But she pumped her legs faster and faster. Even in the dark, she knew where the entrance to the marquee was. She slipped out and ducked into the shadowy trees by the tent.

By the time Mr. Blackwell made it outside, Hinnah was hidden from view.

"I've already called the police, girl! You won't get away with stealing from me!" Mr. Blackwell called out into the night. Though Hinnah knew he must think she was already long gone. He cursed under his breath and slipped back into the marquee. Out of sight.

Hinnah grinned down at the dresses in her arms, finally feeling a sense of accomplishment she hadn't in a long time. Maybe their mission on the *Titanic* was exactly what Hinnah was built for, she thought. Josefa had made the right choice. And so had Hinnah.

NINE

3 DAYS, 14 HOURS, 35 MINUTES
JOSEFA

THE *TITANIC* ROSE in front of them like a giant. All the images Josefa had seen of it in the newspapers didn't do it justice. It was sleek black and seemed to glitter in the sunlight—as if like the *Rubaiyat* it, too, was made of precious jewels. She could only guess at how large the looming ship actually was, because even with her neck strained up, she could barely make out the top of the ship where it disappeared into the blue sky. One thing was for sure—the *Titanic* was magnificent. And just the sight of it sent a thrill through Josefa.

She drew her friends to a secluded corner, away from the throngs of people clamoring to get a glimpse of the ship. She didn't blame them.

"Have you got it?" she asked, turning to Emilie expectantly. The four of them had spent the night in the confines of a train carriage. Josefa had slept restfully, like it was any other night. But now, with the air of Queenstown all around her, Josefa's stomach fluttered with excitement.

Emilie dug around in her bag, searching for what Josefa had asked her to work on for the past few days—documents they would need to board the ship. As Emilie handed them over, Josefa felt her excitement rise even more. It was all she could do to keep the broad grin off her face. Because they were here. And in just a few minutes, they would be boarding the *Titanic*.

They had all changed into clothes befitting their new selves: four women who belonged on the second-class deck of the *Titanic*. They all looked markedly different in the new dresses they had lifted off of Matron O'Neill. Josefa's blue-and-white silk dress wasn't unlike the clothes she had grown up wearing. Still, she didn't mind the reminders of her parents when it was tied up with her dreams. Emilie, too, looked comfortable in the olive-green skirt and blouse Violet had offered her on the train. Hinnah was perhaps the only one who looked like she didn't quite belong in her navy dress, though it was the plainest of all the clothes they had taken from Matron O'Neill.

Violet was the one who embodied her new clothes as if she had never worn anything but lavish things meant for the wealthy. She looked softer than usual in a cream-colored dress that clung to her tightly. She had even donned a feathered hat, which made her look older and more sophisticated, while the rest of them had swept their hair out of their faces and into high buns, less unruly than usual and more befitting ladies in the second class.

Josefa gathered the forged documents into a pile in her

hands. Even Hinnah and Violet stepped closer to catch a glimpse. At the top of the pile was Mlle Sylviane Auclaire, her name written in the upper left corner in perfect cursive strokes. A black-and-white picture alongside the name showed a grim Violet, with her lips pressed together tightly and her blond hair atop her head in a tight bun. Violet grabbed the pile of papers from Josefa, running her hands along the black ink. Like she expected everything to disintegrate with a mere touch.

But obviously it didn't.

Instead, Josefa watched as the real Violet pressed her lips together, just like the one in the picture. "I told you Emilie was the person for the job," Josefa said, looking at Emilie with what she hoped was reassurance. Even from here, Josefa could sense Emilie's nervousness from the way she chewed on her lips. But she met Josefa's glance with a glint in her eyes. Almost like she was enjoying the attention, and the compliments.

"These are good," Violet admitted begrudgingly.

"They're better than good," Josefa said, but she knew that was the most Violet was going to say. She had never been the kind of person to dole out compliments.

"Now, these papers are crucial," Josefa said, drawing them into a tight circle. "And so are the new identities we have to forge. We can't take this lightly . . . we can't afford to get caught."

"Wait . . . ," Violet mumbled. "Shouldn't we inspect all of the papers closely?"

Josefa tried not to heave a sigh. This was, after all, what made Violet such a good partner. She was meticulous, where

Josefa was carefree. They balanced each other out.

"I trust that everything is in order," Josefa said, handing her papers over to Violet. She began to thumb through them, a crease appearing in her brows as she did.

Beside her, Josefa could sense a shift in Emilie. Her shoulders were hunched, her expression tense.

"There's something wrong," Violet said after a few moments had passed. There was a glint of satisfaction in Violet's eye as she held out Josefa's travel papers. Her own black-and-white face stared back at Josefa.

"Everything is perfect," Josefa said. "I don't understand what—"

"Look at the date," Violet said.

Josefa leaned forward, trying to find the date. It was dated to the *9th day of March 1907*.

"These travel papers need to be renewed after five years, Josefa," Violet said, pointing to the British seal at the top and where this rule was clearly written.

"No, I . . . ," Emilie mumbled. She glanced around, as if she expected a new set of travel papers to appear out of thin air. Ones that had no mistakes on them. Emilie shook her head slowly. "I was up so late making these. I must have . . ." She drifted off, her shoulders slumped in embarrassment.

"If you weren't up to the task, you should have told us," Violet said in a no-nonsense voice. "But instead, you're here jeopardizing our mission before we've even started."

"I'm sorry," Emilie said, her voice low but firm. She glanced up to meet Violet's eyes, obviously unwilling to back down from whatever challenge Violet had just issued. "But it's one mistake, and I'm sure that the guards won't even notice the date being off by just a few days. I shouldn't have—"

"You shouldn't have even been invited on this mission," Violet finished for Emilie, crossing her arms over her chest. And even though Violet wasn't much taller than Emilie, she somehow seemed to tower over her in that moment.

"It's a small mistake." Josefa stepped in before Violet and Emilie could say any more hurtful things to each other. She knew it was more than a small mistake—and that it was mistakes like this that were sure to cost them during this mission. But Josefa couldn't help but jump to Emilie's defense. Wasn't it her fault, after all? She should have checked every document carefully and thoroughly. Emilie had never done this before.

"What are we going to do?" Hinnah asked, her eyes nervously darting toward the *Titanic*, looming in the distance. Even from here, they could make out the guards checking everybody's papers. Just a few moments ago, that had felt like the start of Josefa's grand plans. Now it seemed like another obstacle in her path.

Even though Josefa was confident in Violet's ability to talk the two of them out of trouble, she was pretty sure this was one situation even Violet's acting couldn't get them out of.

"I have a plan," she said, as she caught sight of their saving grace in the distance.

* * *

There were many people in this crowd. It was teeming over with people, and Josefa knew that not all of them had come to board this ship. Many of them had simply come here to see the magnificent *Titanic*. Many of them had come to say goodbyes to their loved ones crossing the ocean.

But Josefa had a keen eye, and even from a distance she could make out the woman with dark brown hair stumbling out of her taxi and glancing around at the crowds of ordinary people with distaste written all over her face. This woman was a passenger, otherwise she would not be caught dead here. Even though she looked a few years older than Josefa, she knew this was her best shot.

She led Violet through the crowd as fast as she could, glancing back once to catch sight of Hinnah and Emilie lined up to board the ship.

"What is your plan?" Violet asked.

"Our usual," Josefa said, pointing to the woman in the distance. She had her travel papers ready in her hands. "Now hurry up; we don't have a lot of time."

Thankfully, Violet was just as quick on her feet as Josefa. She approached the woman with her face rearranged into a charming smile while Josefa hung back among the crowd, out of sight.

"Would you like to buy some Irish lace, miss?" Violet asked, her blue eyes blinking innocently. "My mother is selling them as souvenirs. Perfect for your friends in New York!"

The woman glanced at her with narrowed eyes. "Is there something special about Irish lace?"

"Yes, it's world famous. You wouldn't want to leave Ireland without that kind of a souvenir, would you?" Violet asked.

"I suppose not. . . ." The woman stole a glance at her chaperone—an older man who looked even more unimpressed by their surroundings than she did.

"My mother is just over there. You could take a look at what we have to offer." Violet pointed toward an old woman with a basket who was weaving in and out through the crowds.

"We still have time, don't we?" the woman asked her chaperone.

"A little, but you have to hurry," he said, his eyes trained on the ship ahead. There was still a long line of people waiting to board, but Hinnah and Emilie were fast approaching the top of the queue. Josefa knew they might not have a lot of time once she carried out her task.

"I'll be fast," the woman said, giving Violet a quick nod. "Show me the way to this amazing Irish lace."

Violet began to lead the woman through the crowds. Josefa waited for a moment before following behind, easily gliding between people as she caught up to the woman. Violet glanced back just once to catch her eye, and Josefa understood that she meant it was time.

Josefa leaned in as close to the woman as she could, almost brushing her skin as she plucked the papers right out of her hands. She quickly replaced them with her own outdated ones before the woman realized she was missing anything.

The photo on top of these travel papers was perfect. In black and white, Josefa could definitely pass for this woman. She didn't take longer than a second to glance at the papers. Instead, Josefa turned around and began to weave her way through the crowds again, and toward Hinnah and Emilie.

A moment later, she could hear Violet's footsteps running toward them.

"You lost her fast," Josefa commented.

"I just left her with the woman selling wares out of her basket. I didn't wait long enough to see if there was any Irish lace, though. She might be a little disappointed."

"Where did you two *go*?" Hinnah asked in her nervous voice.

Josefa held up the papers she had just stolen in response. "Fixing our problem." She didn't have much longer than that to explain, as the four of them shuffled up the gangway.

Violet pushed in front of them, her eyes alight and charm oozing off her. She had the air of an heiress. She handed the ticket inspector the four tickets. His eyes scanned Violet, before examining the three of them in turn.

"And what are your plans in America?" he asked.

"Well, I have always wanted to visit New York, of course," Violet began with a sigh, as if she had spent her life dreaming of the city. She looked and sounded so unlike the Violet that Josefa knew in that moment—but Josefa was used to this. "Can you believe I have never been there before? All around Europe, of course—and Ireland is charming, but not quite what I'm used to in France. I'm sure you understand."

The man nodded slowly, as if he really didn't understand at all.

"New York, though," Violet continued, her eyes dancing with excitement. "Well, I've heard tales, of course. My father is there on business, and, well, my friends and I are going to visit and—"

The ticket inspector cleared his throat, cutting through Violet's schoolgirl excitement about America. "I'll just have a look at your travel papers if you don't mind," he said. "And then you can be on your way." He glanced past them at the queue of people still waiting to board.

"Of course." Violet passed him her travel papers, and he thumbed through them. Josefa felt Emilie stiffen beside her, but a moment later, the inspector gave a curt nod of his head and handed the papers back.

"This way, madam." He stepped back to let her onto the gangway.

Hinnah followed behind, her papers already at the ready. The inspector nodded once more, allowing her past.

Josefa and Emilie approached next. Josefa flashed the inspector a smile as she handed her papers over. Out of the corner of her eye, Josefa caught sight of the woman she had stolen the papers from. She and her chaperone weren't far away, and her eyes were trained right on Josefa.

"Miss Williams, is that right?" the guard asked, still thumbing through her papers.

"Yes, that's right," Josefa said casually.

"And you're going to America for . . . ?" the man asked.

Beside her, Josefa could feel Emilie tense up. In the small space between them, Josefa reached forward, sliding her fingers between Emilie's. Her palms were warm to the touch, even though the air around them was cool. Josefa gave her hand a gentle squeeze, ignoring the tingle it sent through her, and hoped she communicated something that soothed Emilie.

"We're all traveling together. To New York. Sylviane's father arranged it all." Josefa nodded toward Violet, already on her way up the ship.

The inspector gave one final nod of his head before reaching forward and handing Josefa's papers back. He barely even glanced at Emilie's before waving the two of them through.

Violet paused halfway up the gangway, glancing back at Emilie with a glare. "You were lucky that Josefa and I found a way to fix your mistake. But you might not be so lucky next time. Don't make us regret asking you on this mission."

"Violet," Josefa warned. But Violet barely looked at her before turning away and resuming her ascent onto the ship.

Hinnah, though, paused for a moment, her eyes drifting from Josefa to Emilie. "Don't worry about her. She can be a bit . . ." Hinnah trailed off, like she didn't quite have the words to describe Violet.

"Prickly," Josefa finished off for Hinnah.

"She warms up in time, though," Hinnah added. There was a flush in her cheeks, like she was embarrassed to be saying such things about Violet. Still, she directed a small smile at Josefa and Emilie. A smile was rare enough from Hinnah, and it made her look younger than she usually did. It reminded Josefa that Hinnah was, in fact, younger than all three of them.

Hinnah turned to follow Violet up to the ship.

"Thanks," Emilie mumbled, reaching up to adjust the blue clip in her hair instead of meeting Josefa's eyes. Josefa felt her cheeks redden and looked away from Emilie too—hoping she didn't notice the blush.

"I know this hasn't been easy—won't be easy," Josefa whispered. "But it'll be worth it, I promise."

Emilie only gave her a quick nod before continuing up the gangway. Josefa took a deep breath. She cast one last glance around her—at the crowd of people and the houses rising up behind them. When she turned, she knew she was leaving the green island of Ireland behind her. There was no tug of regret in her belly, just the excitement of slipping onto the glittering ship that carried the object of her most legendary con yet.

If only Josefa's parents could see her now.

TEN

3 DAYS, 13 HOURS, 5 MINUTES
VIOLET

"EXCUSE ME, *WHERE* are your companions?"

When Violet looked up, she found herself face-to-face with a woman who reminded her a little too much of their matron back in Dublin. She wore a conservative black dress that covered almost every inch of her skin from the neck down. Her hair was pulled away from her face, enunciating her sharp jawline and cheekbones, and her lips were pressed into a thin line as she observed Violet.

It took Violet a moment to remember herself and arrange her expression and stature into ones that befitted a vintner heiress. But that must have been enough to cast doubt on her, because the woman stepped closer to Violet, studying her with narrowed eyes.

"My companions?" Violet swept back a stray hair and pulled herself up to her full height. An easy and charming smile formed on her lips, but the woman in front of her didn't seem won over by it.

"I'm the matron of the second class," she said with a frown. "Matron Wallis. I don't think a girl as young as you would be permitted to travel by yourself."

"I'm hardly young." Violet was only seventeen, but she hoped with her hair swept out of her face, she could look at least a year or two older. "Anyhow, I *do* have companions. My father arranged for me to travel all the way to America to continue my studies. He, of course, had the same thoughts as you. A young woman traveling all alone? He wouldn't stand for that, no matter how much I tried to convince him otherwise."

The matron watched Violet closely, and she wasn't sure if Matron Wallis was convinced by her lies or not. Her expression was unreadable.

"Well, in the end, he did arrange some companions for me. They should be right along." She waved a dismissive hand behind her, hoping that the others would stumble up at any moment to assuaage Matron Wallis's suspicions.

To her surprise, that was exactly when Hinnah came into view, her trunk tightly clasped in her hands.

"There's one of them right there!" No sooner had the excited words escaped Violet's lips than Emilie and Josefa appeared in sight too.

Matron Wallis paused to cast a glance over all of them individually, like she would be able to see just by looking if Violet was telling the truth. Violet tried to appear as innocent as she possibly could—her smile firmly in place, her eyes wide with wonder. Still, the matron seemed unsatisfied.

"You're four *girls*," she said.

Violet exchanged a glance with Josefa. "We are, but you have nothing to worry about here."

Matron Wallis shook her head slowly. "Your father arranged for your travel companions to be girls your own age?"

Violet heaved a bored sigh. "Matron Wallis," she said. "Do you know who I am?"

"I have a feeling you're about to tell me."

"I'm Sylviane Auclaire," she said. "My father, Simon Auclaire, owns a wine estate in Pessac. One that I am heir to. He's aware that in America the four of us will be seldom traveling on our own. I assure you, my father isn't concerned about the company I'll be keeping during this journey. . . ." Violet took an extensive pause, a reassuring expression on her face. "So, you have nothing to worry about."

Matron Wallis stared at the four of them again with disapproval. "Four young girls don't belong on a ship like this . . . not on their own."

Violet felt a prickle of anger. The second-class matron surely didn't have the prerogative to kick them off the *Titanic*?

"So, you'll be my responsibility while you're aboard this ship." Matron Wallis caught Violet's eyes, and she seemed to see right through Violet as she said her next words. "Stay out of trouble, or I will find a way to make you stay out of trouble."

With that, she turned around and walked away—no doubt to accost some other poor souls.

Violet waited a moment for Wallis to disappear out of sight, into the crowds of people, before marching inside. She didn't wait to see if the others were following behind, but she could hear the sound of their steady footsteps.

Their tickets had assigned them two cabins side by side, and when Violet stumbled into one of their rooms, Josefa, Hinnah, and Emilie slipped in after her.

"I can't believe we made it." Emilie sighed, leaning her back against the door as if she were already tired.

Hinnah knitted her eyebrows together and pulled at a strand of her black hair.

"I don't think that matron is going to leave us be, if she's anything like Matron O'Neill."

Beside Emilie, Josefa was grinning—her gaze flickering among them all.

"Come on, we knew that this wouldn't be an easy task," she said. "The opportunity of a lifetime requires the hard work of a lifetime."

"I don't know if I'd call lying and sneaking around hard work," Emilie said.

"I would," Violet retorted, taking a seat on the tiny bed in the cabin. "Hard work where it concerns *us* anyway." She raised an eyebrow at Emilie. Violet wasn't surprised that the girl didn't understand that hard work wasn't simply sitting in her room painting all day long. Some of them had to do whatever they could to survive—Emilie would never understand what that felt like.

Emilie frowned and cast her eyes down low. Like she had

nothing to counter Violet's words. That made Violet feel a little better, at least.

"We're here," Josefa said, drawing everyone's attention to her immediately. "We've made it this far."

"We have to be careful," Hinnah said.

"We'll *be* careful," Josefa said, confidence lacing her words. Though *careful* was certainly *not* the word Violet would have used to describe her friend at any given moment. "Let's put away our things and meet at the deck in fifteen minutes. We'll say our final goodbye to Ireland." Josefa's face lit up with excitement, and she didn't wait for a response from the rest of them before slipping out of the room.

Violet wondered for a moment if Josefa hadn't told them the whole truth about this mission. It wasn't rare for Josefa to be confident. But this kind of confidence . . . it felt as if Josefa were overcompensating for something.

But it didn't matter.

Violet could find a way to get the truth out of anyone.

Even Josefa.

ELEVEN

3 DAYS, 12 HOURS, 55 MINUTES
JOSEFA

ALMOST AS SOON as Josefa stepped out onto the deck, her eyes landed on a familiar face across the crowds. His bright blue eyes watched her, with just as much sharpness as they always had.

August Frazier was recognizable to Josefa almost instantly. His signature smirk that reeked of arrogance. The familiar mass of brown curls that sat atop his head. The way he watched Josefa, both observant and ignorant. But he had changed too. In the few years since they had last seen each other, August had grown taller, paler, and there were far too many freckles dotting his face. He had grown so tall, in fact, that when he began to walk toward Josefa, his strides were completely inelegant. As if he hadn't really learned control over his newfound height. But there was something very August about that inelegance too.

Josefa had thought about this moment many times, about seeing August again all these years after his betrayal. About her revenge.

"Fancy seeing you here" were the first words out of August's mouth, as an easy smile replaced his frown. "How long has it been?"

While anyone else would have thought August was delighted to see her, Josefa noticed that his smile didn't quite illuminate his face—like it was something controlled. And that his hands twitched by his sides. Josefa liked that he seemed a little scared.

He should be, she thought.

"Three years," Josefa said.

"Yeah . . . and you still look . . ." He trailed off, taking her in a little too closely. "What are you doing here?" he added after a moment. Josefa didn't miss the nervous way his eyes flitted around.

"I could ask you the same question," Josefa said, though she didn't need to ask him the question at all. Josefa had a pretty good idea why August was here. It's why she'd made boarding the *Titanic* her top priority. Not because of the *Rubaiyat*. Not because of her friends. But because of him, and how he had wronged her all those years ago.

"August." A voice barked from behind them. August glanced over his shoulder for just a moment, and Josefa followed his gaze. A man was looking at the pair of them with a stern expression. And unlike August's, the suit and tie the man wore fit him perfectly. As if they were tailor-made.

"Don't tell me you've gone on the straight and narrow," Josefa said with a raised eyebrow.

August rubbed at the back of his neck, not quite meeting

Josefa's eyes. It was almost as if he were trying to make up his mind on exactly how much to confide in Josefa. On how much he could trust her.

"I wouldn't say that," August mumbled.

"Good. Because I'm not sure if I can even picture an August Frazier who isn't a con man," Josefa said. "I'm guessing all of this"—she gestured to his outfit, so unlike the August she had known: a button-up shirt and black blazer that hung off his shoulder—"is part of some ploy."

"As much as all of *this* is." August nodded at Josefa's outfit. "Or have you finally decided to go back to your life of luxury?"

Josefa's stomach clenched. Not because of what August insinuated. But because he *could* insinuate it at all. At the fact that when they knew each other, she had shared so many intimate parts of herself with him—her past, her family, her fears, her dreams. And now he could speak of it all as if he had some claim to it. Some claim to who she was.

"Do you really think after everything I would go running back to my family?" she asked with a raised eyebrow.

"Well, at least you always had that choice. Unlike some of us." August shrugged his shoulders, as if he were the one who had been wronged all those years ago. As if he had any right to speak of what choices Josefa had, when he had made the choice to betray Josefa and throw her away like she was worth nothing to him.

August glanced back at his employer once more and heaved a sigh. "I have to go."

"I guess there will be time for us to catch up yet," Josefa said with a grin. August didn't look pleased at that, but he didn't look displeased either. He gave a quick nod of his head before disappearing back into the crowds.

Josefa's smile dissipated almost as soon as he was gone, and she took a deep breath. Trying to rid herself of that simmering anger she felt whenever she thought of him. Except now, it was ten times worse. Because August was here. On this ship.

And she was closer to her revenge than she ever had been before.

When Josefa turned around, she spotted Violet approaching through the dispersing crowd. With the ship finally setting off, she was sure everybody was retreating to cabins or beginning to explore all the luxuries that this ship had to offer. She had heard tales of restaurants and cafés, world-class gymnasiums, and more.

"There you are," Violet said once she reached Josefa.

"Any trouble?" Josefa asked.

"No. But I did spot Wallis searching for us."

"Already?" The matron was a problem that she had not accounted for. She couldn't have anticipated that a stranger on the ship would be so concerned about four young women traveling by their lonesome.

"I'm certain Emilie will find a way to make the situation even worse."

Josefa had known that Violet wasn't fond of Emilie when she asked her to join this mission. But she also couldn't have foreseen this odd hostility Violet had developed toward her. Violet took time to warm to people—Josefa knew that. But there was something about Emilie that was making Violet not even attempt to understand or befriend her.

"Emilie is important to this mission, Violetta," Josefa pressed, hoping the nickname that only she used for her friend would soften her. "We wouldn't be here without her."

"She almost jeopardized the mission," Violet insisted. "If it hadn't been for us, would we even be here right now?"

"But it's because of me that she's here. We *need* her," Josefa said.

"But she doesn't need *us*. . . . If she did, she would put in more of an effort. She would pay attention. Not mess up before we even boarded this ship."

Josefa frowned, unsure of how to make Violet see they were all in the same boat, literally and figuratively. They were all desperate for something *more* than their lives in Ireland had ever offered them. Violet seemed determined not to listen to Josefa's defense of Emilie, though.

"Do you not remember what it was like before the two of us became friends?" Josefa asked, because she remembered those days well. When she had nobody left in this world, really. When she trusted no one. She remembered how long it took her to even come around to the idea of Violet.

"That was different," Violet insisted.

"That night when I broke curfew and almost got caught by O'Neill . . . if you hadn't helped me then, I would have never trusted you. We never would have been friends. I thought you were just like everybody else. Only looking out for your own interests. But . . . I was wrong. I should have trusted you from the beginning."

Violet's bright blue eyes bore into Josefa's for a long moment, like she was recalling that night too.

"You and I . . . we were always the same. We always wanted the same thing. But, Emilie . . ."

There wasn't any time for Violet to finish telling Josefa about how different Emilie was from the rest of them, because in the next moment Emilie and Hinnah approached them.

Josefa shook her head, because there was nothing she could do or say to convince Violet about Emilie. She had to come to that on her own.

"I'm going to find us some supplies. We'll need some parchment and pens, because Emilie will need them to forge. It would be great if we could get some rope and twine too. If we get into a sticky situation, they will be useful. And anything else we can get our hands on. We need to be as prepared as possible," Josefa said as soon as the four of them were together once more. "I'm sure there's a storage room somewhere here that will have valuable things."

"I need to send a message before anything else . . . to my brother," Violet said.

"Me too," Emilie chimed in. "I have an important message that needs to be delivered."

Josefa couldn't have set this up more perfectly. Maybe if

Violet and Emilie spent more than five minutes together, Violet would be able to find a kinship with Emilie. All Josefa knew was that the four of them needed to work together for their mission to be successful. And their mission *was* going to be successful.

She pulled out the notebook she had been using to plan everything and thumbed through it. "Hinnah . . . I know that the ship's designer, Thomas Andrews, has a cabin in first class. I'm sure he's going to have something useful there. Something like a map of the ship or blueprints. Whatever will help us get around more easily. Emilie should be able to make a copy of anything you find."

Hinnah gave a furtive nod of her head, even if Josefa could see the crease of worry between her brows. "If he has anything useful there, I'll be able to get it."

"Let's all meet at sundown," Josefa said. "And let's keep away from Wallis."

TWELVE

2:00 P.M.

---

3 DAYS, 12 HOURS, 20 MINUTES
VIOLET

VIOLET COULDN'T BELIEVE her luck. Getting stuck with Emilie was the last thing she wanted to do. She felt as if Josefa had set this up, under some notion that Violet needed to be *nicer* to Emilie.

"So . . . there must be someone you're desperate to get in touch with." Violet wasn't much for small talk, but she did like to know who she was getting in bed with. Right now, she knew little—if anything at all—about Emilie, and she didn't like that.

Emilie simply smiled. "It's more about the message than who I'm contacting."

Violet didn't know what that meant, but she had to admit she was impressed at Emilie's ability to keep her secrets to herself. Maybe that was what Josefa saw in her.

"Who is waiting for you after all of this is over?" Violet tried once more.

Emilie's smile flickered for a moment. "Is there someone waiting for you?" she asked instead of answering. "It must be difficult being away from your friends and family in Croatia."

Violet felt the familiar pang of hurt and regret she always did when she thought of her family.

"It's just my brother," she said finally. "That's why I'm here."

Emilie nodded, like she understood. Like she could *ever* understand. Unlike the rest of them, Emilie had had all the privilege in the world, and that privilege was more than just wealth. She had grown up in a family that cared for and provided for her. She had never been left to fend for herself, unlike the rest of them. It was easy to tell from the way she conducted herself, the way she spoke, the clothes she wore. Violet wondered once more why Emilie had agreed to be here at all.

She stopped in her tracks, facing Emilie with narrowed eyes. "You might not realize this, but Hinnah, Josefa, and I . . . we're not like you," she said. "And we need to succeed. I won't let you jeopardize that for us."

Emilie's honey-brown eyes bore into Violet's—wide and unblinking. That gaze might work on Josefa, but it only sent a prickle of annoyance through Violet. She didn't wait for Emilie's response before turning on her heel and marching up the corridor.

She didn't have long to go before stopping in front of the cabin they had been searching for. Even from outside, Violet could hear the incessant tap, tap, tap of the telegraph service. Never-ending. She didn't know how wireless operators could do it all day. She didn't know how they didn't get a headache, when she was getting one from just a few seconds of listening to that sound.

"Awful sound, isn't it?" Emilie said, approaching Violet from behind.

Violet let out a grunt of agreement. It was as much as she was willing to have in common with Emilie.

They both peered through the doorway into a cramped room, barely big enough to fit more than three people. In fact, if Violet and Emilie took just a few steps they would be on top of the only other person in the room—the man who was tapping away at the transmitter. Beside him was a stack of papers that looked about ready to topple over.

"Um, excuse me?" Violet put on her sweetest, politest voice.

The man put up a finger to hush her. For a minute, none of them spoke as he continued to tap out the message on his telegraph. Finally, after what seemed like an eternity, he turned around, brushing lint off his navy blue sailor's jacket. The man didn't look much older than Violet. He had a round, boyish face, grim as it was tucked away under his sailor's hat.

"Yeah?" He didn't seem pleased to see them. "Can I help you?"

"Um, sir—" Emilie started.

"Jack Phillips," he introduced himself, though there was no pleasantry in his voice.

"Mr. Phillips," Violet cut in. "We just wondered if we could send an urgent message. Well, two." She cast a short glance at Emilie.

Jack heaved a sigh. "Everyone has an urgent message to send," he mumbled, and Violet wasn't sure if the words were for her and Emilie, for himself, or for someone else entirely. "There's pen and paper over there." He pointed to a tiny wooden table pressed against the side of the room. "Write down your messages and add them to the stack; we'll get to them when we get to them."

Violet didn't think that sounded particularly promising, but Jack had already turned around, his finger back to tapping. She considered mentioning her father, and the vineyards she was to be heir to, but thought better of it. She wouldn't want to garner the wrong sort of attention—not now, when they had already run into trouble before the ship even set off.

Emilie piped up of her own accord. "Excuse me, but our messages really are urgent." Violet felt a pulse of anger in her chest, even though she obviously wished that her telegram would be top priority. "And our telegrams are for a little farther out, so if you could—"

Jack interrupted Emilie by turning his sharp gaze on her, a frown plastered to his face.

"Are you first-class passengers?" he asked. "Because it's really only first-class passengers who are allowed to send telegrams."

"Well, we're—"

"Yes, we are," Violet cut in, before Emilie could make things even worse for them. "How else would we have traveled all the way up here? You can check our tickets if you wish, or I'm sure if we call in the matron who welcomed us onto the ship, she would be more than happy to confirm." Violet pasted a charming smile on her lips as she finished speaking, hoping that it exuded first-class confidence, even if everything else about her didn't.

"Well, fine. But I'm afraid there is no way to prioritize your messages." Jack glanced at Emilie with distaste before turning back to his work.

"What was that?" Violet whispered, pulling Emilie to the side and shooting her a death glare.

"I just thought . . . I know you want to send your brother a message, and I wanted to help," Emilie said, her voice wavering.

Violet shook her head, and though all she wanted to do was reprimand Emilie for her foolishness, she knew that here and now wasn't the time or place for it. Not with Jack Phillips already suspicious of them.

"I will not let your ridiculous mistakes cost me my family," she said. With those words, Violet turned away. Grabbing hold of a piece of paper and pen, she began to scribble out her message.

> Dear Marko,
> I'm sending you a promise. Keep it safe. In just a short while I will be back with you again, and we'll have more than we have ever wanted, or will ever need.
> Puno te pozdravljam,
> V

Her anger slowly dissipated, and warmth spread through her as she read over the note. It was the first time she was giving him good news since she had come to Ireland. She would finally be able to fulfill her duty as an older sister: travel back to Croatia, reunite with her brother. And they would take care of each other, like they should have been doing all this time.

With a lightness in her chest, Violet picked up the note and cast a sidelong glance at Emilie. She was still writing, her face scrunched up in contemplation. When Violet glanced at the note with her slender, cursive writing, she could make out only a few words:

. . . coming to Haiti

Find lodging . . . questions . . . payment in a fortnight.

So that was Emilie's plan. The reason why she had agreed to be here. She wanted to travel to Haiti. Violet couldn't imagine for what purpose. Probably the same reason Emilie had come to Dublin—to work on her art. Perhaps the money her father had left her wasn't enough to cover the long journey and stay.

Violet swallowed back her irritation. The *Rubaiyat* meant a new life for her. It meant protection and survival. But to Emilie, it simply meant traveling the world and indulging her own whims. If Violet had any doubts about their differences before, they were certainly dispelled now.

THIRTEEN

2:00 P.M.

3 DAYS, 12 HOURS, 20 MINUTES

HINNAH

HINNAH DUCKED INTO a corridor away from other passengers and toward the smell of freshly cooked chicken. Her stomach rumbled. It had been hours since the last time she'd had a meal, and she had certainly never had a meal the likes of first-class passengers' on the *Titanic*. She would be lying if she said she wasn't at least a little curious about what the tastes of the rich were like, but she was more focused on her task than anything else. The kitchen was where she would find room assignments; she was sure of it.

Hinnah knew the kitchen must be busy, especially since it was just past lunchtime. But even at its busy hours, she couldn't simply barge in unnoticed. She wasn't dressed as kitchen staff.

Instead, she waited by a secluded corner of the corridor for a few moments, just until a steward came by rolling a cart with empty plates and dishes on top. She didn't have much time to make her decision. The next moment, the steward was passing her by, his tired eyes focused on the doors to the kitchen up ahead. Hinnah leaned forward until she was tucked right at the bottom of the cart, next to unopened bottles of wine and empty glasses stacked on top of each other.

The trolley rattled on, but the more time that passed, the louder Hinnah's surroundings seemed to become. Until suddenly, Hinnah seemed to be submerged right into the midst of a kind of hustle and bustle she hadn't really known before. She could hear the low rumblings of people speaking and the shouts of orders being given out. The sizzle of something being cooked and the clinking of cutlery. It was warm here as well, far warmer than it had been out on the deck with the fresh sea air.

Hinnah tried to ignore all that. Instead, she parted the cloth that hid her from view and glanced at the lively kitchen around her. Surely, there must be some kind of a passenger list here. How else would the stewards serve first-class passengers their tea and pastries in the morning?

She took a moment to really study the kitchen. It wasn't a particularly large area, but it was divided into several stations. There were people preparing the food in different stations: those who were cleaning and chopping, and those who were cooking. To another side, the dishes were being washed in rapid succession. And then, right near Hinnah, servers were slipping in and out with rolling carts. If anyone here had a passenger list, this had to be where it was stored.

Just as a server left the kitchen, Hinnah ducked out of her hiding place as quick as a mouse. She knew that at least for a few moments, she could disappear into the disarray of this place without anybody noticing. But if she was here for too long, she would certainly draw attention. There were notes spread out on a counter by the door, but most of them were scribbled orders in various handwriting that Hinnah could barely make out. Used lists that were ready to be thrown away. Hinnah pulled at the drawer right below the counter. And there it was. A bundle of loose papers that contained names, room numbers, and breakfast requests.

Hinnah glanced up and around her. But everybody was too focused on getting lunch out to the passengers. She still had at least a few minutes—or so she hoped. She quickly thumbed through the list, scanning each of the names. Thomas Andrews *had* to be here, she thought, feeling her chest tighten with each name that wasn't his. Until finally, there it was: *Thomas Andrews: Room A-36.*

As Hinnah climbed up to the A deck, she attempted to exude that natural confidence that Josefa and Violet seemed to have, where they could blend into any space without much of an effort.

Of course, it was a lot more difficult to fit in when Hinnah's brown skin immediately set her apart from almost everybody in her vicinity. It had always been true in Dublin, and it was true on this ship.

Hinnah could tell she had entered first class the moment she stepped foot inside. The corridor dividing the rooms was wide enough for half a dozen people to fit through. Lush red carpeting encased the floor, and even though the walls around them were a plain white, the lights in the corridor gave them a beautiful golden glow.

Hinnah tried to shake the shock of it off her. She had never quite been in a place like this before, but she knew that fitting in meant she couldn't look impressed. Let alone awestruck.

Hinnah didn't have to examine the numbers of the cabins for long, because one of the bedrooms that lined the top of the staircase read *A-36* in gold lettering.

Hinnah stepped closer, leaning her ear in to listen for any sound coming from inside the room. She could hear the low hum of the ship's engine, the tinkering of workers, the voices of people in the distance . . . but no noise coming from inside the door. She thought for a moment about the instructions Josefa had given her. Whatever she got from here, she would need to return fast. But if she waited for Emilie, she might not get another opportunity.

So, Hinnah stepped forward and tried the handle of the door, but it was locked. She wasn't surprised. She stood back for a moment, taking the door in once more.

It was constructed with dark wood, and a golden handle matched the gold lettering carved onto it. It was taller than the doors she had seen in the second-class cabins, and the top of the door was lined with what appeared to be glass.

Hinnah reached up on her tiptoes and touched the glass. It was cool on her fingertips, and when pushed, it opened up to let air out. It was a transom dividing the door from the ceiling. It was a narrow space—definitely not built for a person.

Hinnah glanced around the corridor. She could hear noise

coming from the cabins surrounding her, but there was nobody here to see her. She chanced a quick glance down the stairs. There was a couple slowly climbing up, their arms linked together. Hinnah guessed she had one or two minutes until they reached the top.

This might be her only chance. She could see no other way about it.

On her tiptoes once more, Hinnah reached the bottom of the transom—where wood met glass. She pulled herself up slowly until her entire torso was through the narrow gap. It was a close fit, but she managed to pull herself through, landing on the other side with a soft thump.

Hinnah paused for a moment to take in the first-class cabin. It was lavishly decorated—already different from the cabins she and the other girls were to stay in. Wood panels lined the wall, along with intricately patterned wallpaper. The double bed to one side of the room was the largest Hinnah had ever seen, but more impressive than its size were the ruffled hems of its bedsheets and the thick white damask blanket that adorned the bed. If Hinnah didn't know that this was a cabin in a ship, she would be convinced from the decor that she had in fact slipped into the home of some French aristocrat.

Shaking her head, Hinnah got to work. There were papers spread out all over the room. As soon as she glanced at them, she knew she had arrived at the right cabin. There was far too much information about ships and shipbuilding for this room to not belong to Mr. Andrews. But there were papers everywhere:

on top of the bed and the small desk that overlooked the port-hole. Hinnah leafed through them all as fast as she possibly could.

She didn't think Josefa would be particularly interested in the mechanics of shipbuilding, so she pushed all that to the side.

"Come on, come on . . . ," Hinnah mumbled to herself.

Finally, at the very bottom of the papers on the desk, she found a floor plan of the ship. She paused for a moment to study it. This place was even more intricate than she had thought before.

Approaching footsteps stopped Hinnah in her tracks. Fear settled into her bones.

But Hinnah didn't have time to panic. She rolled up the floor plan. Unraveling the ribbon from her own hair, she tied it up quickly, before pressing herself against the side of the door. The footsteps neared the cabin, and Hinnah's breath hitched. If Andrews came in here, Hinnah wasn't sure she would be able to sneak out unseen.

But the footsteps didn't slow down as they neared the cabin. Instead, they sped up and then slowly faded away into the distance.

Hinnah let out a breath of relief, but she knew she might not have long until Thomas Andrews's return. She pulled the door of the cabin open and cast her gaze around to ensure that nobody was waiting for her before stepping outside.

FOURTEEN

---

3 DAYS, 11 HOURS, 50 MINUTES
EMILIE

EMILIE WANTED TO re-create the marvel of the *Titanic*. As if anyone could do that. Least of all her, she thought with a sigh as she traced a finger over the delicate wallpaper. She wanted to study every inch of this beautiful vessel, commit it to memory. She hadn't been able to create anything worthwhile in too long, but she wanted to remember this place for the day that she could again. If that day ever came.

She had already sent a message to her father's friend in Haiti about securing her lodging there, and saying that she had questions about her mother and her family that needed answers. With her share of the money from the *Rubaiyat*, Emilie would finally be able to connect with her Haitian roots—with the family she had never known. She would learn about the place where she was born, not just through her father's eyes, but through her own. And she would learn of her mother from more than the old letters she had left behind and the stories her father loved to tell.

But the thought of the *Rubaiyat* lodged a rock right in her stomach. To see the *Rubaiyat*, to hold it in her hand and admire it for everything that it was, for its craftsmanship, creativity, the magic held within its pages, that was one thing. However it was something quite different to steal it out of the hands of those it belonged to. To see only the value of it after it was torn apart, to use it for the jewels that had been carefully embedded within it.

Emilie didn't have time to keep worrying about her dilemma, though, because a moment later, Josefa came around the corner. She had pulled her dark brown hair up into a bun, and though it helped her fit into these surroundings, it made her look unlike herself. When Josefa's gaze landed on Emilie, her eyes lighting up, Emilie tried to ignore the warmth in her cheeks.

"Did you send your message?" she asked, stepping closer. Emilie wasn't sure why, but her heart sped up at Josefa's sudden closeness. She wanted to believe it was because she had not expected to run into Josefa now, but she wasn't sure if she did believe that.

"Yes," she replied. "Though I'm not sure when it'll be delivered. There are already so many telegrams being sent through."

"No doubt recounting the beauty of this ship," Josefa said wryly.

"Did you manage to get your parchments and pens?" Emilie asked, remembering that's what Josefa had set out to do.

"Not yet. It's . . . a little too easy to get lost around here." There was a wide-eyed wonder in Josefa's face.

She turned around and began marching up the corridor like

she owned the whole ship. "Coming?" she called over her shoulder a moment later.

"I . . . sure," Emilie called back, before shuffling forward to catch up with Josefa. Emilie wasn't sure how she felt accompanying Josefa to steal from the ship's stock. She had had some desperately bad days since her father's passing, and she knew that it wouldn't be long until the rest of her money was used up. But in all her plans for her future, she had never imagined theft would be a part of it. She had envisioned a job, maybe as a teacher or secretary; though it was difficult to find a decent job as a Black woman in Europe, especially one without the protection of her father.

"Have you always done this?" Emilie asked now, curiosity getting the best of her. Josefa turned her head slightly to raise a questioning eyebrow, so Emilie added, "Been a thief."

Josefa quickly glanced around, like she was afraid someone was eavesdropping on their conversation. But nobody was paying attention to them, so Josefa continued leading them forward. "Not always, no."

"So, why did you start?" Emilie pressed.

"Well . . . ," Josefa began slowly with a sigh. "I suppose . . . I stumbled into it. And then I liked it, so I kept doing it."

"So, you do it because it's fun?"

"Everybody needs a hobby," Josefa said, turning to Emilie with a grin.

"Most people's hobbies are things like reading, or riding horses, or . . ."

"Painting," Josefa finished off for her. "Like you. Well, painting is to you as thieving is to me." She paused for a moment in her tracks. Like she expected Emilie to counter that somehow. To deny any truth in it. But Emilie was still trying to wrap her head around that idea: that painting and thievery could have anything in common. One was art . . . the other criminal.

"I've been getting a feel for this place," Josefa said, changing the subject and striding forward once more. "Discreetly, obviously."

"Obviously." Emilie wasn't sure if Josefa knew what being discreet meant.

"So, I've managed to get a look at the second-class cabins," Josefa said, peering around them. Emilie could hear rumblings of sounds coming from everywhere. Murmurs of voices from the cabins surrounding them, the clanking of crews at work, even a low moan of music floating in from somewhere.

"I don't think I've been through here yet, though." Josefa sharply turned a corner until they were on a spacious landing with a rush of people flitting around. A staircase in the middle of the room spiraled toward the upper deck.

The music was louder here, and Emilie's gaze strayed toward the people who climbed up the stairs. Their laughter and cheer seemed to take up more space, somehow more carefree than the rest of the passengers Emilie had encountered. They were draped in expensive clothes and jewelry. The women wore dresses that glittered when they caught the light, and even the men had suits with intricate buttons and gold watches strapped to their wrists.

But it was the staircase that really caught Emilie's eye. She had never seen anything quite like it. It seemed to be shaped like a bell, curving up toward the second floor. The banister was a work of art unlike anything Emilie had seen before, with its wood carved into a pattern Emilie couldn't make out from this distance.

"Upstairs?" Emilie asked.

"I think that's first class," Josefa said. When Emilie gazed back at Josefa, there was a twinkle in her eyes. "I don't think we should risk that . . . yet." It was the *yet* that made Emilie's stomach twist with worry.

"This way." As Josefa wove past people, Emilie tried her best to keep up. Around the staircase and to a set of plain double doors.

"I think we should go in there," Josefa leaned in to whisper. "No fancy guests in sight."

Emilie tried to ignore her nerves. "There might be workers. Sailors . . . I don't know." Emilie looked down at herself. The dress she wore was plain. It certainly wasn't fit for a first-class passenger, but she doubted anybody would believe she was a worker on this ship either.

"We won't get caught." Josefa shrugged, as if not getting caught was simply a matter of willpower. "Trust me."

Emilie didn't get a chance to reply before Josefa pushed the door open and strode inside. Emilie glanced back at the crowd behind them, before creeping behind Josefa into a dimly lit narrow corridor.

Josefa nudged open the door to the room nearest to them, but it was just a narrow bathroom. She shook her head, undeterred, and proceeded to the next door. Emilie stepped past her, trying the door on the other side of the corridor. At first, the door wouldn't budge as she pulled on the knob. Emilie stepped back, wondering if it was locked.

"Did you find anything?" Josefa asked, appearing beside her.

"It's locked," Emilie said.

"Something important must be in here, then." Josefa seemed alight with excitement as she reached for the doorknob and gave it a tug. The door gave a shudder, but it was definitely locked.

Josefa didn't seem bothered by that. She pulled something out from her pockets—it looked like a metallic hook—and began to jiggle it inside the keyhole.

There was nobody in this little corridor but the two of them. Still, Emilie could feel her body tense.

"Just give me . . . one . . . more . . . second." At her last word, a click sounded. Josefa shot Emilie a grin and pulled the door open. "Ta-da!" She took a little bow, as if this was all a performance to her.

There was almost something endearing about it. Emilie could see the appeal of it all right then, beside Josefa—of a kind of life she had never known or envisioned before. And she thought maybe it was because of Josefa, because it would mean being by her side, experiencing the thrill of it all. Emilie tried to put that thought out of her head. Instead, she stepped into the room, side by side with Josefa. The room in front of her was littered with unmarked boxes.

"This must be it!" Josefa exclaimed. "I'm sure we can find what we need here."

Emilie pulled open one box only to find it filled to the brim with cigarette cartons. Another held needles and thread.

"What about this?" she asked.

Josefa tilted her head up and observed Emilie with a curious look. "That could come in useful." It was clearly not her top priority. "The parchment and pens should be our first priority. When Hinnah comes back from her trip into Andrews's room, you'll need them to make copies. And for later too. Nobody pulls off a mission like this without having to jot down a few things."

Of course, Emilie had no idea what a mission like this needed. She slipped the needle and thread into the pockets of her petticoat before sifting through more of the boxes. She came upon everything from food and drink to rope and twine.

"Parchment and pens!" Josefa exclaimed from a deep corner of the room.

"So . . . why did you want me on this mission?" Emilie asked after a moment.

"Because of your artistic talent!" Josefa replied a little too fast, a little too brightly. "Nobody else I know possesses that kind of skill."

"Why did you think I would say yes?" Emilie pressed.

"Why wouldn't you say yes?" Josefa asked.

"I'm serious," Emilie said. "It's . . . not like we'd ever even spoken before."

Josefa's smile flickered. Something in her expression shifted, and she stepped closer. Her facade of pride and confidence had been replaced with a strange vulnerability. "Well, just because we'd never spoken didn't mean I hadn't noticed you," she said. "And . . . I had always hoped that . . ."

Josefa stopped short at the sound of approaching footsteps. Emilie turned toward the door with wide eyes.

But Josefa didn't seem fazed.

"They're probably just going past," she reassured Emilie. But no sooner had the words left Josefa's lips than they heard the doorknob twisting.

Emilie's breath caught in her throat. They were completely exposed in this place. It was an open room with nowhere to hide. They would be caught immediately. The mission would be thwarted before it had even begun and—

Josefa grabbed hold of Emilie and pulled her against a shelf that stood nearby, pressed a little too close to the wall. But Josefa and Emilie somehow managed to squeeze into whatever space there was between the shelf and wall.

"They'll see us," Emilie whispered. If anybody walked toward the end of the room, they would just have to look right to spot them.

"We'll be fine," Josefa said. There was so much certainty in her voice that Emilie swallowed down her fear. There was nothing else to do anyway as the door swung open with a creak.

Footsteps circled around the room, and Emilie could hear the sound of the boxes being pawed through.

She pressed her eyes closed and tried to ignore her increasing pulse.

"You okay in there?" a deep voice called from a distance.

"Just looking for a smoke." This voice, gruff and older, was a little too close for comfort. "Want one?"

"Like you even have to ask," the first voice said. There was a low laugh. More rustling around the boxes.

Emilie peeked her eyes open, only to find Josefa's brilliant blue eyes peering right into her. She was so close that Emilie could smell the scent of the sea on her—tinted with the aroma of jasmine. She was so close that Emilie could feel how her body expanded and contracted with every breath she took. She was so close that she was sure Josefa could hear her pounding heart—except now it was beating fast for a completely different reason. If Emilie or Josefa, or both, leaned forward just a few inches, there would be no space left between them at all.

The door closed with a thump, the sound reverberating around the room. Josefa and Emilie stood there for a moment longer—a moment too long. But then Josefa slipped out of the tiny space. She tucked a strand of hair back into her bun and adjusted her dress, though there was nothing wrong with it.

"We should probably get back before anybody else comes in here," Josefa said, not meeting Emilie's gaze. Her voice a little breathless.

Emilie cleared her throat. "Yes, definitely."

They gathered up the supplies they had found into their arms—as many as they could manage—and ducked out of the storage room.

All the while, Emilie kept thinking about what had passed between them mere minutes ago. And what Josefa had been about to confess.

FIFTEEN

---

3 DAYS, 12 HOURS, 5 MINUTES

VIOLET

VIOLET WAS GLAD she'd ditched Emilie after leaving the wireless operator's cabin. She didn't need an amateur weighing her down, not when she had her eyes trained on her goal.

Josefa had told Violet about the man who was in possession of the *Rubaiyat*. But Violet still had to figure out where he could be found and how to coax the necessary information out of him.

She paused by the entrance to the second-class decks. A clerk in uniform stood outside the doors, beaming at passengers slipping by. Surely if anybody could give her the information she needed, it would be a clerk.

Violet brushed a stray lock of hair away from her face and pasted on a smile.

"Excuse me?"

The man glanced up to meet Violet's eyes. "Yes, madam? How can I help you?"

"I'm terribly sorry, but . . . I'm supposed to meet with Mr.

Lake, but I can't seem to find him anywhere, and, well, I'm not sure where he's staying," she said.

"Mr. Clayton Lake?" the clerk asked. Violet tried not to let her excitement show as she nodded.

"That's the one."

The clerk frowned. "He's at the café with some colleagues," he said, eyeing Violet with some suspicion.

"Well, of course he is," she said casually. "That's why I've been running around this ship searching for him, because I'm late. They won't wait for me, and . . ." Violet heaved a sigh. "My father will be so disappointed if I miss this. He has important business with Mr. Lake and . . . I'm really supposed to speak to him. He's a busy man, and I was so lucky to get this opportunity to dine with him."

The clerk raised an eyebrow, studying Violet closely. "I can let Mr. Lake know that your father was searching for him. His name would be Mr. . . ."

Violet stifled her annoyance with the softest smile she could muster, one that befitted a lady of her stature. She was growing increasingly tired of this idea that women like her could not conduct business or travel alone. If only they knew Violet had been fending for herself since she was a child.

"Simon Auclaire of the Pessac wine estate. He is figuring out important affairs at home," Violet replied. "He arranged for me to handle his business while on this ship. However, if you can't help me, I'll find someone who can." Violet took a step back. "Of course . . . if I miss this meeting, I will have to write to my father about the man who kept me from it. I don't think he, or Mr. Lake, will be very happy about that." She took another step back from him, her expression brightening.

The clerk stepped forward as if to stop Violet in her tracks. "There'll be no need for that, madam," he said. "Mr. Lake is at the Café Parisien with some clients and his assistant. I didn't realize that . . . anyone else was supposed to join them, or that you were Mr. Auclaire's daughter."

A steady stream of panic accompanied the clerk's words, like he was afraid of the power that Violet held over him.

"Thank you." She gave a firm nod of her head before pushing past him.

As Violet made her way to the restaurant, she glanced down at herself. She was still dressed up as an heiress, in her cream-colored dress and her feathered hat. The clerk had said Mr. Lake was having lunch with *clients*. Somehow, Violet didn't think Sylviane Auclaire was the right person for this job.

If even the clerk had questioned her right to dine with them as a young woman, she doubted Mr. Clayton Lake and his companions would be any more accepting—even if she was the heiress to a French wine estate.

Violet didn't have to search long to find the tiny storage room beside the Café Parisien, filled with waitress uniforms. She quickly changed into a black dress and white apron and stepped outside looking as innocent as possible.

The outfit was itchier than anything she had worn and had a distinctively musty smell, like it had been stored away for a little too long. Most of Violet's clothes were worn down and stitched back together with her own fingers, but they certainly did not itch or smell like this. Still, with a grin, Violet slipped into the Café Parisien.

The café was already full and bustling with life. Wicker furniture lined the room, each table filled with first-class guests who were too busy drinking, eating, and laughing to notice Violet's presence. On the far side of the café, wide windows overlooked the vast blue ocean and clear skies in front of them. Violet had never visited Paris, but with the low sound of soothing music and the slight accent of the waiters, she felt like she had stepped into the city.

Violet slipped in between the tables and chairs, keeping her eyes and ears peeled. She had no idea what Mr. Clayton Lake looked like, and it was difficult to pick out anybody among this sea of faces. All the men wore the same kind of suits, and all the women wore elegant dresses.

As Violet wove in and out, exchanging polite nods, floating almost invisibly among the rich, she picked up tidbits of conversations.

". . . expecting five hundred guests at the wedding. Five hundred! Can you believe that?"

". . . and tried to convince me they were real. As if I don't know what real pearls look like."

Violet had to bite her tongue to keep from rolling her eyes. She tried not to think about all the girls in the boardinghouse struggling to make ends meet. Hinnah almost getting thrown out for making a livelihood. Violet barely having the money to support herself and her brother. While these people were rolling in riches and reveling in showing off their wealth.

Finally, she heard the words she had been searching for.

". . . entrusted with the *Rubaiyat*. Very trying business, but of course, we are the best at it."

Violet spotted the speaker almost immediately, sliding over to the edge of the café where a group of men sat huddled together. The man who was discussing the *Rubaiyat* had a pale, round face. Mr. Clayton Lake, Violet assumed. He smirked, as if the *Rubaiyat* were a prize he had won.

Not if she had anything to do with it.

Beside him sat a boy with a full head of brown curls, devouring his meal in a way that Violet had never seen someone wealthy eat. It was more the behavior of someone who had known leaner times.

As Violet took in the pair of them for a moment, she realized that she wasn't the only person who was out of place here. While Mr. Lake's lavish suit allowed him to blend in with the rest of his wealthy companions, the boy's suit set him apart. It looked as expensive as anybody else's in this café, but there was a worn quality about it. And it looked a little too big, like the suit hadn't been made for him at all.

Violet picked up a pitcher of water from a nearby table and stepped toward Mr. Lake's table gingerly. As close as she dared.

"Of course, it is as amazing as everyone says it is. Better, even. There's something new to admire about it every time I look at it, which is often. You can't have a prize like that in your possession and not be almost hypnotized by it. I've taken to reading one of Khayyam's marvelous poems every night." One of the other men at the table nodded sagely, as if he understood exactly what was being said about the *Rubaiyat*. This man's suit was perfectly tailored, and its buttons glinted gold when they caught the light.

Violet wondered if this other man was a buyer, or simply another person interested in the marvel of the *Rubaiyat*. Josefa had said that the *Rubaiyat* was supposed to be delivered to America for a buyer. That was why she had brought them here, because she thought nobody would miss it on this ship, not until they had reached their destination, at least. And by then, Josefa had assured them, it would be too late.

But maybe Josefa's information was wrong, and maybe they needed more than whatever replica Emilie could conjure up.

"Sir . . ." It was the boy who spoke, his voice deeper than Violet would have guessed. At first glance, he had looked much too young, almost drowning in his suit. But upon closer inspection, Violet realized that he must be the same age as her, if not older. Despite his youthful features, he was tall and gangly, and this close Violet could make out a prickle of stubble on his chin.

"August, please. This is business." Mr. Lake didn't even look at the boy. But the boy had turned slightly to glance at Violet.

She stepped even closer, beaming at the group of men. "Can

I get you gentlemen anything? A refill of water?"

Mr. Lake pushed forward his own empty glass, barely glancing up at her. Even the boy next to him seemed to have lost interest as he tucked into his food ravenously once more.

Violet leaned forward, slowly pouring water into Mr. Lake's glass.

"So they must be paying handsomely for it," the other man continued, as if Violet weren't there at all.

"Of course." Mr. Lake nodded with a small smile. "And this is why I've been entrusted with bringing it to New York. I have experience. It's not the first time I've transported something of such value."

"If I were to let you auction off some of our valuables . . . ," the man continued solemnly, "I would have to know your safety precautions. More than your desire to read poetry every night."

Mr. Lake laughed like this was the funniest joke he had ever heard. He even glanced at August, who let out a little bit of a laugh—not quite befitting his stature.

"Of course, I had to ensure that it was protected," Mr. Lake said. "It's tucked away in my cabin in an unbreakable safe."

"As unbreakable as this ship is unsinkable," the boy pitched in this time, swallowing down the last of his food.

"It was my assistant's suggestion, yes." Mr. Lake glanced at the boy with some admiration flickering in his eyes. "August Frazier . . . he's been a great asset since I hired him. A great asset to this job."

Violet silently stepped to the other side of the table, filling up every glass in sight and trying to stay the invisible waitress.

"And if, say, someone else wanted to take a look at this rare *Rubaiyat*?" one of the men at the table leaned forward to ask. "Would that be off the table?"

"That can be arranged," Mr. Lake said, smiling.

"Excuse me, waitress!" The call from the table on the right seemed to break the spell. Suddenly, Mr. Lake seemed all too aware of Violet. His eyes were sharp as they took her in.

She didn't drop the pretense—she couldn't. Instead, she let the smile flicker on her lips before she shuffled toward the next table. As graceful as any waitress could be.

As Violet took the orders of this new set of passengers, she tried to keep an ear on the conversation between Lake and his dining fellows, but it was as if he were all too aware now that they were in a public place. Their conversation fell to a hush, and their table seemed closed off. Violet knew she couldn't easily slip back in. Not when Lake had noticed her. Had *seen* her.

She itched to learn more about the *Rubaiyat*, but she knew she had lost her chance.

So, after compiling the orders from the next table, Violet slipped past Lake and his guests. Past the crowd at the café and all the way outside. But all throughout, she couldn't help but feel a prickle on her back. As if someone was watching her.

But when she turned around to try to figure out who it was, there were too many people. All of them uninterested in a waitress going about her day.

Violet shook her head. Maybe it was simply paranoia from

Mr. Lake catching sight of her before she had all the information she needed. But as she slipped out the door of the café, she finally spotted a head of curls ducking out of her sight.

Lake's assistant: August Frazier.

He had been watching her.

SIXTEEN

3 DAYS, 11 HOURS, 20 MINUTES
EMILIE

EMILIE WAS STILL sorting through the supplies that they had taken from the storage room when the door to her cabin burst open. She jumped to a stand. But it wasn't the matron—she supposed Matron Wallis probably didn't have permission to barge into passengers' cabins, at least not in second class. It was only Hinnah, breathing hard but looking strangely triumphant.

"Where's Josefa?" she asked.

"Not here," Emilie said, before her eyes landed on the rolled-up paper that Hinnah was clasping in her hands. "What's that?"

"Floor plans of the ship." A grin spread across Hinnah's lips as she stumbled up to the table in the middle of the room and began to unfurl it.

"What?" Emilie leaped forward, only to find zigzagging lines detailing the ship in front of her. "Wow." She turned to Hinnah with an admiring gaze. "This must have been difficult to get."

Emilie didn't know much about Hinnah. Just that there were many rumors about what Hinnah got up to when she wasn't at the circus. She had never believed any of them. Hinnah seemed little more than a timid girl trying to make sense of circumstances she'd never expected herself to be in. Not unlike Emilie. But now Emilie felt like she was seeing a new side of Hinnah. Someone more than the quiet, meek girl who seemed afraid to occupy space. Someone who had talent beyond what Emilie had ever really imagined.

"We need to make a copy," Hinnah said. "I think Mr. Andrews will miss this if it's not back with him soon." Emilie nodded and turned to the parchments and pens that she and Josefa had taken from the ship's storage.

"How long do you think it's going to take?" Hinnah's voice was tinged with anxiety.

"How long do you think we have?" Emilie asked.

"I'm not sure. He's probably dining in one of the restaurants, but it's well past lunchtime by now."

If Emilie knew anything about the men in first class, it was that they enjoyed their long lunches. She remembered a time when she and her father would spend their lunches with important people, and while he spoke about wondrous things like art and business, Emilie listened with rapt attention. Trying to soak up all the information that she could. Those lunches would last for hours.

But Emilie couldn't risk anything here.

"Give me a few minutes," she said, taking a deep breath as she pulled a chair close to the table.

It wasn't easy work. If only because it wasn't the kind of work that Emilie was used to doing. It was much more meticulous than painting. She had to get down every detail precisely. If she missed anything at all, she was sure that it would come back to hurt them later.

Still, there was something strangely wonderful in the process of copying the floor plan, in studying something so intricate and detailed. For a little while, Emilie didn't feel that thick anxiety sitting in her stomach. She could almost forget about all the things that had been worrying her for the past few days.

It was easier to work fast without those worries. And soon, she was putting down her pens. She took one last look at the floor plan that Hinnah had given her and the one that she had created. There was nothing amiss; she was sure of it.

"Wow." Hinnah studied Emilie's work with wide-eyed appreciation. "You really are good."

Emilie bit back a smile and handed the floor plan back to Hinnah. "You'll be okay returning this by yourself? I could . . . accompany you, if you wanted." She wasn't sure how much help she could really provide, but she didn't like the thought of Hinnah putting herself at risk all alone.

"It'll be easy." Hinnah grinned, like she had done this a thousand times before. For all Emilie knew, she had.

"Okay . . ." Emilie sighed. "Just . . . be careful."

She watched as Hinnah slipped out of sight, her mind reeling back to Josefa all too easily. If Emilie was being honest with herself, it had been difficult to not think about her. Not just since their moment in the storage room, not just since Josefa asked her on this mission. But maybe from that first day the two of them had spotted each other.

It had been her first week in Dublin, and Emilie was still figuring out how to cope with her father not being a part of her life anymore. In those days, she made it her mission to go everywhere her father had once spoken of—like fulfilling this dream of his could somehow bring him back.

During one of her days walking around the city, Emilie had seen her: a flash of her dark brown hair. Her overconfident grin. The quick work of her hands as she slipped something out of a stranger's pocket and ducked out of sight. Then Emilie blinked, and Josefa was gone. Like she had never been there in the first place.

She had never seen anything like that before. Of course, there were pickpockets in Paris. There were pickpockets everywhere—but Emilie hadn't seen one at work like that before. And certainly not one who looked like Josefa.

Later, at the boardinghouse, Emilie spotted Josefa in the dining hall in deep conversation with Violet. For a moment, she had wondered if she was a figment of her imagination. But she wasn't—and the more Emilie asked around about her, the more she realized that the girl she had seen on the streets couldn't be anyone other than Josefa.

Emilie couldn't help but wonder how Josefa could always pull her out of her grief, show her a new way to life that she had never considered before. She had done it then on the streets of Dublin, and she was doing it now. She didn't even know it.

Emilie turned back to the copy of the plan she had made. Meticulously detailed and perfect, like nothing she had done in a long time. She reached up to touch the blue clip in her hair—a birthday present her father had given her years ago. He told her it had belonged to her mother, and in the paintings he created of her, it was always there, perfect against her dark brown curls. Having it with her was the only source of comfort Emilie had these days.

Except—it wasn't there.

Emilie glanced at her reflection in the mirror of the cabin, hoping that the hair clip was tangled in her curls. But it was nowhere.

Emilie had lost it.

She had lost her only connection to her parents.

SEVENTEEN

3 DAYS, 7 HOURS, 25 MINUTES

JOSEFA

BY THE TIME Josefa strode into their cabin after sundown, Violet, Hinnah, and Emilie were already there waiting.

"Well . . . how did it go?" she asked, glancing at each of her friends in turn. "Hinnah . . . did you manage to get into Thomas Andrews's room?"

Hinnah sat up straighter, a smile illuminating her face.

"I managed to find the floor plans to the *Titanic*."

"Brilliant!" Hinnah was almost glowing from Josefa's compliment when she turned to Emilie.

"And Emilie made a perfect copy."

Violet tucked a lock of hair away from her face. "I know where the *Rubaiyat* is."

Her statement obviously had the effect she intended, because a hush fell over the room.

"And you waited *this* long to tell us?" Josefa asked, stepping closer to Violet.

"It was off of your information," Violet said slowly. "Mr. Clayton Lake . . . and his assistant, August Frazier."

Josefa's fingers clenched into a fist, as if of their own accord. But she kept her face neutral. Even if blood was pounding in her ears just at the sound of that name.

"Go on," she encouraged with a nod.

"They were at the Café Parisien, having lunch with someone important, I suppose. Mr. Lake was a little too eager to let everyone know that he had the *Rubaiyat* in his possession."

Josefa frowned. "And . . . August?"

Violet met Josefa's eyes; something unreadable flickered there for a moment. Then she leaned back on the bed as if she hadn't found Josefa's question unusual. "Well, he's just an assistant, but he also seemed more . . . aware. He was paying attention to me."

Josefa's stomach clenched. She knew August was the kind of person who paid attention to even the minuscule things. But she didn't think he would notice Violet so quickly. Josefa could already see the thread of her carefully constructed plans coming undone, and she couldn't have that.

"You'll have to stay out of his way," Josefa said. "We don't know much about him, and if he gets even an inkling of what we're up to, it could ruin the entire mission," Josefa said.

"Don't worry; I wasn't planning on befriending him," Violet joked, but she seemed to be looking at Josefa a little too closely now.

"Where are they keeping the book?" Josefa pressed, changing the subject.

"Well, from what I could gather," Violet began slowly, her eyebrows drawn together in thought, "Mr. Lake is an auctioneer. You were right, he already has a buyer in America, but that doesn't stop him from having loose lips. He and his assistant seemed to want to impress. But . . . Mr. Lake said he has an unbreakable safe in his stateroom where he's keeping the *Rubaiyat*."

"How do we get inside?" The gears in Josefa's head were already turning. She slipped out her notebook and jotted down Violet's information. The breaking in was the easy part. It was the rest that always proved to be difficult. That was what required a thought-out plan, and people who could think on their feet too.

"Did you expect Lake to give me instructions on how to steal the *Rubaiyat*?" Violet asked, rolling her eyes. "There was only so much I could hear before they noticed me hovering."

"So we just have to figure out how to get into Lake's stateroom. We've done that before," Hinnah said. Josefa shot her a grin. Hinnah was right: they *had* broken in and out of places before. But the *Titanic* was full of people, and there was no way to simply run off with their loot. They had to be careful. Discreet.

"If we break in and Lake alerts someone . . . Wallis is already watching us. Can you imagine what would happen?" Emilie asked.

"Nothing is without its risks," Violet scoffed, glancing at Emilie with a frown. "But . . . don't worry, we won't have to break into the stateroom yet. Lake and Frazier are the only two people who have access to the *Rubaiyat*. And I think I know how we can get close to them."

When Josefa looked up and met Violet's gaze, there was a twinkle in her eyes.

"What did you have in mind?" Josefa pressed.

"If we can get an invitation to dine in first class . . ." Violet began. "That should get us close enough to them to figure out more."

Josefa nodded slowly, a plan taking shape in her head. Getting into first class *had* to be the first step. And she was sure once they were invited to dinner there, Josefa could get all the information she needed out of August.

"I'm sure Sylviane Auclaire could easily get invited to dinner in first class," Josefa said to Violet, her smile widening.

"I'm sure that she could," Violet agreed.

"What about us?" Hinnah asked, edging forward in her seat. This was one of the things Josefa loved about Hinnah—she was always keen to please, though she often tried not to show it.

"Well, the floor plans of the *Titanic* are going to be helpful," Josefa said, thinking aloud. "But we need an alternate way to get around the ship. If my research is right, we might be able to get around through the vents."

"I can have a look at the vents and see if we can travel through them," Hinnah said with a look of fierce determination.

Josefa's eyes drifted from Hinnah to Emilie. She tried to ignore the rise in her pulse as Emilie's brown eyes gazed into hers. Her mind was already flashing back to the storage room, where she and Emilie had been close enough to . . .

But she shook that thought out of her head before it could take ahold of her. Josefa had never really found the words to explain to anyone that her contempt for a life married to some man was less to do with *marriage* and more to do with the man. She had always assumed that it was one more thing that marked her as someone who would never belong in her family. She would have never dared speak the thought aloud to her parents, who were always more concerned with properness than anything else. But once she left her finishing school, she met enough women with an attraction to other women that Josefa didn't think it was the strangest thing about her. But somehow she doubted that she would get so lucky that Emilie had the same inclination for women as her.

There was no doubt in Josefa's mind that their shared moment in the storage room was only something she had built up in her head. That Josefa was the only one whose breath had caught in her throat at their closeness. Emilie thought of Josefa as a friend—if even that.

More important, Josefa had to remind herself that she needed Emilie for this mission to be successful. She couldn't succumb to whatever feelings she had developed for her over the course of the past few weeks. It was, after all, only superficial attraction.

"If I can get ahold of some images of the *Rubaiyat*, do you think you can begin making a copy?" she asked Emilie.

Emilie's face didn't give anything away as she nodded, keeping her gaze steadily on Josefa. She wondered for a moment if Emilie knew that Josefa's heart raced just at the sight of her. She broke off eye contact and nodded firmly. She had to focus on the task at hand. Feelings only ever got in the way.

"So then it's settled. Tomorrow, we'll be one step closer to the *Rubaiyat*."

Josefa stirred awake in the middle of the night, unsure of what had woken her up. But when she glanced around her cabin, she noticed that Emilie's bed was empty.

Josefa slipped out from under the covers and outside their cabin, spotting Emilie turning the corner ahead. It felt strange to follow behind her wordlessly—especially after what had happened between the two of them in the storage room. Though Josefa didn't really know what that was.

Instead, Josefa heaved a sigh and rushed forward, calling to Emilie as loudly as she could without drawing attention. "Emilie!"

After her fifth time calling her name, Emilie finally turned, her eyes wide at the sight of Josefa.

"What are you doing here?" she whispered.

"What are *you* doing here?" Josefa asked. "I thought I was the one with a penchant for sneaking out at all hours of the night."

Emilie almost smiled but seemed to hold back at the last minute. There was something strange about her expression now. Something unlike herself.

"I . . . lost something," she said finally with a sigh. "I've been trying to find it ever since I realized it was gone, but . . . I can't." Her voice wavered, and Josefa could see the sparkle of unshed tears in her eyes. She had never wanted to touch someone so badly before. To comfort her. She wanted to pull Emilie into her arms, to somehow make everything okay again.

But Josefa had never been good at those sorts of things.

"What did you lose?" she asked. Emilie reached up to touch her hair before answering, as if by instinct. And Josefa knew.

"It was this hair clip. It's . . . silly, but . . . it was a present from my father, and he told me it used to belong to my mother when she was still alive. It's really the only thing I have left of my family now. And I don't know what happened to it. I've been all around the ship, and it's just . . . gone." She shook her head like she already knew it was hopeless.

"We'll find it," Josefa said. "Trust me, I'm very good at finding things." Which wasn't technically true—Josefa was good at "finding" things that didn't belong to her.

"I don't even remember if I had it when we boarded the ship. What if it's back in Dublin? Or on the train? Or Queenstown? Or—"

Josefa leaned forward this time, trying to ignore the flutter in her stomach as she brushed back a strand of Emilie's hair. "You had it right before we boarded the ship," she said. "I remember. So it must be here. And I *will* find it for you."

Emilie did smile this time, though it was a watery one. It tugged at the strings of Josefa's heart, and just like that, she knew that she would scour the entire ship for Emilie's hair clip if she had to.

EIGHTEEN

2 DAYS, 14 HOURS, 50 MINUTES
VIOLET

VIOLET EXAMINED HERSELF carefully in the mirror of the cabin. While she'd had trouble falling asleep last night, none of her fatigue showed on her face this morning. She wore a low-cut red blouse and a plain black skirt. It might not be the fanciest thing that Violet owned, but the cut of the outfit and the way the colors complemented Violet's pale white skin had always proved to be a popular combination. Violet wore it only when she wished to draw attention to herself.

She stood, and after taking one final look at her made-up face, Violet turned—only to hear a ripping sound pierce the air.

"Oh no." Emilie, who had been watching her get ready, was on her feet before Violet could even glance down. The bottom of her skirt, caught on the chair, had ripped when Violet turned.

"I'm sure you can wear something else," Emilie said as she examined the rip in the cloth. It was deep, traveling almost to Violet's thigh. It was unsalvageable. "Or I can fix it."

"You can fix it?" Violet asked.

Emilie didn't wait for her to say more. She dug into a box of items she and Josefa had lifted from the storage room yesterday. After a moment, she pulled out a needle and a spool of thread.

Violet knew she probably shouldn't be impressed as Emilie quickly sewed up the tear in her skirt. These were the kind of skills that any woman of Emilie's stature was expected to know. Simple skills. Feminine skills.

Skills that Violet had never learned because of her dysfunctional family. And because she had left home so early.

"You know, you're really very good at this," Emilie mumbled as she worked.

It was a compliment, but it sent a prickle of annoyance through Violet all the same.

"I have to be. If I want to survive."

Emilie must not have been accustomed to hearing the blunt truth, because her face fell. But Violet wasn't here to protect the feelings of a rich girl who was finally getting a taste of the real world, even if the sight of Emilie's expression shifting from warm happiness to cold disappointment unsettled her stomach.

At least Emilie was quick to learn, because a minute later, she had rearranged her expression into something resembling a smile, though it didn't quite reach her eyes. "Well, let's hear your French accent, then."

Violet chuckled before putting on a ridiculous mockery of

an accent that sent Emilie into a fit of giggles.

"You're not winning anybody over with that," Emilie said, once she had finally settled down. She was slowly pulling the needle in and out through the skirt, and Violet could feel the ghost of Emilie's touch on her skin.

"Well, I'll just use you as my inspiration," Violet said. "Though you don't have much of a French accent at all, do you?"

"I haven't been in France for a while now. And . . . well, when you're a bit different, you have to do what you can to fit in as fast as you can."

"Different?"

Emilie paused her work for a moment. She glanced up to meet Violet's gaze with a raised eyebrow.

"Oh." Violet hadn't given much thought to Emilie being Black. She supposed it must mean that she stood out from most everyone in Dublin, and now on this ship. She didn't know how that might affect her. Violet had always assumed that Emilie's father's wealth and status meant that she must have spent her life wanting for nothing. Unlike her.

But Violet wondered if they had more in common than she had realized.

"After my father died, I didn't really have anybody else to lean on," Emilie said slowly, pulling the thread through the end of Violet's skirt. "His family didn't approve of his marriage with my mother. She passed away in Haiti when I was just a baby. He brought me to France because he thought it would give me more opportunities, a better life. And it did, I suppose. But . . . I always knew I was different." Emilie heaved a sigh.

"I traveled around Europe after he passed away . . . to Switzerland, then Portugal. To study art. And it made me realize more than ever that having my father there used to be a kind of protection that I didn't really have anymore." Emilie pressed her lips together, as if she were recalling unpleasant memories of her time there. "And then the boardinghouse in Ireland . . . I felt a little more myself there. Everyone seemed too busy worrying about themselves to worry much about me. Still, the French accent just accentuated my differences."

Violet nodded. "I had to lose my Croatian accent too. People don't always take kindly to differences."

"No, they don't." Emilie stood up, dusting herself off. "There," she said simply, meeting Violet's gaze with a smile. And it was as if they reached some kind of understanding.

Maybe Emilie wasn't up to the tasks that the rest of them were. Maybe she couldn't charm or outwit people at the drop of a hat. But Violet was beginning to realize that her skills were necessary during this mission. And she felt a strange surge of protectiveness, too, as she took Emilie in. The same kind of protectiveness that thoughts of Marko filled her with. After all, everybody needed someone to look out for them.

Violet wove through the crowd on the A deck, nodding politely at passersby. All the while, her eyes searched for someone. She wasn't sure who she was looking for yet, but she had always been good at picking out the kind of people who were a little too gullible. She needed someone who was young, but not too young. Someone with bright eyes and keen interest. Someone eager to impress.

Finally, her eyes landed on a young man who looked to be in his early twenties. He was carefully listening to the group of much older men around him. But while they looked completely at ease with each other, he seemed a little out of place. Possibly because of his age, Violet guessed.

She made her way toward the railings at the top of the deck, leaning against the metal and taking in the horizon where the sky bled into the ocean. Turning her head slightly, she waited until the man caught her eye. Violet smiled wryly before she quickly glanced away once more.

The man, or boy really, was exactly what Violet had hoped he would be. Younger than his peers and obviously searching for someone like Violet—someone he could show off for. Because only a few minutes later, he had excused himself and made his way toward Violet. She studied him from the corner of her eyes. He was tall, though not much taller than Violet herself. He had a strong jaw and a sharp nose, though neither of those things made him look less boyish among his company of older men. His fair hair was parted perfectly in the middle, and he wore a white shirt and black coat, which were both perfectly pressed.

"It's a beautiful day, isn't it?" he said with a distinctly American accent. As he rested his elbow right beside Violet's hands, she had to stop herself from pulling away from the railing.

Instead, she offered him another shy smile.

"It is," she agreed, turning away to look out at the horizon once more.

"I'm Peter Fischer," he offered. "I don't think I saw you at dinner last night. I know I would have noticed."

Violet let out a little laugh that sounded unlike herself. She knew it was the kind of laugh men fawned over: high-pitched and girlish. "There are hundreds of people on this ship. I hardly think you would have noticed *me*."

"I've noticed you now."

Violet wished she could blush on command. Instead, she settled for a furtive glance in his direction that she hoped conveyed that she was flustered.

"You know, I'm rather well-traveled; I've been all around the world, met all kinds of women. Still, I noticed you here on this ship." Peter volunteered this information before Violet could even ask. There was a grin on his lips, and he had edged a little too close to her.

"This is my first time traveling somewhere so far away," Violet said. "I can't imagine going all over the world."

"My father is a businessman, and I'm helping him. His work requires a lot of travel, and it's why we were in the British Isles. And now finally we're on our way back home."

"And I'm sure you'll be off on another adventure soon after," Violet said with a dreamy sigh. "It must be so wonderful."

"It is pretty great," Peter said, glancing back at Violet curiously. "I don't think I caught your name?"

"Sylviane Auclaire," Violet offered.

"And you're traveling to New York all on your own?"

"Not quite," she replied. "I'm traveling with some of my friends."

"Do you have business in New York?"

"I'm hoping to continue my studies there. My father . . . he owns a wine estate in Pessac." *That* seemed to get his attention, even more than Violet's playful coyness. He stood up straighter, turning almost completely to face Violet. She pretended that she hadn't noticed his change in demeanor. Instead, she looked ahead, as if speaking about being heiress to a French wine estate was nothing out of the ordinary for her.

"My father wanted me to stay and finish my studies in France. But I've always dreamed of traveling to New York. He has to finish up his affairs before he can join me there."

"Pessac . . . that must be beautiful." Peter couldn't keep his admiration out of his voice.

"Our wine is simply the best in all of France. And there is nothing more beautiful than the vineyards of Pessac," Violet said. "The only place that perhaps comes close to rivaling it is Italy, and its rolling hills."

Peter hummed thoughtfully at that.

"You don't agree?" Violet asked in mock horror.

"Italy is certainly stunning," Peter agreed slowly. "But can it rival the beauty of Spain? Or Greece? Perhaps *that* is what can rival your beautiful vineyards of Pessac."

"I may not be as well traveled as you, Mr. Fischer, but I can assure you Spain and Greece do not comes close to our beautiful Pessac, and on that I will remain unmoved," Violet teased.

"I do think I can change your mind," Peter said. "Though perhaps I'll require a little aid with that." He glanced over at the group of men he had been with, none of whom seemed to have noticed his absence.

"Sadly for you, I have promised my companions I will be joining them soon," Violet said, leaning away from the railing and Peter.

"Oh . . ." Peter's expression darkened. "I had really hoped we could continue our conversation. I can't let you go around believing it is only Italy that can rival your beloved France in beauty. Perhaps I will see you at dinner tonight?"

Violet tried to keep the excitement from her voice as she heaved a deep sigh.

"Well, second-class passengers aren't invited to dine with first-class passengers. So, I don't see how that would be possible."

"Your father did not get you a first-class suite?" Peter asked.

"He thought it would be better for me and my companions to share cabins in second class, under Matron Wallis's watchful eye. She knows my mother."

Peter grinned, all his perfectly white teeth showing. "Ah, I understand how fathers can be. But don't worry. You will be *my* guest at dinner."

Violet hesitated, glancing down at her feet instead of up at Peter. "I'm not sure. I wouldn't really know anyone there other than you."

"You can bring one of your friends," Peter offered up on his own.

"Are you sure?" Violet asked, glancing up to meet his eyes inquiringly. "I don't want to put you out."

"Of course," Peter said. "I look forward to continuing our conversation."

He reached for her hand and brushed a kiss against the back of it. Violet smiled through the ordeal like she genuinely enjoyed the admiration of strange men.

"Until then," Peter said, meeting her gaze.

"Until tonight."

NINETEEN

2 DAYS, 6 HOURS, 20 MINUTES
JOSEFA

THE FIRST TIME Josefa stole was not some grand heist. It wasn't some con she had planned for weeks and months. She remembered how it was raining in London. So hard that Josefa could hear the fat raindrops hit the ground.

She knew that she if she were still at Blackwood boarding school, she would be shuffled inside to the dormitory she shared with four other girls. But Josefa had just been expelled, and instead of feeling worry or desperation, she felt elated.

Out of the corner of her eye, Josefa spotted a man who reminded her a little of her father. He was climbing out of his car and pulling out an umbrella to make the short walk to his house, a beautiful redbrick building that almost looked out of place in the middle of that dreary day.

Josefa wasn't sure what had flitted through her mind in that moment. But she knew she had nothing but the clothes on her back. More than that, she was so caught up in her freedom she didn't really *think* at all. She saw a man from money who was momentarily distracted.

Josefa rushed forward, and before the man had a chance to realize what had happened, she had grabbed the wallet from his pocket. She was already halfway down the road by the time he figured out what Josefa had done. He gave chase, his footfalls heavy behind her. A thrill ran up Josefa's spine. She remembered the thumping of blood in her ears as she pumped her legs faster and faster—until there was barely any breath left in her lungs. She turned this way and that, barely able to see anything in the rain.

When she finally stopped to catch her breath, Josefa glanced behind her. There was no sign of the man anymore. She had no idea when she had lost him. But she grinned. No, she remembered thinking: *This* was freedom.

Amid the wealthy of the *Titanic*, perhaps some of the richest Europeans and Americans of their time, Josefa felt that familiar thrill run up her spine.

At her grin, Violet turned to shoot her a glare.

"If you don't stop smiling like a crocodile about to kill its prey, we're going to get caught," Violet whispered, giving Josefa a quick jab with her elbow.

"Do you see Mr. Lake?" Josefa leaned down to whisper to Violet, while casting a watchful eye around the room. She recognized a few people, including John Jacob Astor, one of the richest men in the whole world. She had seen his picture in the papers.

The woman he was speaking to, though, was unfamiliar. She was clad in a beautiful blue sequined dress with a strap hanging off the shoulders and a necklace of pearls looped around her neck. Josefa's fingers itched at the idea of all the wealth simply dangling off people in this place. She just had to walk by John Astor and his companion in order to get her hands on that pearl necklace. It looked as if it could fetch her quite a bit of money.

"That's Lady Duff Gordon," Violet leaned down to whisper. Her voice was clouded with astonishment, like she couldn't quite believe who she was seeing.

"Who?" Josefa eyed the woman once more, studying her easy laugh and the way she fit into this place as if it belonged to her.

"She only designs the most beautiful dresses in the whole world. Her advertisements are everywhere," Violet said chidingly. Josefa frowned. She guessed the most beautiful dresses in the world also came with a pretty price tag.

"Well, do you see who she's speaking to? John Astor. He's one of the richest men in the world."

Violet shook her head, like she couldn't quite believe where she was and who she was surrounded by. It did feel a little surreal, even to Josefa.

"Don't ogle. We need to fit in," Violet snapped at Josefa a moment later.

"I wasn't ogling," Josefa said defensively, though she definitely had been. More important, she had been *pining*. She had to remind herself that there was more at stake. After the *Rubaiyat*, the pearls on Lady Gordon's neck would look like nothing.

As they wove through people at the dining hall, Violet suddenly grabbed hold of Josefa's hand and squeezed. "There he is," she whispered. Josefa followed Violet's gaze to the balding man with a round face and a laugh that reached them even through the crowds.

Violet winced. "He's not very good at subtlety."

"That's good for us, though," Josefa reminded her.

Violet nodded in agreement. She was watching him closely. But Josefa was more interested in the boy who stood beside him: August Frazier.

"Violet, you should go find Fischer. Keep up appearances. I'm going to take care of August."

Violet paused, turning to observe Josefa with a small frown. "Josefa . . ." There was a warning in her voice, and Josefa wondered for a moment if some form of reprimand was coming. But instead, Violet simply said, "Whatever it is you're up to, be careful."

"I always am."

Shaking her head, Violet left Josefa's side before disappearing into the throng of people. From across the room, August caught Josefa's eye. She held his gaze, letting a smile grace her lips.

August began to slowly approach Josefa, a frown hardening his youthful looks. With his eyebrows furrowed and his jaw clenched, he could have passed for the peers he had been keeping company on this ship. It was far from the August Josefa used to know—one with fair hair from the sunlight, which had now darkened to a dusty brown, and bright eyes full of excitement and mischief, which had been replaced by a look beyond his years. He broke eye contact with Josefa only to occasionally nod at passing dinner guests with gracious smiles.

But Josefa stood stock-still, never letting her eyes wander away from this boy from her past.

Just three years back, August had been Josefa's best friend. The person she trusted most in the whole world. She had met him after her expulsion from boarding school, when she still tried to appease her parents by writing them long letters filled with lies about her life.

"You know, your parents are going to figure out you're not the proper lady you're pretending to be, sooner or later." August had loved to make that point, over and over again.

August was used to life on the streets. He had been surviving on pickpocketing and thieving for far longer than her. During those days, she used to latch on to his words like they were gospel. He used to act like his words *were* gospel.

"I think I'd prefer it if they figured it out later rather than sooner." Josefa was finishing off her latest letter to her mother. She had detailed adventures in Wales, the beautiful greenery, and the sound of the ocean. She had obviously left out the fact that she and August had broken into the homes of multiple wealthy people, pawning their jewelry and trinkets for enough money for a train ticket to Scotland, along with lodging and food for the next while.

"If you weren't such a stellar thief, I would recommend

you become a writer. You are definitely something at spinning tales." Josefa felt a tinge of warm pride at August's compliment. She didn't even mind that he had read her letter over her shoulder without permission. But the idea of being able to do something different than what was expected of her always sent a thrill through Josefa. Folding up the letter and stuffing it in an envelope, Josefa turned to August with a smile.

"You know, in Scotland, we should do something big." Josefa had been thinking about this for some time. She was tiring of petty thievery and selling trinkets for a livelihood. What she really wanted was to feel that thrill of danger, of almost being on the brink of something, of taking a risk that made her feel something she hadn't felt before. She wanted a challenge.

"I thought I was the one who planned these jobs." August raised an eyebrow. Josefa could tell he wasn't really mad from the way his lips tugged at the corner, like he was trying not to smile.

"Yes, well. You've taught me well enough. I think I'm capable of planning something."

August did smile then, holding her gaze. "You definitely are."

The swell of pride in Josefa's chest was less to do with August's approval and more to do with her own abilities.

Of course, August had to ruin everything.

One moment, Josefa was feeling that swell of pride; the next August leaned a little too close. So close that Josefa could feel his breath on her.

She leaned as far back as her chair would allow.

"What are you doing?" she asked, even as she knew exactly

what he had been doing. Josefa thought they were friends, but August obviously had a slightly different idea.

"I thought . . ." He leaned back, blinking as if he had just woken from a dream. Josefa desperately attempted to avoid his gaze, but August began to dig around his scattered belongings. Finally, he took out a worn-out leather-bound book. "This is . . . for you. A present."

"A present?" Josefa wasn't sure what to think of that after he had almost tried to kiss her. She didn't want to give August the wrong idea, but she was afraid he already had the wrong idea.

"Open it," he urged. "It's for you."

Josefa carefully opened the leather-bound cover to find August's handwriting scrawled onto the grainy yellow paper. The first page contained a short poem about a girl with "chestnut hair and blue eyes."

"I wrote them myself." August's voice was laced with pride—as if he thought there was something wonderful about gifting someone a book of poetry out of the blue.

"They're . . . about me?" Josefa asked, flipping through the pages. They were all filled with poems in the same handwriting. Every single one seemed to be about her. And—as far as Josefa was concerned—they were all awful. Not just because Josefa had never been keen on poetry, but because she had never considered August anything other than a friend.

"August . . ." She wasn't sure how to gently let him down. She didn't know how long he had harbored these feelings. It must have been for a while if he had managed to procure a whole book of poetry from them. "I don't think I can take this. . . ." She closed the book once more, avoiding August's gaze as she attempted to slide it back toward him.

"But I wrote them for you. You have to take them."

"August . . . I'm sorry," Josefa mumbled, though she didn't really feel sorry at all. Her cheeks warmed at the idea that all this time she had thought she and August were best friends, partners in crime, even. While August had been thinking they were more.

She tried to bite down her discomfort by standing up and grabbing the envelope for her mother. "I should send this off."

August didn't bring up the book of poetry or his feelings for Josefa again, though he had left the book with her. Maybe he hoped his words would somehow change her mind, but she had never even taken the time to peruse them.

When August came to her two days later with a job, Josefa was sure all had been forgiven and forgotten. They had been through too much together to let something as silly as feelings stand in the way. He still wore that easy smile that he always had around her.

"So you'll go in through the window and let me in," he explained. "And whatever we manage to sell will help with your big plans in Scotland."

Josefa smiled. He had taken Scotland seriously after all.

Under the blanket of the night sky, Josefa had found her way through an opening in the window of the house August had led her to. She had nearly crashed into the coffee table as she landed, barely managing not to make a ruckus as her feet thudded against the wood floor. Elegance had never really been Josefa's thing.

Josefa took a look around the dark room, letting her eyes adjust before opening the door for August. But she didn't get a chance.

The next minute, the door flung open. Two policemen shone a bright light in her face. It blinded Josefa. She couldn't even make out their features as one of them pulled at Josefa's arms, handcuffing them behind her back. The metal handcuff dug into her skin painfully. She had to bite her tongue to keep from crying out loud.

"I think there's been . . ." Josefa cut herself short when she noticed the third figure by the door: August.

He was watching her with an expression that Josefa couldn't figure out. One that she had never seen on him before.

Now, as August strolled up to her in the middle of the *Titanic*, his expression was different still. Easygoing, with a hint of something like restlessness. "I would have expected you to be busy finding your mark," he said as a way of greeting. "Instead, it almost feels like you're here for me."

"You wish," Josefa scoffed.

"So why *are* you here?" he asked. And for a moment, his eyes flickered to the side of the room, where Josefa spotted Violet's bright blond hair ducking out of sight. "Because I'm sure I've seen your friends around."

"She's hardly my friend," Josefa said. "Probably in the same way you and I were hardly friends once upon a time."

To her surprise, August almost seemed embarrassed about that. He shifted weight from one foot to the other, his cheeks tinting slightly pink. "I guess you're still holding on to that."

Josefa almost wanted to laugh. Of course she was holding on to it. How could she forget how her only friend, the person she had trusted with everything, had betrayed her? Simply because she hadn't returned his affections. Because she had turned him down when he tried to kiss her, he had sold her out to the police.

Josefa was never going to forget that, let alone forgive it.

But to August, she simply smiled through a lie. "You know I've never been one for grudges."

August didn't look convinced. "So, it's just coincidence that we're both on this ship at the same time?"

"I could be asking you the same question. Why are *you* here? Apparently, it's not because you're being a good assistant to Mr. Lake."

August glanced over his shoulder, as if he were afraid his boss was eavesdropping on their conversation. But he was a little too busy entertaining people on the other side of the room to worry about what August was up to.

"I *know* you're here for all of this. You've never been able to resist," August said, gesturing at the space around them: the imported carpet, the twinkling chandelier, the decadent smell and feel of wealth emanating from the room.

"Did you ever think . . . ," Josefa said, keeping her eyes

trained on August, "that you're the reason I wanted all this?"

August straightened up, the grin disappearing off his face as if Josefa had flicked a switch. He blinked at Josefa, his eyebrows scrunching together. Like she was a puzzle that he couldn't figure out. "Me?" he asked. "You were running cons long before I came along."

"Sure, but . . . I didn't really *enjoy* any of it until you showed me the ropes. Until you taught me what I was capable of."

Her words had the effect that Josefa wanted, because some of the tension seemed to leave August's body. He leaned forward a little and ran a hand through his messy curls. "I really thought . . . you would still be angry."

Josefa smiled, though that was the last thing she wanted to do. "It was a long time ago. You did what you had to do. You cut me loose when things got complicated. I would have done the same thing," she said. "So . . . now that you know that the past is behind us, tell me the truth. What is your game plan with Lake?"

August's gaze flicked to Mr. Lake once more. He seemed to consider something before he turned back to Josefa. This time, his eyes were alight. *This* was the August that Josefa had known. The one who was always brimming with secrets— secrets that only Josefa had been privy to once.

"Mr. Lake has something I want," he said slowly.

"So you're working him, eh? I guess you're not meant for the straight and narrow path after all," Josefa said.

August smirked. "I did think about actually trying

it—briefly," he said. "Working for Mr. Lake is nice . . . great, even. But . . ."

". . . it's not as great as what you want?" Josefa asked.

August shared a look with Josefa, like there was a private joke between them. Like they were friends again, the way they used to be before everything. When a single look could convey more than words. It sent a thrill through Josefa.

Men were too easy to fool.

"It's not like Lake's assistant is a dream job anyway. And I already have someone lined up in New York." August shrugged, like there was nothing else to it. Like he had any qualms about cheating someone out of a deal.

"And I'm sure you've got all your meticulous plans too—detailing how you're going to do it," Josefa said. She knew how August prided himself on being calculated about his cons. If there was one thing she was glad to have picked up from her friendship with August, it was his penchant for thinking things through.

"It hasn't been easy, since Lake works me day and night," August said. "But I manage to slip away every morning to the reading and writing room on the ship. It's barely used by anyone, so he never distracts me there."

"So what's worth risking your neck for?" Josefa asked finally.

"Trust me, it's worth it," August said. "Worth more than you can ever imagine."

Josefa raised an eyebrow. "I'm sure." Then she tucked back a loose strand of her hair. August's eyes followed her, before darting toward Lake again. Josefa could almost see the gears turning in his head, the calculations he must have been doing.

A moment later, August leaned close. His lips brushed Josefa's ear as he whispered, "Meet me tomorrow night, and I'll show you."

TWENTY

2 DAYS, 5 HOURS, 10 MINUTES
HINNAH

HINNAH HAD BEEN studying the floor plans for what felt like hours. With Josefa and Violet off to dinner, leaving only her and Emilie in their cabin, it was much easier to focus. Before Josefa left, she had exchanged a meaningful glance with Hinnah.

"Tonight might be the perfect night to check out the vents and figure out if we can get around through them," she said.

Emilie was set up on a desk of her own to one side of the room, carefully poring over the auction pamphlet that Josefa had managed to grab from Lake's briefcase earlier that day.

Hinnah considered what Josefa had said. She studied their cabin slowly. It took a few moments of searching before she finally found what she was looking for. Hinnah got up, grabbed the chair she had just left, and pulled it up beside the two single beds. Balancing herself carefully, Hinnah stepped onto the chair and reached up on her tiptoes. A small metal grate almost blended into the wall, but Hinnah pressed her hands into the cool steel. She moved it aside slowly until she could peer into the vent that it blocked.

When she leaned down to place the metal grate on the floor, it scraped loudly. Emilie's head jerked up, and she caught Hinnah's gaze.

"What are you doing?" Curiosity illuminated her face.

Hinnah hesitated for a moment. "I'm going to climb up into the vent," Hinnah admitted, pointing to the small opening in the wall.

Emilie studied it with a terse frown. "Are you sure you can fit in there? It's a bit tight."

Hinnah smiled. While Josefa and Violet were well versed in Hinnah's abilities, Emilie obviously still hadn't seen enough. "Don't worry. Compared to some of the spaces I've found myself squeezed into, this vent is basically a mansion."

"Do you want help?" Emilie asked.

Hinnah hesitated again, her gaze resting on Emilie. She had been doing things by herself for so long that Emilie's offer to help seemed strange. Even when she, Josefa, and Violet worked together, everything was carefully planned in advance. Hinnah had her role, and Violet and Josefa had theirs.

"I mean . . . I'm used to this. It's my job, so . . ." Hinnah trailed off, setting the metal grate carefully on the floor.

When she looked up, Emilie had left her chair and was studying the vent with a thoughtful expression.

"Have you always worked in the circus?" she asked. "Even in India?"

Hinnah shook her head slowly. "In India . . . well, I was just a kid."

"Yeah." Emilie sighed. "I was a kid in France as well, and I was just a baby when I left Haiti. Do you miss it? India?"

Hinnah frowned, tilting her head down as if she were taking in the green carpeting of their cabin. Did she miss India? She missed certain things. Like the food and the call to adhan at different times of day. She missed the intricate clothes, and the sound of churis and nupurs, the feel of them against her skin. But there were so many things she absolutely didn't miss at all. Like her family's disdain of Hinnah's body, and how they always seemed ashamed of her. Or how they were content to stay quiet and mind their own business instead of fighting back against the British like the revolutionaries risking their lives for freedom on the streets.

Maybe that was what had drawn Hinnah to Ireland. What had led her to stay longer than she had stayed anywhere else. She felt a kinship to the people there. They were all looking for their freedom from the British too.

"India isn't so different, you know," Hinnah said finally. "But I guess I miss . . . my ammi's cooking. She made really good food, but . . . you can't really find the right ingredients in Ireland." This was, Hinnah thought, the most she had spoken about her home since she left. The people at the circus were never curious—they preferred to keep the past buried in the past. Josefa and Violet, too, seemed afraid of the past in some ways.

Hinnah was surprised that speaking of her family didn't

bring any pain. Instead, the memories it conjured up were tinted with happiness.

"Are you going to go back when this is all over?" Emilie asked tentatively. "Your parents must miss you."

Hinnah bit her lip. She had known that sooner or later someone would ask her that question. Or they'd ask her why she left. Violet and Josefa had some inkling of it, but nobody *really* knew. Hinnah kept it hidden away, tucked into the back of her mind where she couldn't remember it anymore. Though she still thought of it often when she tossed and turned at night, willing sleep to come to her. It was one of the reasons why she loved being a part of the circus. It was so rigorous that she didn't have the time to think about what had happened. She didn't have the time to dwell, even in the darkness of the night as she tried to sleep. She was too tuckered out most of the time, too busy thinking about the bruises new circus tricks often left her with.

"My parents kicked me out," Hinnah said, carefully choosing her words. "I don't think I'll be going back there again." The words sat heavy between them for a moment. Emilie looked at her with sympathy written all over her face. And maybe some regret about having asked the question in the first place.

"I only had my father, and since he passed, I don't really have anywhere or anyone to go to, either," Emilie said slowly. "It's not the same thing, but—"

"I know." Hinnah nodded. She hadn't been so sure about Emilie at first, but she was beginning to like her. She was realizing that Emilie was just as put-together as the rest of them—which was not at all.

She thought back to her last night in Dublin and how she had almost gotten caught. She could have asked for Josefa and Violet's help then—but she didn't. Maybe she had been wrong. So, Hinnah did the unthinkable. "I *could* use your help, you know," she said.

Emilie visibly brightened at that. "Really?"

"Well . . . I want to chart a path through these vents," Hinnah said. "I'm not sure where they go . . . how far they go . . . how far they can take us."

"You want me to come with you?" Emilie glanced up at the narrow space that marked the entrance to the vent. She didn't look particularly thrilled with the idea of it.

Hinnah chuckled, shaking her head. "I don't think you're ready for that yet." She knew that Emilie would be able to get in with no issues—she was petite. All skin and bones. But it wasn't easy to move around in a crawl space like that.

"I'm going to go up, but I need someone to help me map it out."

"I can do that." Emilie grabbed hold of the floor plan and marked the opening of the vent in the very cabin they were standing in.

"Okay." Hinnah nodded, feeling a strange warmth flooding her as she turned again toward the vent. She climbed up slowly, the metal chafing against her legs and elbows. It was a tight fit, but she managed to squeeze through into the crawl space. She crawled farther in, the darkness enveloping her. But there was something calming about the thought that Emilie was waiting for her back in their cabin.

It almost reminded her of the kind of solace a home was supposed to give you. The comfort of knowing someone is there for you—for better or for worse. Hinnah hadn't felt that for a long time. With her family, back in India, she wasn't sure if it was ever really like that. But Hinnah was beginning to realize that maybe there was more to family than blood.

Hinnah came up above a grate through which she could hear voices. Peering down, she saw two women gossiping about a woman who had been sleeping with several men instead of marrying. They sounded scandalized at the thought, and Hinnah had to smile. Both because of the ridiculousness of it and because she was sure she knew the exact path the vents were taking her through.

If she had remembered the floor plans correctly, she was sure that the vents could lead her to almost anywhere on this ship. She just had to be careful.

Hinnah paused above another grate, where she spotted a familiar face. Matron Wallis was deep in conversation with one of the ship's clerks. Hinnah leaned forward, trying to listen and make out what they were saying.

". . . in the first-class dining hall," the clerk finished off with a nod of his head.

Matron Wallis seemed to consider his words for a moment with a frown. "I was just about to make my way there," she said finally. "I'll keep an eye out for anyone unusual."

Hinnah's pulse quickened at the words. Wallis wasn't supposed to go down to the first-class dining hall. She was supposed to stay here, in the confines of the second class, where Violet and Josefa didn't have to worry about her.

Hinnah knew she didn't have time to hesitate. Instead, she hurried back the way that she had come. Crawling through the vents so fast that she could feel the skin of her arms bruise and redden from the impact. But she was used to sustaining injuries from her time at the circus. It was simply part of being an athlete—being a performer like she was.

"That was fast," Emilie said cheerfully as soon as she spotted Hinnah. She was ready with parchment and pens to create her outline of the map of the vents.

"Matron Wallis is going to the first-class dining hall," Hinnah said, her words coming out in a jumbled rush.

Emilie only blinked at her for a moment, like she was having difficulty understanding Hinnah's words.

"Why would she—"

"I don't know," Hinnah cut her off, pacing back and forth in their small cabin. "But we have to do something. If Wallis sees Josefa and Violet in there, she'll ruin our plans."

"We have to warn them," Emilie said.

"No." Hinnah shook her head slowly because she knew what they had to do. The problem was, Hinnah and Emilie were not the people for the task at hand. "We have to stop Wallis."

TWENTY-ONE

9:40 P.M.

2 DAYS, 4 HOURS, 40 MINUTES

EMILIE

HINNAH DASHED OUT of the cabin before Emilie could even process what she had said. They had to stop Matron Wallis, but Emilie had no idea how. She wasn't the person who came up with daring plans or quick escapes. She was the girl who thought through every decision carefully.

But she dashed out after Hinnah regardless, her thoughts flashing wildly in her mind. So fast she could barely process any of them.

"Where are we going?" she asked, aware that the sound of their footsteps seemed too loud against the floor.

"I'm not sure," Hinnah said, though she didn't slow down. She had that determined look on her face—the same one she had had when she returned with the floor plans to the ship.

"What are we going to do?" Emilie pressed.

"I don't know that either." Hinnah shook her head. Emilie could see the panic in her face. She felt it in herself as well. A steady thrum of it rising up through her chest, making all her

156

thoughts seem fuzzy and out of focus. How did Josefa do this? How did she *enjoy* it? But there was a small thread of excitement through Emilie's panic too. She wondered if *this* feeling was what Josefa was talking about.

The two of them thundered past familiar cabins until they finally spotted Matron Wallis in the distance. Thankfully, she didn't seem to be in a rush to get to the first-class dining hall. Instead, she was checking in on nearby passengers—like she had all the time in the world.

Emilie wished *they* had all the time in the world.

"We need to find a way to distract her," Hinnah said, glancing around as if a distraction were going to pop out at any moment now. Emilie glanced around, too, but there was nothing that she could think of that would attract Wallis's attention.

She had to think like Josefa—not like herself. A painter who had whiled away months trying to find the right way to finish the perfect painting of the river Liffey. What would Josefa do in this moment? How would she figure out how to distract the matron and keep her from going up to the first-class dining hall?

"Matron Wallis!" Emilie wasn't sure who had called for her, but from the way Hinnah was blinking at her, she realized it was her. In front of them, Wallis turned around, her eyes set into a steely glare.

"What are you two doing here?" she asked. No doubt she was remembering their first conversation on the ship, when

Wallis had all but threatened them. Emilie wasn't sure what kind of power the matron had on this ship, but she was sure that if she got caught in a lie here, she would be responsible for jeopardizing their plans.

"My friend . . ." Emilie turned to Hinnah, a stricken expression on her face. "She suddenly fell very ill."

Hinnah's face already had a sickly pallor—probably from crawling through the vents and rushing after Matron Wallis.

Wallis slowly approached the two of them, and Hinnah bent down, holding on to her stomach as if she really *were* sick. "What's wrong with her?" she asked, narrowing her eyes.

"I'm not sure," Emilie said, leaning forward to rest her hand on Hinnah's shoulder in what she hoped seemed like worry. "But . . . I wasn't sure who could help her. There were no other stewardesses around."

The matron looked from Hinnah to Emilie.

Emilie tried to ignore the erratic beat of her pulse and the fact that her own stomach roiled with anxiety. She chewed on her lips nervously—forgetting that she was supposed to act like the worried friend.

But Wallis seemed convinced.

"This is why girls like you need a chaperone," she mumbled. Her voice had an undertone of annoyance, but Emilie could tell that she really didn't mind that much. "If there was someone here to help you, they would have known to take you right to the hospital on the ship."

"The hospital?" Emilie asked.

"It's not far from here. Are you okay to walk?" Wallis asked, glancing at Hinnah with concern.

Hinnah simply gave a quick nod of her head, while Emilie grabbed hold of her arm. As if to help guide her through the hallway.

The three of them passed by the grand staircase leading up to first class, and Emilie and Hinnah exchanged a nervous glance between them. Emilie knew they were thinking the same thing: they hoped their little act had bought Josefa and Violet enough time to get out of there.

TWENTY-TWO

2 DAYS, 4 HOURS, 30 MINUTES
VIOLET

VIOLET KNEW WHAT the plan was, but watching Josefa and August across the room, she felt like she had had the rug pulled from underneath her. Josefa had assured them all that once Violet got them invited to the first-class dinner, she would be able to charm August into showing her the *Rubaiyat*. It was why she had insisted she needed to get dressed up—to lure August with her feminine wiles.

But watching them, studying the strong familiarity between them, Violet wondered if they weren't the ones being conned. If she wasn't the one in the dark here.

"Sylviane?" When Violet turned to meet Peter's gaze, she realized he must have been trying to get her attention for at least a few minutes.

She let a smile grace her lips. "I'm so sorry," she mumbled. "It's just . . . I'm feeling a little . . . unwell."

"Let me get you a drink," he said, calling to a passing waiter.

Violet used the opportunity to affix her gaze on Josefa once more. Only to note that August had leaned forward, so close to Josefa she wondered for a moment what their relationship was.

Then he seemed to whisper something in her ear, before turning around and making his way toward Lake.

To anyone else, Josefa looked composed, but Violet knew she had succeeded. A slow smile appeared on her face, and her gait was a little too jovial.

"Here you are," Peter mumbled as one of the waiters filled up her glass to the brim. Violet gave him a smile, already plotting for a way to leave this dinner behind to try to figure out what Josefa was hiding from her.

"Are we ready to leave?" Violet whispered to Josefa, the moment she had managed to extract herself from Peter Fischer. She was tired of dining with the rich and famous of the first class. More important, she was tiring of Peter Fischer, who had spent most of the night singing his own praises—which were not many, and not particularly impressive, if Violet said so herself.

Josefa took a sip from her overflowing champagne flute. "I don't know. I'm feeling quite at home here."

Violet tried not to roll her eyes. Josefa was already a little tipsy, and she knew they didn't need to draw any more attention to themselves.

"How did things go with Frazier?" Violet asked instead.

"Perfectly," Josefa said with a dreamy sigh. "I told you I could handle him."

"But I don't understand what the plan is here," Violet said. "You think he's really just going to show you the book?"

"He promised me he would," Josefa said with a lopsided grin.

Violet sighed and glanced across the room. August and Lake were deep in conversation with a group of other men. Violet recognized some of them from the Café Parisien, but most of them were strangers to her.

By the time she glanced back, Josefa was halfway through another glass of champagne. Violet tried to bite down her irritation as she grabbed the half-empty flute from her and placed it on the table between them. The last thing she needed was to take care of a drunk Josefa.

"We need to get back to our cabin," Violet said, tugging Josefa up to stand. She flashed a charming smile at anybody who caught their eye as she and Josefa slowly made their way out of the first-class dining area.

But not before she felt that familiar prickle on her back— like somebody was watching her. And just like last time, when she turned around, she caught August's blue eyes boring into them. Violet felt a shiver run down her spine as she pulled Josefa along and out of the dining hall.

"What are you keeping from me?" Violet asked Josefa almost as soon as they had left the dining hall.

"Nothing," she said, but Violet knew she was lying. Like she had been from the beginning of this mission. There was something about August; Violet could tell from the way Josefa's entire demeanor seemed to change every time his name came up.

"Then why are we so focused on August?" Violet pressed. She hoped that Josefa's inhibitions being down meant that she would let something slip. But despite how much she had had to drink, it was like speaking about August brought back Josefa's focus. She looked at Violet with her sharp blue eyes, a frown pulling at her lips.

"He's Lake's assistant. Why else?" She sounded flippant, like this was all a coincidence. But Violet knew it couldn't be.

Josefa pushed past Violet and down the stairs back to second class.

"We're risking a lot for this mission," Violet said, following after her. "And you're making it even more dangerous. First you invite Emilie, who is an amateur at best."

In front of her, Josefa's shoulders stiffened at her words. But Violet didn't care. She was getting tired of Josefa's antics, especially when they were getting in the way of her plans to reunite with Marko. She wouldn't let anyone do that. Not even her best friend and her ridiculous crush.

"And now it's this guy who obviously means *something* and—"

Violet cut herself off when she spotted a familiar figure approaching in the distance. She had changed out of her conservative black dress into an evening gown, but there was no mistaking Wallis's full head of hair and her confident strut.

If she spotted the two of them here, she would have some choice questions for them.

"We need to hide," Josefa said before Violet could. Instead

of taking the remaining steps down the stairs, they hurried back up the way they had come. They waited in the shadows, holding their breath, hoping that the matron wasn't about to come up to first class.

To their surprise, two more figures followed after the matron—Emilie trotted behind her with long strides, almost dragging a slower Hinnah beside her.

Violet's stomach dropped at the sight of them. What had happened? But more important, were they caught?

"Is it much farther?" Emilie said in the distance. Her voice had a nervousness to it that irritated Violet, especially now.

"It's just down here," Matron Wallis said, glancing back at the two of them. To Violet's surprise, she actually seemed . . . concerned. Not angry, for once. The three of them passed by the grand staircase and disappeared outside onto the deck.

"What was that?" Violet asked as she and Josefa ducked out of the shadows and crept down the staircase slowly. Violet kept her eyes on the doors leading outside the entire time. As if any moment now Matron Wallis would come traipsing back.

"No idea," Josefa said. "We should hurry and get back to our cabins."

"You don't think we should go after them?" Violet asked.

Josefa shook her head. "I don't think so. I think they're okay."

Violet usually trusted Josefa's instincts without a second thought. But something about this journey—this mission—and Josefa's secret was making her doubt her friend. She didn't want to. Still, Violet nodded her head. Choosing to trust that Emilie and Hinnah could deal with Matron Wallis by themselves.

The two of them left first class and slipped into second, where everything was much less lavish. The lights weren't covered in gold-plated casing, and the carpet was a dull green instead of vibrant red. The walls had patterned wallpaper instead of that iridescent white of first class. But it was still far grander and more beautiful than any place Violet had ever really been to before.

"August and I have a past," Josefa said as they approached their cabins. She was looking down at the carpeted hallway, not at Violet, as she said this.

"You do?" Violet asked, even though she had suspected as much.

"I want to tell you, Violet; I *do*," Josefa said, finally meeting Violet's eyes. She almost looked sad, and Violet had never seen Josefa look sad before. "But it's . . . complicated, and I'm not sure if I'm ready yet. But you *have* to trust me. About August. About this mission. About Emilie."

"I do," Violet said, though she wasn't so sure if she meant that completely. "But you can't keep lying to us and expect us to trust you. There's so much at stake. We *need* to trust you."

"I know," Josefa said with a nod of her head. Violet nodded too. She wasn't happy that she still knew little to nothing about August Frazier—but at least she knew that Josefa wouldn't continue to lie to them. Even if she couldn't tell her the whole truth just yet. Violet trusted Josefa enough to know that the truth would come when the time was right.

TWENTY-THREE

10:05 P.M.

---

2 DAYS, 4 HOURS, 15 MINUTES
EMILIE

"WHAT HAPPENED TO you two?" These were the words that greeted Emilie and Hinnah as soon as they stepped back into their cabin.

"Matron Wallis." Hinnah sighed.

"She didn't find you, did she?" Emilie asked.

Violet and Josefa shook their heads simultaneously.

"She was about to head to the first-class dining hall . . . Emilie and I found a way to distract her," Hinnah explained, glancing at Emilie with admiration in her eyes. Wallis had escorted the two girls all the way to the ship's hospital before going back the way she had come. She hadn't asked too many questions—thanks to the pained expression on Hinnah's face and Emilie's clear worry for her.

"*You* found a way to distract her?" Violet asked in a disbelieving voice. The question was technically for the both of them, but Violet's eyes were studying Emilie. Like she couldn't

166

quite believe someone like Emilie could think on her feet as she had.

Emilie couldn't even blame Violet for being doubtful. She hadn't thought she and Hinnah could pull it off. She was still not entirely sure *how* they had done it.

"*We* did," Emilie said, meeting Violet's gaze head-on. And if she wasn't mistaken, she could see a flicker of respect in Violet's eyes before she looked away.

"What about the two of you?" Hinnah asked. "Did you do what you needed to do?"

"Obviously." Josefa grinned.

"And now I'm ready for bed," Violet said, standing. She didn't wait for anybody else before slipping out. They could hear the click of the door as she stepped into their second cabin.

"We should make sure we stay out of Wallis's way until we put our plan into action tomorrow evening. Stay out of everyone's way, really," Josefa said.

Hinnah gave a nod of agreement and followed after Violet. Then it was just Josefa and Emilie in the enclosed room.

Josefa shuffled to the table where Emilie had been copying pages of the *Rubaiyat* from the leaflet that Josefa had stolen that morning.

She ran her fingers over Emilie's work, a strange kind of determination on her face.

Emilie watched Josefa with bated breath, trying not to think about the way the air in the room suddenly felt thick with something she couldn't explain. It was exactly how it had felt the last time Emilie and Josefa were alone.

"What's this?" Josefa asked, her fingers running over the pages.

"The copy of the *Rubaiyat*, remember?" Emilie pulled out the auction pamphlet Josefa had gotten for her earlier that day and waved it in front of Josefa.

"Oh, right. Yes . . . Wow." She stared at Emilie's pages with wide eyes, like it was the first time she had seen anything like it. "It looks so . . . real. You're amazing."

Emilie's cheeks grew hot, and she tucked the pages aside swiftly.

"Are you drunk?" she asked, changing the subject. Josefa's cheeks were a little too pink, her eyes a little too bright. And though Josefa was not known for her meekness, her sudden admiration and boisterousness were not things Emilie would usually ascribe to her.

"No!" Josefa exclaimed defensively. "I'm just . . . a little . . . I had a few drinks," she admitted. Josefa dropped slowly and sat against the wall of the cabin. Emilie gingerly slid down beside her. She felt the chill from the cold floor seeping into her, even through her clothes. And she felt the sway of the water underneath the ship. She tipped her head back and closed her eyes for a moment. There was something strangely peaceful about the silence.

"How did you learn?" Josefa asked after a long moment.

When Emilie opened her eyes, Josefa was staring right at her.

"Learn?"

"Art? Calligraphy? All that?" She nodded at the desk. "Who taught you?"

"My father." Emilie shrugged. "He was an art historian. Art has just always been around me, for as long as I've been alive, really. And he used to paint as well. I don't think I've ever not . . ." She shook her head. "Not been doing this."

"So you always wanted to be an artist?" Josefa seemed confused at the thought.

Emilie had to smile. "I guess. Art was . . . how I related to the world around me."

"Was?"

Emilie turned away from Josefa's questioning eyes and pulled her knees up to her chest. "Ever since my father died, it's all felt a bit . . . pointless," she said. "Like . . . I don't really know what I'm doing anymore. Or everything I'm doing somehow feels wrong." Emilie didn't even know how to explain to Josefa the feeling of creating a painting and seeing a void. "It's like . . . something crucial is missing from everything I've been doing. Like maybe whatever talent I once had just disappeared with him." It felt strange to voice it aloud after months of these thoughts festering in her mind.

"It definitely hasn't." Josefa's tone had an aggressive confidence in it. Like she knew Emilie's art through and through— even better than she did. "I've *seen* your work. You're the most talented artist I know."

Emilie turned to her with a smirk. "And how many artists do you know?"

Josefa smiled too, rolling her eyes. "Okay, so . . . I don't have a wide repertoire of artist contacts. But . . . I know you're talented. In case you weren't aware, I've seen the paintings people admire enough to spend hundreds of thousands on. They're nothing compared to what you've done."

Emilie felt a bubble of pride rise up within her—and a tingle in her stomach. Josefa had a way of making Emilie see herself differently.

"What about you, then?" Emilie asked. "I can't imagine pulling off grand heists has always been part of the plan."

Josefa giggled, making Emilie smile. There was something carefree about her laugh. Josefa had never been controlled like Violet, never so careful that she wouldn't let anything slip. But Emilie had realized that she had walls up around her too.

Maybe tonight, Emilie could finally see the Josefa that existed behind her mask of confidence.

"I guess . . . ," Josefa began slowly. "My parents had a plan for me. I never stuck to it. They wanted me to get an education and be exactly like them. They wanted me to find a man of good stature to marry." Josefa emphasized the words like they were preposterous. "But that wasn't what I wanted. I just wanted to . . ." She trailed off, like she was searching for the appropriate words. "I wanted to *feel* something," she said finally. "My parents had a nice and proper life, but they didn't seem happy. They were just . . . uninspired. Resigned. That's not what I want."

"Do you only feel something when you break the law?" Emilie asked.

"No," she answered without hesitation, and Emilie could feel a rush of heat creeping up her neck. "But there's nothing like that rush when you know that there's something at stake. When you're doing something you're absolutely not supposed to and knowing that at any moment you could get caught. That rush makes me feel . . . alive."

"Are you ever afraid?"

"Of what?"

Emilie felt something inside her unravel. "Of . . . *everything*. Making a mistake. Losing control. Failing."

Josefa reached out and held Emilie's hand. It took Emilie by surprise, but at the same time she didn't want Josefa to let go. "There is something I'm afraid of."

A strange openness crossed Josefa's face. It made her look softer somehow. "I'm afraid of regret. Regretting the things I haven't done because I was too scared. Or too timid. Or because I doubted myself."

Josefa leaned her head back against the wall, squeezing Emilie's hand. "I just want every moment in my life to matter. Am I making any sense?"

Emilie had never thought about life the way Josefa put it. About every moment mattering. But being here with Josefa, on the cabin floor of the *Titanic*, holding her hand, was a moment that Emilie knew would be etched on her heart forever.

It was terrifying, the idea of living the way Josefa did. Seeking out what you wanted and seizing it, without looking back.

Maybe Emilie needed Josefa in a way that she never realized before.

"Yes," she replied, lacing her fingers through Josefa's. "I think it makes perfect sense."

TWENTY-FOUR

10:30 P.M.

2 DAYS, 3 HOURS, 50 MINUTES

JOSEFA

JOSEFA WATCHED EMILIE'S quietly contemplative face as she stared into the distance, their hands still intertwined. It reminded her of Emilie when she painted. There was something dreamy about it—as if Emilie had been transported to another place that existed only in her mind.

Josefa had to admit she hadn't been entirely honest with Emilie. Maybe she hadn't even been entirely honest with herself.

There had been so many times—too many times maybe—where Josefa had stopped in her tracks to catch Emilie at her work. Watched her from a hidden corner of the boardinghouse or caught a glimpse of her from outside her window. Those were moments when Josefa had wanted to approach Emilie, but she couldn't bring herself to do it. She'd been too afraid. Emilie seemed so out of her league, and the way she examined everything so thoroughly—it intimidated Josefa. Emilie was an artist and artists were observant. If she got too close to Josefa, would Emilie see some of the cracks in her armor? Would she see all the insecurities that Josefa liked to pretend didn't exist?

But now, sitting here shoulder to shoulder with Emilie, she could feel that pang of regret that she hated. Josefa should have let down her guard with Emilie sooner.

Emilie turned to Josefa, breaking the silence after what felt like hours.

"Whenever I'm not sure how to feel, I start painting or drawing," Emilie said. "It helps me make sense of my emotions. . . . Or . . . it did, I suppose. Lately, I just feel so aimless. Like I don't have a purpose."

"But you do," Josefa said.

She turned to hold Josefa's gaze. "You sound so certain."

"That's because I follow my instincts," Josefa said, her lips curling up into a smile.

"And your instincts are always right?"

"No, but the odds are in my favor when I listen to what my gut is telling me," Josefa answered. "For instance, my gut is telling me that your paintings capture the essence of you. I could imagine them in the houses of people like John Astor and Lady Duff Gordon. Or in a gallery, long after we've left this world behind, collecting the admiration of people from near and far."

Josefa was baring her soul here, but the more Emilie's eyes lit up, the more words kept tumbling out of her mouth. "There's something about your work that would make people stop and search their hearts in ways they hadn't before."

"So . . . are you . . . one of those people?" Emilie asked.

Josefa took a deep breath. The dizziness from the champagne was traveling to her chest. "Yes."

She searched her heart now. Being in the presence of Emilie. In their closeness in this small cabin. In the way that everything in this ship, in the world, seemed to have fallen away, leaving only Josefa and Emilie behind. There was a serenity and stillness that filled her up with warmth.

"Do you want me to teach you?" Emilie asked softly.

"Teach me what?"

Emilie smiled. "How to do calligraphy?"

Josefa grinned back. "I'd like that."

She watched as Emilie laid the sheets of leftover paper on the floor and began to draw her pen over one slowly. Josefa loved how Emilie's face contorted into a look of concentration. Her eyebrows pulled together, lips arranged into a frown, eyes focused on the page in front of her, and jaw set.

"You're supposed to be watching the calligraphy." Emilie's lips quirked up at the corners as she said this. Josefa felt a blush creeping up her neck, and she turned her eyes back to the page.

Emilie sat up as she reached the end of the blank page.

Then she reached out her hand and held Josefa's arm delicately. Not looking up, Emilie began to trace the words from the *Rubaiyat* right onto Josefa's skin. She could feel every stroke of Emilie's pen, sending a shiver up her spine.

She didn't know why, but Josefa's mind reeled back to a poem she had once read by Omar Khayyam himself. A poem that she had been forced to learn by a tutor she detested. At that time, she had hated it; she had hated Omar Khayyam for forcing her to memorize the words. But on this ship, with the moonlight bathing them in its silver glow, with Emilie curling the verses onto her arm, his poem was beginning to take hold in her mind.

Josefa recited the words softly—meant only for her and Emilie's ears, like a secret that they could hold between them: "'Make the most of what we yet may spend, before we too into the Dust descend.'"

TWENTY-FIVE

11:00 P.M.

---

2 DAYS, 3 HOURS, 20 MINUTES

EMILIE

EMILIE PULLED AWAY from Josefa. Sharp, cold air rushed in to fill the space between them.

She remembered the poem. "'A Jug of Wine, a Loaf of Bread—and Thou.'"

A familiar gnaw of guilt grew in her chest. How could Josefa recite the words of Omar Khayyam and not understand the weight of what they were planning to do?

She wanted to say this to Josefa. She felt that if she did not confess it all to her, her doubts, her fears, she would never get the chance again. And she dreaded what that could mean for the two of them. She feared Josefa would never trust her again—that this would be the end of their friendship. And the beginning of something else between them could never happen after that.

"Josefa . . . ," Emilie said, and Josefa looked up; her blue eyes were even brighter bathed in the light of the moon.

"Yes?"

For a moment, silence pressed around them. Not the silence

of awkwardness or even unspoken words. Just a silence filled with possibility.

Emilie could only manage to say, "You're not going to learn calligraphy until you try it yourself, you know."

Josefa smiled, though there was a hint of sadness behind it. Like she had expected Emilie to say something else.

Emilie had wanted to say something else, but she was terrified of how Josefa would react if she told her the truth: Emilie didn't want to do this anymore.

She didn't want to destroy a priceless piece of art, no matter what it would mean for the four of them. She didn't know how Josefa would look at her if she admitted that.

Somehow, even with Josefa right in front of her, with Violet and Hinnah in the next cabin sleeping soundly, Emilie felt lonelier than ever. Because if she told Josefa the truth, Emilie knew she would not be a part of them anymore. A part of something Josefa held dear.

"I guess I should practice," Josefa finally said.

"I guess you should."

Josefa picked up Emilie's pen and crawled closer. She reached for Emilie's palm and touched the tip of the pen against her skin. She slowly wrote the words of Omar Khayyam's poem.

It was nothing like Emilie's work. It was messy, and carefree.

It took Emilie's breath away.

Emilie didn't know when the two of them fell asleep. Somewhere in the middle of the night, with Josefa's hands clasping hers, and ink trailing the floor of the cabin.

TWENTY-SIX

APRIL 13, 1912, 8:30 A.M.

1 DAY, 17 HOURS, 50 MINUTES

HINNAH

"**WHERE ARE YOU** going?" Hinnah asked when she spotted Violet already dressed the next morning. Tonight, Josefa would pull off the first part of their plan—and help them get one step closer to securing the *Rubaiyat*. After Josefa enticed August, they would finally get a glimpse of the book and set everything in motion. But the plan didn't require Violet to be up and about so bright and early in the morning.

"I have to go to the wireless operator's cabin," Violet said, barely glancing at Hinnah.

"Josefa said we should stay out of everybody's way today."

To her surprise, Violet bristled at that. "I'm going whether Josefa wants me to or not," she said. "And anyway, I know how to take care of myself and stay out of trouble."

"But if something goes wrong then—"

"Nothing will go wrong, Hinnah. You and I were perfectly okay taking care of ourselves before Josefa came along," Violet said. Hinnah realized that she had probably walked herself into an argument between Josefa and Violet that she didn't want any part in. But she also didn't want Violet to wander the ship all by herself.

"Can I come?" Hinnah was already climbing out of bed, ready to accompany Violet.

"If you want," Violet said with a shrug of her shoulders. The two of them slipped out of their cabin.

"Are you sending a message to your brother?" Hinnah asked after a moment.

Violet shook her head slowly. "I'm actually hoping he's sent a message to me."

"You must miss him," Hinnah said softly. Hinnah was an only child, though she had many cousins. After her parents cast her out, Hinnah had wished she had someone like Violet—a sister who put her first.

"My brother needs me," Violet said. "And . . . I need him." Her voice was small, like there was something unspoken behind her words.

"Wallis," Violet hissed before Hinnah could respond, and the two of them took the next turn and ducked into a nearby corridor. "How are we meant to get around without her pouncing on us?" Violet asked after a moment.

"This is why we shouldn't have left our cabin . . . ," Hinnah said, but when Violet turned to glare at her, Hinnah simply smiled. "I know another path to the wireless operator's cabin." She began to lead the way toward the other side of the ship. It was a longer path, but she was confident they would avoid any run-ins with Wallis. After last night, they definitely didn't need to see any more of her.

"It must have been hard to leave," Hinnah said as they walked. "It's not the same, but . . . leaving my family behind wasn't easy either." She took a deep breath as she thought back to her parents. She didn't really like to speak of them, but she supposed it was unfair of her to ask about Violet's brother without sharing anything about her own family. "They didn't always accept me, but . . . I guess I love them all the same."

"It *was* difficult to leave," Violet said. "And . . . I shouldn't have done it." Hinnah was surprised to hear strain in Violet's voice, like she couldn't bear to speak about her family.

Before Hinnah could say anything, Violet continued. Almost like she had held all of this inside her for a long time and the words were now bursting out of her. "I had wanted to get away from my father for such a long time. He had all these dreams about . . . how in Zagreb he would finally make something of himself, without my mother and brother weighing him down. But without them, it was just him and me, and all of his anger and failure bottled up inside of him. So, when I finally had the opportunity and resources to leave, I did. I've never regretted that." Violet paused, as if she were thinking back to that time now.

"I used to think when I finally left him, I would find my way back to my brother. I would reunite with him, once and for all. But . . ." Violet shook her head slowly, like she wasn't sure how to finish her story. "I wanted to find my way in the world. I had these grand dreams of traveling outside of Croatia and finding a home for myself that finally fit. Then I could reunite with Marko. When I could give us the home that we deserved."

Violet heaved a sigh. "I didn't realize how hard it would be. And then . . . I couldn't go back. I never had the money to travel so far again. Things have just gotten worse for Marko, and it's all my fault. I was . . . selfish." There was guilt entrenched in each word Violet spoke. Hinnah could almost feel it.

She reached forward and rested her hand on Violet's shoulder. The two of them stopped in their tracks as Hinnah tried to figure out the words to reassure Violet. Hinnah didn't know how to tell her how lucky Marko was to have family like her. How anybody would be lucky to have family like Violet.

"You've thought this the entire time? That you're selfish?" Hinnah asked instead, because she couldn't believe Violet could ever think that of herself. Hinnah had seen again and again Violet's generosity with those she cared about. When she wasn't sending money back to Marko, she was looking out for Hinnah or helping Josefa. It was clear to Hinnah that Violet had spent so long taking care of others, she didn't even realize what true selfishness entailed.

"I *am* selfish," Violet insisted.

But Hinnah shook her head vigorously. "You were thinking of him the entire time. You left because you wanted to give him a home."

"But I couldn't. I haven't been able to. Maybe after this I—"

"You do everything you can to help him," Hinnah said. "We all know that. Whenever you have money, you send it to Marko. Even if it means being late on rent or going hungry for a few nights."

"But I left him . . . ," Violet said, anguish in her expression. "Just like everyone else. Like your family left—"

Hinnah took a sharp breath, and Violet cut herself off. She cast a furtive glance at Hinnah, like she was afraid of being reprimanded. Hinnah hadn't expected Violet to bring up her family. She didn't really understand how Violet could ever compare herself with Hinnah's parents.

But she supposed she couldn't be that surprised. Violet didn't know what had really happened. The reason why Hinnah was cast out.

"I . . . had this friend. . . ." She thought back to her only real friend in India. A boy named Reza she'd played with since she was a little kid. When they were children, it was okay for them to be friends. But the older Hinnah grew, the more her body developed, the less "proper" it was for Hinnah to spend time with Reza.

"He was having a difficult time at home. His father . . . he didn't treat him well. My parents didn't approve of our friendship, but I was the only person he ever confided in. Sometimes his father flew into these fits of rage. . . . I knew he needed me. So, I told him that he could come to our house whenever he needed to. He could climb up through the balcony into my bedroom, and he would always be welcome there. He would be safe there. He never took me up on it until . . . one day, he did."

Hinnah remembered it as clearly as if it had happened yesterday. She had just returned from her cousin's wedding. She was still wearing her gold saree, the one that her mother hated because it showed off too much skin. She stumbled into her bedroom only to find Reza lounging on her bed. She shut the door behind her and rushed toward him. "Are you okay? Are you hurt?"

"I'm fine." Reza had always put on a brave face. He batted her away with a grin—like it was normal for him to show up in her bedroom. "It wasn't as easy to climb in here as you made it seem, you know. I had to get past guards."

"You should expect some guards . . . ," Hinnah said, still taking her friend in. There were no bruises or cuts on him, but she knew something bad had to have happened for Reza to be here. She sat down beside him, slowly taking the glass churis off her hands. She knew Reza would confide in her when he felt comfortable.

But he never got the chance. Moments later, Hinnah's ammi stumbled in, Hinnah's shoes in her hand. "Hinnah, you left your—" Her eyes went from Hinnah to Reza, and even before anybody had spoken, Hinnah could see the connections her ammi was making in her head.

"I tried to explain why he was there," Hinnah said. "I thought my parents would understand, but they didn't. They . . . assumed the worst. It never mattered what had really happened. Just what they thought had happened. Or what they worried

people would think or say. Their reputation was more important to them than I was."

"And that was it?" Violet asked, disbelief lacing her words.

Hinnah was surprised to hear a tremble in her voice as she
said, "That was it." She had never spoken the whole story aloud
to anybody. "Sometimes I think about all of the things that
could have been different. But I don't think it really matters.
My parents always wanted me to be someone else. They didn't
like that I had grown up so fast, that I looked sixteen when I
was still only twelve. I couldn't have ever changed any of that."

Silence washed over them for a moment as Hinnah tried to
blink away her tears. She had cried over her family too many
times already. She wanted to put them in her past, because she
was forging a new future for herself now. One where she had
people who loved her for who she was—like Violet.

"What about your friend?" Violet asked. "Was he safe?"

"At least for that night . . . ," Hinnah said. "I've written
to him a few times, but he's never written back. I asked him
to leave with me, but he wouldn't." That was the only regret
Hinnah had. If she could go back and change things, she would
persuade Reza to come away with her too.

TWENTY-SEVEN

---

1 DAY, 17 HOURS, 20 MINUTES
VIOLET

VIOLET WOULD HAVE never guessed that Hinnah was the bravest person of all four of them. But there was bravery—not just in what she had endured, but what she had taken away from it. She may have been the youngest among them, but the things life had dealt her somehow made her appear the oldest.

The two of them were only steps away from the wireless operator's cabin now, but Violet couldn't go toward it. She was turning Hinnah's story over and over in her head.

"Will you go back and find your friend?" she asked. "After all of this?"

Hinnah shook her head again. "I don't think so. I want . . ." She trailed off, like she wasn't really sure what she wanted at all. "I want a future," she said finally. "One where I make the rules for myself. I want . . . that freedom."

Violet could understand that. After everything Hinnah had been through, she deserved to be happy.

"You know, you'd be welcome to come with me to Croatia," she said, realizing that she meant it. "With me, and Marko."

Hinnah smiled, and it seemed to illuminate her. "Really?"

Violet shrugged, though now that she had said the words aloud she felt even more eager about her offer. She could already imagine their life—her, Hinnah, Marko. They would make a strange family, but a perfect one. "I'm not sure about circuses in Croatia, but . . . yes, if you wanted to."

"If I wanted to," Hinnah mumbled under her breath, like she was really considering Violet's offer. "I've never been to Croatia."

It was Violet's turn to smile. Even though Hinnah hadn't given her a resounding yes, it was enough to fill Violet with satisfaction. They would both have the futures they had always wanted soon—and they would be side by side to achieve it.

There was a message from Marko waiting for Violet. Even though it had been only days since she'd read Marko's last letter, somehow it felt like an eternity. The message was scribbled in Jack Phillips's messy, barely legible handwriting, but it still filled Violet up with joy.

Can't wait to see you, it's been so long. —Marko

Violet was finally going to be reunited with Marko; his message confirmed that. Nothing could take away from the happiness she felt at that realization.

Jack the wireless operator pulled off his headphones with a groan, stopping his work for a minute to glare at the machine in front of him.

"Everything all right?" Violet asked, though she knew she was supposed to be blending into the background. She certainly shouldn't be striking up conversations that could potentially risk their mission. She knew that if she let her guard down, or if he suspected she wasn't who she said she was, things could go awry.

"Nothing, ma'am. Just a lot of messages." He waved her off, like she was nothing, before picking up his headphones and listening to the noise coming from it hesitantly. Grabbing a pen, he began to scribble something out, mumbling under his breath.

"Ice report in lat. forty-two degrees north to forty-one degrees twenty-five minutes north, long. Forty-nine degrees west to long. Fifty degrees thirty minutes west. Saw much heavy pack ice and great number large icebergs, yeah, yeah, yeah, like I haven't got enough messages to send." He finished his message and went right back to tapping, this time with an angry scowl on his face.

Violet frowned. Icebergs certainly didn't sound promising, but Jack didn't seem worried about it. Maybe this was a common enough message for wireless operators on ships to receive.

She picked up her message, clutching it close to her chest like it was the most precious thing in the world. And when she met Hinnah's eyes, twin smiles blossomed on their faces.

TWENTY-EIGHT

9:10 A.M.

1 DAY, 17 HOURS, 10 MINUTES

JOSEFA

"**WE NEED TO** get ready for tonight." The four of them had gathered in her cabin, and Josefa was desperate to distract herself from the hammering in her head and her memories of last night. "Everything has to go according to plan."

Josefa opened up her notebook, the one she had been using to keep track of everything. Step one was already completed: August had agreed to show her the book. The rest of it hinged on tonight: step two.

"I have everything ready," Emilie said. From the desk she was working at last night, she brandished a perfectly copied page of the *Rubaiyat*. When she handed it to Josefa, their fingertips touched for just a moment. And Josefa had to pretend that it didn't send tingles down her body.

Instead, she took hold of the page and studied it carefully, trying very hard not to think about Emilie and the night before.

"This is perfect," she said. "August will never suspect a thing."

"And once August thinks he's responsible for ruining the book, he's going to do everything in his power to keep it safe and sound and away from anybody's eyes, especially Lake's," Violet chimed in with a nod.

"Making it easy for us to figure out how to make the swap, and for August to take the fall," Josefa finished off, biting down her grin. She had been carrying around more than just her anger at August. She even had the journal of poetry he had once given her, before she rejected him. And he betrayed her. And now it wouldn't be long until August got a taste of his own medicine.

"What should we do until tonight?" an ever-eager Violet asked. "Are there any more supplies we need? Or is there something that—"

"No." Josefa cut her off with a shake of her head. "The best thing we can do is split up and lie low. Keep an eye around us to make sure nothing will disrupt our plans tonight. But otherwise, stay out of everyone's way. Especially Wallis, Lake, and August."

Outside on the sundeck, Josefa's thoughts were interrupted by Matron Wallis caught up in a conversation with one of the other passengers. For once, there was no frown pasted on her face. But there was something else about her—something that had drawn Josefa's eyes.

In the matron's hair was a clip glinting bright blue in the sunlight. One that looked eerily familiar.

It was Emilie's. Wallis must have found it after Emilie lost it. She must be holding on to it until she found the owner. Josefa had to tell Emilie. She was about to turn back to find Emilie when she realized what going up to the matron and asking for the clip might mean. Would she give it to them without asking any questions? What proof did they have that this clip belonged to them? Wallis was already suspicious of them, and somehow Josefa knew that asking about this clip would make her all the more suspicious. After all, she may have found it in a part of the ship they weren't even supposed to be in.

But Josefa couldn't just leave the hair clip with her. Losing it had devastated Emilie, and Josefa had promised her she would find it. Return it to her.

Now was her chance.

Josefa didn't think she was someone with great self-control, but she had done well to keep her hands firmly away from the pockets of the rich on board this ship.

But this was different.

There was a little voice in Josefa's head reminding her of the risk, but she ignored it. There was an even louder voice reminding her of Emilie and how much this hair clip meant to her.

She found herself striding toward Matron Wallis. Her face was turned away from Josefa. She was deep in conversation. Distracted.

Josefa's lips pulled into a grin. This was far too easy.

One moment, the aquamarine clip was firmly fastened to Wallis's brown hair; the next it was carefully nestled in Josefa's closed fist. Wallis hadn't even noticed her presence. And Josefa didn't give her a chance to.

She crossed the deck, weaving through the people there. All the while, she couldn't wipe the smile off her face.

TWENTY-NINE

1 DAY, 12 HOURS, 50 MINUTES
EMILIE

IF EMILIE WASN'T mistaken, the man perched in one corner of the third-class saloon, looking more interested in the people than the food, was none other than Francis Davis Millet. Emilie had never met him before, but she had seen his work. She had seen his portrait too, though looking at him now, she wasn't sure it did him justice.

She hadn't come to the saloon searching for him. She had come to seek inspiration for her painting of the *Titanic*, because she wanted to study as much of this ship as she could. Even though Josefa had asked them to lie low. And she couldn't ignore the famous painter her father had admired so much. Seeing him here felt like a sign.

Francis sat in a secluded corner, broken away from the crowded saloon. Still, his keen eyes observed the people he had separated himself from. While everyone else chatted away to their dining companions, Francis was silent and observant.

Emilie wondered if it would be rude to approach him. It was

clear to her that he wasn't searching for company. But before she could make up her mind, he caught Emilie's curious gaze. A smile flickered on his lips. It made him look younger than his years.

Emilie found her feet carrying her past the crowds and right toward him. "Excuse me? Are you Francis Davis Millet?" She felt a little foolish asking the question, but his smile widened.

"I didn't realize anybody would recognize who I was," he said.

"My father . . . he really loved your work," Emilie explained. Then she quickly added, "Me too, of course."

Francis let out a chuckle and patted the empty chair beside him. "Care to join me?"

Emilie slipped into the seat he had offered her. He had already turned away, his eyes flitting around the room. Emilie took this in curiously. There was nothing exciting happening in this saloon. Yet Francis's face would suggest he was watching something exhilarating unfolding in front of his eyes.

"I'm sorry . . . is there a reason why you're watching these people?"

Francis chuckled again but didn't turn back to Emilie. "It's interesting to see all the different personalities such a small space can hold. Observing people is one of the great joys in life."

Emilie didn't quite agree, but she supposed there could be something inspiring about the everyday lives of the people in this saloon. One could find inspiration in the smallest, most banal things. At least, that was something her father had taught her.

"So, your father? He's on this ship?"

"No . . . but he is—was—an art historian. So I've learned a lot about art from him."

"I can imagine. Not every day you meet a young lady such as yourself with an interest in art."

"Well, my father taught me his love of art. All kinds of art. Paintings and poetry. He used to share all of that with me. He helped me see the world a little bit better, I guess," she said. "We even used to paint together."

"Oh, yes?" Francis didn't seem surprised at the admission, merely curious.

"Yes, though lately, it hasn't been so easy to paint."

"An artist's block? I get those sometimes myself. This helps."

"Watching people?"

"Observing them," he corrected her. "It helps bring your art to life when you understand people."

Emilie heaved a sigh. She tried to see what he saw in this crowded saloon, but all she noticed were ordinary people, going about their lives. She wished she could speak to someone about what was *really* bothering her. How she couldn't get Josefa out of her mind. And how she couldn't bear to do the one thing Josefa had set out to do either.

"I think my problem," Emilie said slowly, "is that I'm not working on what I want to. Have you ever had to paint something because you know it's going to benefit you? It'll bring you money or fame; it'll help you lead a better life. But maybe it makes you a worse person? It takes something from you?"

Francis finally met her gaze. She wondered if the question was too much. Or if it even made any sense at all. It barely made sense to her, and she knew what she was confused about was no painting.

"Sometimes we have to do things that we don't want to do, yes," Francis said. "Practicality is important. But . . . if you don't follow your heart as an artist, it makes sense that you have a block. Art is so much about pouring out your soul, your very being, onto the canvas. If you're not being true to yourself, how can you be true to your art?"

But being true to yourself often came with a cost; Emilie knew that all too well.

"What if . . . other people are counting on you? For this thing that is practical but maybe not right? Other people who you care about?"

"If they cared about you, would they not want you to do what makes you happy?" Francis asked with a raised eyebrow. "Would they want you to do this even if it, as you put it, took something away from you?"

Emilie considered this. Would Josefa or Hinnah or Violet understand why she didn't want to complete their mission anymore? Would they understand that destroying the *Rubaiyat*'s bookbinding felt like a betrayal of everything she stood for? Would they care?

She wasn't so sure about that.

THIRTY

1 DAY, 3 HOURS, 20 MINUTES
JOSEFA

"IS THIS MUCH dressing up absolutely necessary?" Josefa asked. It was evening, and Josefa found herself sitting in a chair, wearing a dress that made her skin itch. Hinnah brushed her hair slowly, picking and parting and pulling, while Josefa tried not to groan from frustration. Violet dabbed at her face with powder and rouge—just enough to enhance her appearance, but not enough to make it seem like she was wearing any makeup at all.

"I know it's not your favorite thing to do, but if you want August Frazier to be putty in your hands, then yes," Violet said with a shrug.

In the mirror, Josefa watched herself transform from her usual self into the kind of girl that she knew August Frazier was mad about, although as far as she knew August Frazier was mad about any girl in a skirt. But she supposed she should help him see what he had really been missing out on.

"My mother would have loved this," Josefa said after a moment. "Dressing me up was her favorite thing to do."

"Is that what you were getting away from when you ran away from boarding school? Pretty dresses?" Violet asked with a roll of her eyes.

"Of course not, but . . . this whole thing." She waved at the mirror in front of her, at the fact that she suddenly looked like a completely different version of herself. She almost looked like a younger version of her mother, and that thought sent a shudder down her spine. "It's so . . . utterly . . . boring. And people spend so much time on it. My mother loved it so much she would offer me a new dress every birthday, and I would have to spend my time picking out stitching and patterns and hemlines. It was awful."

"I like it," Hinnah said. And when Josefa glanced at her, she was smiling like she really did enjoy it.

"My mother liked these kinds of things too, but . . . she never helped me pick out nice dresses. She only ever wanted to cover me up; that was the most important thing a piece of clothing could do for me. I would have loved to go shopping with a mother like yours, Josefa." Hinnah shrugged, like she hadn't just said something preposterous, but Josefa guessed maybe her hatred of dressing up was less to do with the dressing up itself and more about the rules her parents had made up for her. All the constrictions of her previous life.

"Are we quite finished?" Josefa asked as Violet lined her eyes with just a dash of kohl. She stood back, observing Josefa with pursed lips.

"I think you're ready to go." She turned to Hinnah, like she was asking for her approval too.

Hinnah nodded. "You look nice."

"Great!" Josefa was up in an instant, brushing a strand of loose hair out of her face. She was going to stroll right out, but then she caught Emilie's eye.

"You look beautiful, Josefa," she said with a small smile.

And just like that, Josefa felt the bottom drop out of her stomach.

"Th-thanks." Clearing her throat, Josefa turned away, toward the door. Her hands shook in the lace gloves Violet had slipped onto them earlier. A moment ago, everything had seemed easy. Josefa had done this a million times. Well, not this, precisely. But she wasn't unused to the lying and the stealing. But suddenly, something about all of this felt different.

It seemed to only then dawn on her how big what they were trying to do was. How much rested on her tonight. She couldn't get her breathing to return to normal as she slipped out the door. All the while, a single thought repeated itself in her mind: *I have to succeed.*

Josefa's nerves were at an all-time high. Even with the fresh ocean air and the sprinkling of stars on the canopy of black above her, she felt her heart beating so fast that she was surprised it didn't burst out of her chest. She willed her hands to still themselves from shaking. She willed her breath to come out normally, rather than the unsteady sharp intakes that led her all the way from their cabin to the promenade.

She had never been this nervous before. In fact, usually before a job, Josefa felt little but the familiar thrill running up her spine. But tonight was different. Josefa had been waiting for this moment for years. Ever since that night August had left her to fend for herself. That night when Josefa had learned she couldn't trust anyone—not really. And that was the very same night Josefa had promised herself revenge.

Now she was finally going to keep her promise to herself.

It was past midnight, and August had yet to arrive. With each passing second, it seemed that her heart beat faster. She wasn't sure how much longer she would be able to keep her nervousness at bay. There were a million anxious questions running through her head: What if August had decided it wasn't worth the risk? What if August had gotten caught by Mr. Lake on his way out? What if, what if, what if?

When she finally spotted August's tall, lanky form and his full head of brown hair in the darkness, she let out a breath of relief. She thought of Hinnah, Violet, and Emilie, and it stilled the nerves inside her somewhat. She had done this before, she reminded herself. She was Josefa Herron. She had broken into grand estates, stolen precious jewelry and trinkets, among other things . . . more important, she had gotten away with it all. She could best August.

"I've been waiting here and it's cold, you know," Josefa stated when August was finally within earshot. He clutched the book to his body, hiding it from view. Like he was afraid of showing his hand all at once. "What took you so long?"

"I had to get it out of Mr. Lake's safe. Couldn't have him suspecting me," August said, coming to a stop in front of her. His eyes traveling down the length of her slowly. "You didn't have to get dressed up on my account." But he smirked in a way that told Josefa that he was glad that she had.

"Your ego is bigger than this ship," Josefa said. "What have you got to show me, then?"

"Hang on!" August tucked the book away from Josefa's reach. "You don't want to hear about how I bravely managed to foil Mr. Lake's security measures to get this for you? He's a Sotheby's auctioneer. He's been trusted with this in his safekeeping. Do you know what that means? It means this is the most precious thing on this entire ship. Maybe more precious than the ship itself. And I've gone and brought it here for you."

"Oh, wow, my hero!" Josefa exclaimed, trying not to let the sarcasm steep too deeply into her words.

"You know, it wasn't easy to gain Mr. Lake's trust. With everything I've had going on."

"Well, you did. And now you've apparently got the most precious thing in this world in your possession," Josefa pointed out. She was itching to get the book in her hands, but she couldn't just grab it. She couldn't let on to August how much she really wanted it.

August shook his head, a laugh escaping him. "You don't

even understand how valuable this is, Josefa," he said. He exchanged the book from the hand tucked behind his back to the one near Josefa. She could see it as clear as day through the glint of moonlight. Josefa took a sharp breath. It was more beautiful than she could have imagined. Intricate patterns in glittering gold lined the cover. The patterns were so detailed that just one glance gave away little. She needed to see more.

August watched her closely, like he was examining her reaction.

"The *Rubaiyat*," he said with a grin. Like she didn't already know. "It's probably the rarest, most sought-after book in the world."

"And somehow it's in your hands." Josefa didn't want to seem too eager, but it was difficult not to reach for the book immediately.

"Technically, in Mr. Lake's." August shrugged. "But it'll be mine soon; don't you worry."

Josefa reached out a hand, meeting August's gaze to ask for permission, though she really didn't care for it. He reached the book out farther toward her, like he *was* giving her permission.

August was so close now. The *Rubaiyat* was so close. Josefa could make out the beautiful peacock-feathered cover, green and gold and unlike anything she had seen before.

Josefa's fingers tingled with the need to reach forward and feel it, so she did. It was cool and hard to the touch. Josefa could feel the hairs on her arms rise with anticipation and excitement.

She had waited for this moment for so long, and now it was finally here.

But just as her hand touched the *Rubaiyat*, August shifted. Like he had been waiting for something too. There was already so little space between them, and when August leaned forward, everything seemed to happen in the blink of an eye. One minute Josefa was relishing the touch of the *Rubaiyat*; the next August was closing the gap between them. Coming closer and closer. Until his lips were pressed to hers.

For a second, everything seemed to still. Then, Josefa stumbled back, trying to steady herself against whatever she could. The noise of a paper ripping echoed into the night.

When she found her balance again, Josefa could see only the piece of paper hanging from her hands. The words of an Omar Khayyam poem etched into it. A part of August's priceless book.

August—face red and blotchy with anger—was staring right at her.

For a moment there was only the sound of absolute silence.

Then Josefa stuttered out the only words she could. "August, I'm so—I'm so sorry." It didn't seem like enough, but it was all she could really offer. August wasn't even looking at Josefa anymore.

"I risked everything to bring this to you." August's voice was quiet, but that didn't stop the pure rage in it.

"I know, and I didn't mean to—"

"Do you understand how long it took me to build trust with Lake? How long it took me to get this job? And now . . ."

"August, I can help you fix it," Josefa offered with pleading eyes. "It was a mistake, and we'll find a way to—"

"You'll pay for this, Josefa," August said. When he finally looked up, his face was contorted into an expression of pure rage and something like hopelessness. Without sparing Josefa another glance, August turned on his heels and rushed away. His hurried footsteps echoed in the quiet of the night.

Josefa leaned against the railing of the deck. She was still clutching the page from the *Rubaiyat* in her hands. As if it meant anything at all without the rest of it.

She dropped the piece of paper and watched as it floated down all the way from the ship. She watched as it met with the sea crashing against the ship, slowly dissipating into nothingness.

THIRTY-ONE

1 DAY, 2 HOURS, 20 MINUTES
HINNAH

HINNAH COULD SEE darkness as she peered out the porthole. Nothing distinguishing sky and ocean, other than the moon and a blanket of twinkling stars. It was better to look out there than at Violet.

Violet's strange vulnerability from earlier this morning had disappeared. It was replaced with her usual wall of stoic tension.

While Josefa carried out the plan, there was nothing for them to do, really, but wait. Somehow, Violet was having the most difficulty with the suspense.

"She'll be back soon," Emilie reassured her. "It's only been a little while."

"I know," Violet said, though the knowledge didn't seem to ease her tension. She stood up from the bed she and Emilie had been sharing and began to pace the room slowly. As if that would bring Josefa back faster.

"She's done this a thousand times," Hinnah offered. "And this is her plan."

"I *know*." But Violet was getting more and more agitated with each passing moment. "It's just . . . there's something about him. August."

At this, Emilie glanced up. Her eyes flickered to Hinnah, a question in them.

"What about him?" she asked.

"I don't know." Violet shook her head.

"Isn't he just Lake's assistant? Foolish enough to trust Josefa?" Hinnah asked. That was how Josefa had described him, anyway. Though Josefa could fool most people.

Before Violet could share any more, though, a knock sounded on the cabin door.

Hinnah turned away from the porthole. Emilie leaped up from the bed, and Violet took a step toward the door.

"Josefa wouldn't knock," Violet said, stating the obvious.

"It's midnight," Hinnah mumbled.

The knock sounded again. Louder this time.

"Open the door, ladies." It was Wallis's voice on the other side. "I have something I wish to discuss with the four of you."

The three of them exchanged a glance. Hinnah tried to ignore the way her stomach twisted. She knew they would have to contend with Matron Wallis eventually . . . she hoped that Josefa and Violet had a plan for that. But from the thunderstruck expression on Violet's face, she didn't think they did.

Violet cast a sweeping glance across the cabin.

"Follow my lead," she said, her stern expression flickering

from Hinnah to Emilie for a moment before she flung the door open.

Wallis stood at the threshold of the cabin, arms crossed over her chest.

"It's a little late for a visit, Matron," Violet said, her voice sweet but tired. She stifled a yawn, covering her mouth with her hands to overexaggerate it.

"This is not a social call." Wallis's eyes swept over the room. From Violet, to Emilie, and finally to Hinnah.

Hinnah tried her best not to look guilty—but she wasn't sure how that was supposed to look.

"I have reason to believe that one of you is a thief."

"Excuse me?" Violet asked, feigning shock. Hinnah ran through all her interactions with other passengers, trying to figure out if there was a moment she had slipped up. She didn't want to be the reason for Wallis's suspicion.

"Something very valuable has gone missing, and I seem to remember one of you stalking around in the vicinity when it happened," Wallis said. She marched deeper into the cabin, her eyes traveling around the room. "You might as well fess up."

"I can assure you, it wasn't us," Violet said firmly, blinking her wide blue eyes. "But if we hear something, we'll certainly let you know."

Wallis didn't seem to be paying much attention to Violet, though. Instead, she neared Hinnah. Maybe she sensed Hinnah's nervousness. Because her stomach was still in knots, and despite a chill in the air, she could feel beads of sweat on her forehead.

"There were four of you," Wallis said to Hinnah. Then she promptly swung around to face Emilie. "Where is your other friend?"

"She's—" But Wallis cut Violet off with a raised finger. It was as if she knew that Violet could talk her way out of anything. Like she could smell weakness on Hinnah and Emilie, because her questioning eyes were staring right at them.

"She just went for a walk," Hinnah supplied. "She's been having trouble sleeping, and she thought . . . the fresh air . . . it would clear her head."

"It can get claustrophobic in these cabins," Emilie added with a nod. She was blinking a little too much, but Matron Wallis didn't seem to notice.

"Does it really matter?" Violet asked. "We can tell you that she certainly hasn't stolen anything. And—"

"So, you wouldn't mind if we checked your belongings?" Wallis asked with a smile that didn't seem to reach her eyes. "And if I waited for your friend to return?"

"What was stolen?" Violet pressed instead of answering her question.

"I hope something I won't find in your possession," Wallis said. She didn't wait for the three of them to give their permission before stepping over to the desk pushed up against the wall.

When Hinnah glanced at Violet, she simply nodded. But

Hinnah knew what that meant immediately. They didn't have time to waste.

Violet was the closest to the door, and she slipped out first, followed by Emilie. Hinnah cast a last glance at Wallis poring over their materials, her eyebrows scrunched together. Then she turned and fled.

"We need to find Josefa, so she doesn't go back to the cabin," Violet said as the three of them ducked into the nearest corridor. None of them slowed down. Hinnah knew they had minutes—maybe even less than that—until Wallis would call for security to find them.

"We should go toward the promenade," Emilie said. "That's where she is."

But Hinnah shook her head. "We can't all go in the same direction," she said. "That will definitely get us caught immediately." The sound of approaching footsteps was not far behind them. They rushed around another corner. On to a new corridor filled with cabins. Hinnah could glean from Violet's expression that the gears in her head were turning. But Hinnah was the one who knew this ship inside out. She hoped Violet wouldn't mind as she began whispering instructions.

"We should split up. Emilie, you should find Josefa. Violet, you go the opposite direction."

"What about you?" Violet asked.

"I'm going to distract them," Hinnah said.

"Hinnah." There was concern in Violet's voice, but Hinnah just smiled.

"I'm a fast runner, trust me." If there was one thing Hinnah was confident about, it was her ability to outrun pretty much anybody.

As Emilie ducked down a corridor to the left, and Violet toward the right, Hinnah slowed down. She needed Wallis to see that she was here. That she should be the one they had to come after.

Moments later, the door at the end of the corridor opened up. Wallis and a convoy of guards slipped inside. The matron didn't seem angry, really. But there was nothing pleasant in her expression as she took Hinnah in.

"I knew the four of you girls were trouble," she said. "Four girls traveling alone like this . . . it *always* spells trouble."

Hinnah simply grinned before turning around and sprinting right up the corridor.

By now, she had memorized the floor plans of the ship. She was still in second class, and she had to ensure that she could keep the guards away from the others for as long as possible. She turned a corner and swung through a set of double doors into the service corridor.

Hinnah could still hear footsteps following behind, though she had left the guards far enough back that she couldn't see them anymore. Exactly what Hinnah wanted. She dashed through the corridor until she stepped out onto the deck. The chill of the air sent a new rush of adrenaline through her. Hinnah could climb up onto the first-class promenade or she could climb down. There was space between the railings where she could place her feet. She had done this type of thing a million times. Of course, in the circus, it wasn't icy water waiting beneath her if she slipped up. She glanced now at the black water below, before lifting up her skirts and tying them around her waist. Climbing was much easier in the clothes that she wore at the circus, but this would have to do.

There was little space, but Hinnah managed to grab the gap between the railings and pull herself up. She climbed slowly until she landed on her feet on the deck above. Hinnah glanced down for only a moment at the space she had left behind. Nobody had seen her climb up; she was sure of that. At least luck was on her side now.

She turned around, stepping away from the edge of the ship, leaving confused guards below.

Time to find her friends.

THIRTY-TWO

12:10 A.M.

1 DAY, 2 HOURS, 10 MINUTES
EMILIE

EMILIE HAD NEVER run so fast before. She didn't even know she had the ability to run this fast, but she had only a few minutes before Hinnah's plans to distract Matron Wallis and her guards would fall apart.

She had to get to Josefa.

Copying the floor plan of the *Titanic* meant that Emilie was well-versed on the layout of the ship. It wasn't long until the promenade was in her sight. She couldn't make out anyone on the deck. She feared that she was too late—maybe Josefa had already turned back to their cabin. Maybe she had already been taken by Matron Wallis.

Or worse. What if Emilie was too early and Josefa hadn't even finished carrying out their plans?

But there was little time to worry about all these things. She barreled forward until the light of the moon illuminated Josefa. She stood by the edge of the ship, her hands stretched out to the ocean. It was only when Emilie had almost reached her that Josefa turned. There was confusion etched onto every part of her face.

"Emilie?"

"We need . . . to go," Emilie said, coming to a stop in front of her. She was already out of breath and could speak only in between puffed breaths. "Wallis . . . is looking . . . for us."

"Wallis?" Josefa asked. Emilie could see Josefa had more questions, but Emilie didn't have time to answer them all. Or any of them. Any moment now, Matron Wallis and her guards could catch up to them. Instead of answering, Emilie reached forward and grabbed Josefa's hands. She tugged until Josefa followed behind her.

"We need a place to hide," Emilie said, thinking aloud. If they could take refuge somewhere for a little while, maybe the matron would give up.

"Why is Wallis looking for us? Why are we running?" Josefa asked.

"Come on." Instead of answering her, Emilie tugged Josefa's hand harder. They rushed past familiar cabins and rooms and up a staircase. Emilie wasn't sure if she was paranoid when she heard approaching footsteps and murmuring voices behind them, but she didn't chance a backward glance. Their pursuers might not have caught sight of them yet, but if she slowed down they would.

Emilie turned a corner only to find a door leading into a darkly lit corridor.

"In here," she whispered, turning the doorknob and shoving

Josefa inside. She followed behind, closing the door with a soft click. It was too dark to see anything, and the hallway was barely wide enough to house the both of them. Gingerly, they made their way from the door toward the other end of the corridor. The whole time, Emilie could hear little but the sound of their own breathing. She wondered for a moment if there was another way out of here, or if she had just trapped them both here. This was a ship, after all, and there weren't many places they could go.

"Where are Hinnah and Violet?" Josefa asked Emilie in a hushed whisper. They pressed themselves against the wall, out of sight from the door. Their knees brushed against each other, and all Emilie wanted to do was lay her head down on Josefa's shoulder and forget that she had spent the last twenty minutes running from the guards. But she couldn't do that, for more reasons than she could count.

"I don't know," Emilie replied softly. "Hinnah said she was going to distract them . . . give us a chance to find you and get away. We split up, and I came to find you."

"So, they could be anywhere." Josefa sighed. She didn't seem pleased with those chances.

"They could have even been caught." The words made Emilie's throat go dry. Josefa must have heard the fear in her voice because her hands found Emilie's.

For a moment, Emilie was comforted by their entwined fingers. But there was a cold fear creeping inside her too. One that she couldn't ignore. Wallis said that something had been stolen. She had suspected them, even without any proof.

Josefa had asked them to steer clear of everyone, but Emilie hadn't listened. And even though she knew she had been careful, though she was sure she hadn't let anything slip to Francis Davis Millet, doubt had been niggling at the back of her mind. She had broken Josefa's rules. Worse—she had let her guard down. She had asked Francis Davis Millet for advice. Even though they had spoken only about art, she couldn't help but worry she had given something away. Something that had made him realize she didn't belong here.

With the truth of her mistakes weighing on her, Emilie couldn't bear to sit in this dark corridor with Josefa's hands in hers. She turned to Josefa, a confession on the tip of her tongue.

But then footsteps sounded right outside the door to the corridor. Instead of telling Josefa the truth, Emilie instinctively crawled closer to her. Josefa's fingers pressed even tighter against Emilie's palm.

"They must be around here somewhere," a gruff guard's voice said. If they simply pushed the door open, they would be able to spot Josefa and Emilie huddled together. There was enough light outside to pour in and illuminate their hidden forms.

Josefa nudged Emilie until she glanced at her. Her eyes had adjusted enough to the dark to make out Josefa's form.

Josefa reached a finger to her lips before slowly standing. She pulled Emilie up along with her. They began to inch toward the end of the corridor. Emilie hoped that there was another exit. If not—she didn't want to think about it.

Josefa must have spotted something because her expression changed from somber to excited. She rushed forward, until they had reached the door at the very end of the corridor.

Josefa pushed, but nothing happened.

"Shit, locked," she mumbled under her breath. Her eyebrows scrunched together for a moment, while Emilie kept glancing back. If they didn't come up with a plan, they would definitely be caught in the next few minutes.

But Josefa didn't seem too worried. She reached into her dress, pulling out the hook she had used to unlock the storage room the other day.

Josefa slipped it into the keyhole. She bent down as she worked. The sound of the pick scraping against the keyhole was hollow and metallic, and to Emilie sounded deafening. Emilie held her breath, but the guards didn't come inside.

"Aha!" Josefa exclaimed as the lock gave a soft click. "Let's go." She swung the door open, and to both their dismay, it creaked loudly enough to fill the corridor. In the next moment, the entrance they had come through swung open. The guards spotted them almost immediately, but Josefa tugged Emilie along and outside. They were out on the deck once more, the sea air greeting them sharply with its biting cold.

"There you are!" Violet and Hinnah were only a few feet away from them. They were both breathing a little too fast like they, too, had been running up until this very moment. Still, Violet glanced at them victoriously, while Hinnah searched the deck with worried eyes, as if she expected a guard to pop out at them at any moment.

Hinnah was right to worry.

"They're right behind us!" Josefa exclaimed. "Come on!" Without even stopping to acknowledge the other two girls, Josefa and Emilie turned another corner and ran down another set of stairs.

"We thought we'd lost them!" Violet's voice floated down from somewhere behind them. Somehow, she barely sounded breathless. Emilie was having a hard enough time running with her dress. Her lungs and her legs ached, but she had to keep pushing.

They found themselves in the steerage deck. Josefa led them past the cabins and down another set of stairs. They were going deeper and deeper into the ship, and Emilie was afraid that Josefa was leading them to a dead end.

"I know where we can go," Hinnah cried from right beside Emilie. "Down into the boiler room. They won't expect us to go there."

"Are you sure about that?" Josefa asked.

"We don't have time to argue!" Violet exclaimed. "Lead the way, Hinnah!"

Hinnah strode forward easily. Josefa didn't look happy as she fell back and let Hinnah guide them from the steerage deck and to more darkness. There were workers here who passed them curious glances as they rushed forward, but nobody seemed particularly interested. Maybe a little annoyed at the disturbance, Emilie thought, but nothing like Matron Wallis.

They climbed down a set of stairs to the boiler room. Metal grates lined the floor, and massive boilers lined the walls. With the stuffy heat, Emilie could feel the press of a headache on her temples and beads of sweat forming along her forehead. She could only imagine how much worse it was for Josefa, who was still dressed up from her meeting with August.

"What are you doing down here?" one of the workers, a man with sweat drenching his shirt, asked them with a frown.

Hinnah kept moving forward, past the man and leading them farther into the room.

"They're still coming." Violet's voice was filled with hopelessness.

Emilie could hear the guards above them. In just a few moments, they would be down here. And the four of them would be cornered. There was no escape route that Emilie could see.

After all of that, after days of sneaking around and planning and hard work. After everything. *This* was how their mission would end?

THIRTY-THREE

1 DAY, 2 HOURS, 0 MINUTES
JOSEFA

"**THERE HAS TO** be another way out of here," Josefa said, impressed with how unwavering her voice sounded as she glanced around the room. She tried to ignore the heat caving in on her from everywhere and block out the steady sound of footsteps behind them. She just didn't understand *how* the four of them had ended up in this situation.

"There is," Hinnah said, turning to them with fierce determination on her face. In the blink of an eye, she was down on her elbows, pulling open a barely visible metal grate on the ground.

"It's the vents," she explained. "I've been through them, and I think I know where this leads. And they'll never look for us there."

"Brilliant," Violet whispered, even as her eyes flickered between the doors they came through and the gaping, dark vent that opened up in front of them. "Let's hurry."

Hinnah climbed through the narrow hole with no problems.

Josefa dove in after her, squeezing her dress in with her somehow. The vent smelled musty and horrible. As if something had died in this place. It creaked with the weight of them. Josefa hoped that it could hold the four of them as she moved forward, keeping her eyes trained on Hinnah. She could already hear the sound of the guards in the boiler room they had just left behind.

After what felt like hours, Josefa could finally see light in front of them. Hinnah seemed to crawl faster, finally reaching a metal grate, which she pulled open. Hinnah glanced down before turning to Josefa.

"It's a bit of a jump," she warned Josefa. "Follow my lead." Before Josefa could say anything more, Hinnah flew through the air and landed smoothly on the ground with only a soft thud.

She glanced up from the floor of the mail room she had led them to. "Be careful," she warned. "I can give you a hand, if you want."

"I'll be fine," Josefa called down. She tried to copy Hinnah's movements closely, but there must have been more skill to Hinnah's work than Josefa realized. Instead of dropping to the ground smoothly, she landed against one of the bags of mail. She groaned, rubbing at her back, which was already throbbing a little. At least mail was softer than the ground.

Emilie and Violet followed after the two of them, sticking their landings with Hinnah's help. Then it was just the four of them and the stuffy mail room.

"Are you sure we'll be safe here?" Violet turned to Hinnah

with a raised eyebrow. "They might come searching for us."

"They'll probably look around the boiler room," Hinnah said. "I don't think they'll come here, though. It's a completely different part of the ship. We'll be safe."

"I don't know what we'd do without you, Hinnah," Josefa said, beaming at her with pride. She couldn't have been happier that Hinnah was with them at this moment. Josefa had always known that Hinnah would be crucial to their mission. But she hadn't realized just *how* crucial.

A soft whimper sounded beside Josefa. She turned to find Emilie huddled against a mail bag, tears streaming down her face. She was rapidly trying to brush them away but failed as more kept coming.

"Emilie?" she asked. Hinnah and Violet turned toward her too. The three of them edged closer to Emilie, shuffling onto their knees on the cold ground until they surrounded her.

"They're not going to find us here, Emilie," Violet offered. The softness of her voice surprised even Josefa.

"Everything will be fine," Hinnah said reassuringly.

"It's not that." Emilie wiped at her face harshly. Josefa had never seen Emilie like this. Her composed exterior was completely gone, leaving behind only vulnerability. She had caught a glimpse of this last night, but not to this extent. "It's . . . it's my fault."

"What's your fault?" Hinnah asked, at the same time that Violet asked, "How is it your fault?"

Josefa crawled closer still to Emilie, until she was right

beside her. "What's going on?" she asked, brushing aside some of her tears.

Emilie sniffled and slowly she began her story. "There was an artist in the dining saloon. I recognized him and I told him . . . well, I thought I was being secretive, but I guess he must have figured it out. I was just . . . I was confused about what I was supposed to do. My father and I used to read Omar Khayyam's poetry together. He is one of my favorite poets. What we're doing . . . it feels like a betrayal. To myself. To what I believe in. The *Rubaiyat* is not just a book. It's art. Irreplaceable. How can I destroy that?"

"And you told all this to someone on the ship?" Violet's voice now had a sharp edge.

Emilie hung her head in shame. "I thought he could help me figure out what I should do. If I should go through with it or not. I never said anything about the *Rubaiyat*. I never even told him my name or mentioned any of you. I don't know how he figured it out."

Josefa took in her confession. She didn't believe for a moment that Emilie's conversation with anyone could lead to Wallis chasing them through the ship.

"Wallis was looking for us, right?" Josefa asked, meeting each of their gazes.

"Yeah. She said one of us was a thief," Violet said.

"She said that . . . we were thieves?" Josefa pressed. "Or . . . that we had stolen something?"

"What difference does it make?" Hinnah asked.

Josefa sighed. She couldn't believe she had been so foolish. She knew that it had been a risk, but she had taken it anyway. Now she was watching Emilie blame herself for Josefa's mistakes.

She dug into her pocket and pulled out the blue hair clip. The one that Emilie had lost and Josefa had gotten back. She had envisioned this moment differently.

Still, she turned to Emilie. "I got this back for you," she said. For some reason, she couldn't meet her eyes as she pinned the blue clip to its usual place. As always, the brilliant blue color looked iridescent against Emilie's ink-black hair and her golden-brown skin.

"Matron Wallis had it, and . . . I stole it from her. It's my fault we're here, not yours," Josefa explained slowly. "I knew it was a big risk, but you were so upset when you lost it. I knew how much it meant to you. I didn't think the matron would suspect us. I was careful. I just thought . . . I don't know what I thought."

Josefa shook her head. Lately, she had been thinking with her heart rather than her head. The worst thing was, she wasn't sure if that was the worst thing.

Emilie touched the hair clip gently, like she was ensuring it was real.

Her eyes were still watery, but the last of the tears had been washed away, leaving a trail on her cheeks.

Before Josefa knew it, Emilie threw her arms around Josefa, pulling her into a hug. Josefa breathed in the scent of her. It was tinted with the musty smell of the vents they had just climbed through. But that didn't bother Josefa.

Out of the corner of her eye, she could see Violet and Hinnah exchanging a glance. Josefa pulled away from Emilie, putting some distance between them. That didn't help with the blush in her cheeks or the heat rising through her entire body, but it was a start.

Josefa turned to Violet and Hinnah. She was the reason they were here, instead of in a cozy cabin, fast asleep. "I'm sorry. I shouldn't have taken a risk like that."

Hinnah looked at her sympathetically, but Violet crossed her arms over her chest, her eyes narrowed as she studied Josefa.

"You told me to trust you, and now you're the one putting us in jeopardy," she said.

Josefa would have been defensive—but Violet was right. Josefa *had* told Violet to trust her, over and over again. And she had taken a risk because of her heart. Not thinking about anybody else.

"I'm sorry," she said. "I know it's not an excuse, but I knew how important this was to Emilie. If you had lost your father's pocket watch, Violet, I think I would have done the same thing."

"And it would have been just as stupid a risk," Violet retorted. She took a deep breath, like she was trying to keep her anger at bay. "Josefa, I think . . . you owe us an explanation."

Josefa had known Violet would demand this eventually. But she had been hoping it would be later. After the *Rubaiyat* was safe and sound in her hands. After she had already won and

Violet could see how the risk was all worth it. Not like this, when she had put all of them in jeopardy. When all their careful planning had been thrown out the window because of one mistake.

"Violet, we've had a long night, and—"

"You've been lying to us," Violet cut her off. "You told me to trust you, and I did. Now we're here, and our plans are ruined. You owe me the truth." At the last minute, she glanced at Hinnah and Emilie, like she had just remembered it wasn't simply the two of them anymore. "You owe all of us the truth."

It was the last thing she wanted to do, but Josefa knew it was time.

"August and I used to know each other. A long time ago." Her voice was laced with more bitterness than she wanted. Even though it had been years, their vicious parting had stayed with Josefa. "When we were friends, we used to do what the four of us are doing now. We used to steal, con, pull off heists. I didn't know much about all of this before I met August. He taught me how to pull off a job. He had been doing it much longer than me. Then one day he showed me this book. . . ."

Josefa brandished it now from the pocket of her petticoat to show her friends. She always kept it on her person, to remind herself of how August had wronged her. And how she needed to get him back.

"It was some kind of profession of his love for me, I suppose. It was filled with poems he had written himself. It was . . . well, ridiculous. I had never had any feelings for him; I don't know how he could have had any for me either. I turned him down, but I really believed our friendship was stronger than some flimsy confession of feelings. But the next time August planned a job, I found out it was all just a trick. He led me there to get caught by the police."

When Josefa closed her eyes, she could still see the jail cell where she had spent the night. August had been her only friend then. She'd had nobody else to turn to. She had sworn her revenge that very night, with anger simmering in her veins. She knew that one day her chance to get back at August would present itself.

"I promised the police that I was a student at a prestigious school and cried some pretty tears. They believed me, brought me back to school instead of keeping me in jail, and I managed to slip away. But by then August had taken everything. He was gone. . . . All he left me was his ridiculous book of poetry and my anger at his betrayal," Josefa explained.

"So that's why we're here." Violet considered Josefa studiously, as if she were seeing her in some new light.

Josefa heaved a sigh. "It's part of the reason. . . . I've always tried to be aware of August's whereabouts, but it wasn't easy. When I found out he got a job with Mr. Lake, I knew this was my chance . . . and then it got even better. He was going to be on the *Titanic*, supposedly protecting one of the most precious things to exist. It was like he was giving me my revenge on a silver platter."

Josefa could tell Violet wasn't impressed with her explanation. She exchanged a glance with Hinnah and Emilie, and Josefa wasn't sure what Violet's expression meant.

"You should have told us," Violet said, a bite of anger in her voice.

"I was afraid . . . I thought . . . you would try and talk me out of it."

Violet shook her head slowly, like she couldn't believe the words out of Josefa's lips. "You told us to trust you. But you never trusted us, Josefa."

And Josefa had nothing to say back to that because Violet was right. She was Josefa's best friend—she was the person Josefa trusted the most in the world. But she had kept this a secret, even when Violet deserved to know the truth.

"We're putting everything at risk for this mission. The lives we had in Dublin. My future life with my brother." Violet had never directed her anger at Josefa like this before. Even in the early days of their friendship, Josefa had known Violet trusted her, respected her.

"Hinnah left her life in the circus for this. For you. Because we trusted you." When Josefa glanced at Hinnah, she looked away, like it was too much to even meet her gaze.

Hinnah had never been one to express anger, so Josefa supposed Violet was expressing it for her.

"I'm sorry," Josefa said. "But you don't know what it's like to have someone betray your trust like that. And I couldn't . . .

couldn't even imagine what I would do if you stopped me from going after him."

"Well, I think we all know what it's like to be betrayed by a friend now," Violet said, settling Josefa with the kind of cold glare that sent a chill right through her.

"Come on, Hinnah; let's get some sleep," she said, taking hold of her and turning their backs on Josefa. They settled into the farthest corner, as if trying to get as far away from her as possible. And even though Josefa wanted to defend herself, apologize, make things better, she heaved a sigh and turned away.

Maybe a good night's sleep would help everyone.

THIRTY-FOUR

3:00 A.M.

---

23 HOURS, 20 MINUTES
EMILIE

WHEN EMILIE WOKE up, she forgot for a moment about everything that had happened the day before. Then her eyes adjusted to the mail room and the gentle sounds of her friends breathing as they slept.

Except Josefa.

Instead of sleeping, Josefa was in the farthest corner of the mail room all by herself. Emilie came to a stand, slowly shuffling toward her.

"What are you doing?" she whispered.

Josefa startled at the sound, her eyes wide, but when they landed on Emilie, she seemed to settle quickly. She patted the ground next to her and shifted to make room for her. She had papers spread out all around her and a pen in her hand.

"I'm trying to work out a new plan . . . it's a bit weird without my notebook," Josefa whispered. "But if we don't figure something out soon, all of this will have been for nothing."

Emilie peered at what Josefa had written out so far, but they were words and diagrams scribbled in such messy penmanship that Emilie couldn't make anything out. There was something very Josefa about that, though.

"You shouldn't have gotten the hair clip for me," Emilie said after a moment.

Josefa turned to her with a frown, her eyes traveling from Emilie's face to the clip still fastened to her hair. "I thought that you—"

"I know what you thought," Emilie said, though she wasn't sure what Josefa's thought process was at any given moment. "And it means a lot that you did. But now . . . everything is . . ."

". . . ruined," Josefa finished off. "It doesn't matter. I promised that I would find it for you, so I did."

"Even though you had to take it from Matron Wallis," Emilie pointed out.

Josefa shrugged. "It was important to you."

"Like this is important to you," Emilie said with a sigh. "The whole thing with August . . . his betrayal." She shook her head. She had been thinking about it. Hadn't been able to stop thinking about it. She couldn't imagine how it must have felt to be betrayed by the only person you trusted. "Do you think we're the same, me and August?"

Josefa's eyebrows shot up into her hair, like she couldn't even understand the question. "You and August are nothing alike."

"But . . . I don't want to steal the *Rubaiyat*. I don't want to ruin it. I kept that from you all this time. I almost told a stranger

230

our entire plan and ruined everything. I almost betrayed you."

"But you wouldn't." There was so much conviction in Josefa's voice that it was difficult to argue against that. "August is selfish. I'm not sure he was ever really my friend. But you . . . you want to preserve something important to you. You're the furthest from August a person can get." Josefa was looking at her in a way nobody had ever looked at Emilie before.

Emilie realized that the two of them had unwittingly edged so close together that there was barely any space left between them at all. Josefa's hands reached forward, slowly cupping Emilie's face. Emilie felt an exhilarating shiver run down her spine at the touch.

She wondered if this was what Josefa meant when she said that she wanted to make every moment matter, because Emilie was sure she had never felt like this before.

"'Make the most of what we yet may spend, Before we too into the Dust descend.'" Omar Khayyam's words on Josefa's lips sounded like some kind of magic.

It felt like nothing and nobody existed but the two of them. Emilie leaned forward and pulled Josefa close. Until their lips touched, and her hands tangled in Josefa's hair, and her arms wrapped around the small of her back. All of Emilie's thoughts slowly faded away into nothingness. Until there was nothing but her and Josefa pressed together. The smell of her like jasmine and metal. The taste of her like cinnamon and salt water.

When they finally pulled apart, Emilie could barely think.

When Emilie glanced up to meet Josefa's eyes, there was no overconfidence in them. No glint of self-assuredness or mischief. It was as if Josefa's walls had finally come down. "I'm really sorry, Emilie."

"For what?"

There was a flicker of a smile in her expression. "Because I'd wanted to talk to you for so long. Because I needed a reason to get to know you."

"And you thought a complicated and dangerous mission on a journey across the Atlantic was the best way to do it?" Emilie asked.

Josefa shrugged. "I thought that if it wasn't . . . you would say no. So why did you say yes, if you don't want to destroy the *Rubaiyat*?"

"I don't know . . . ," Emilie mumbled. "I guess . . . I wanted to see it. I thought it was a once-in-a-lifetime opportunity, and if my father were there, he would hate for me to miss that chance. To see, to touch, something so precious. So rare."

"So it was just because of him?" Josefa asked, looking at her as she always did—as if she could see right through her. As if she could see Emilie better than she could see herself. And when Josefa looked at her like that, Emilie was sure that she could, because ever since her father's passing, she hadn't felt like a complete person anymore. She felt like fragments of herself that she was still trying to piece together, but Josefa had made her feel more herself than anyone else ever had.

"It wasn't just because of him . . . it was because Omar

Khayyam's poetry had always meant so much to me. It was because . . . because . . ." Emilie wasn't sure how to say the words aloud. "Because every time we spoke, you made me feel something I hadn't in a long time. You made me feel hopeful, made me see myself in a different way."

Josefa tilted her head, like she hadn't expected Emilie to say that. "You make me see myself in a different way too," she said finally. Emilie reached forward in the distance between them, linking their fingers together. There was some strange comfort in that. In Josefa's presence by her side in this dark, lonely room so far away from the rest of the people on the ship.

"Tell me about your plans," Emilie said after a moment.

"What about—"

Emilie cut Josefa off with a shake of her head. "It's not about the *Rubaiyat*," she said, because she was beginning to realize it wasn't. Maybe her father wouldn't have been happy to see the *Rubaiyat* destroyed, but Emilie knew that art was more than that. "Omar Khayyam's poetry will live on forever . . . whatever happens to the *Rubaiyat*."

And if Emilie could have Josefa, if she could feel whole again, it was worth it.

THIRTY-FIVE

6:45 A.M.

19 HOURS, 35 MINUTES
HINNAH

"HINNAH, WAKE UP!" Violet's voice woke Hinnah with a start. She glanced up at her friend, a blur against the mail room. For a moment, she wasn't sure what she was doing here. Then she remembered everything that had happened last night.

"I need your help," Violet whispered.

Hinnah rubbed sleep out of her eyes, trying to register Violet's words. "My help?"

"I can't stay here with Josefa, not after everything she lied to us about," she said. That jolted Hinnah right out of her sleep. She sat upright, glancing around. But Josefa and Emilie were on the other side of the mail room, suspiciously close to each other as they slept.

"Violet . . . what about the mission?" Hinnah asked. As far as she knew, Violet would do anything for the mission. She would do anything to go back to Marko.

"If Josefa keeps lying to us, how are we supposed to pull it off successfully?" Violet asked, and Hinnah had to admit it was a fair question. How were they supposed to put their trust in Josefa when she had been lying to them from the beginning? Hinnah wasn't close to Josefa—other than working together a few times, they had barely spoken before boarding the *Titanic*. But if even she felt hurt by Josefa's betrayal, Hinnah couldn't imagine what Violet must be feeling.

"So what do you want to do?" Hinnah asked, wondering if she would regret the question.

"You and I are going to come up with our own plan to steal the *Rubaiyat*." Violet's voice was firm, her gaze unflinching. And Hinnah wondered how much of this was coming from Violet's anger at Josefa, and how much from a place of clarity.

"What about Josefa's plans?" Hinnah asked.

"It doesn't matter," Violet said. "Because she's not going to be a part of our mission."

Even as Hinnah led Violet through the vents, she had some serious doubts.

"Are you sure this is the only way?" Hinnah asked for the umpteenth time since they had sneaked out of the mail room, leaving the sleeping Emilie and Josefa behind. "I mean, Josefa apologized. And Emilie didn't even do anything wrong."

"Hinnah, you're far too forgiving," Violet said with an exasperated sigh. "Josefa only apologized because she got caught in her lies. And Emilie . . . maybe she hasn't done anything wrong, but she would just further jeopardize our mission. You and I are the only ones who can pull this off. Now, are you with me or not?"

Hinnah still had her doubts. Grave doubts. But she wasn't going to voice them aloud when Violet seemed so determined. And she could see where Violet was coming from—Josefa probably wouldn't have told them about her history with August if Violet hadn't demanded the truth from her.

She led the way forward, trying to ignore the burns on her skin as it scraped against the cold metal. She had studied the maps of the ship inside and out, so she knew where Violet wanted to go and how to get them there. She just wasn't entirely sure of Violet's plans once they got past the vents.

Still, Hinnah paused at an opening that led to a first-floor corridor, right outside the reading and writing room.

She glanced back at Violet hesitantly. "Your clothes look a bit slept in," she mumbled, studying the way Violet's plain white blouse and black skirts were creased around the edges. It was certainly not an outfit that a first-class lady would wear.

Violet glanced down at herself, too, but she wasn't dissuaded. "Hinnah, I can handle myself. Trust me."

Hinnah crawled out of the vents first, ensuring that nobody was around as she helped Violet down too.

"You need to stay here and make sure that nobody spots us," Violet instructed Hinnah as she brushed dust off her clothes. Hinnah thought that was the least of Violet's problems. In addition to her crumpled-up clothes, Violet's hair was in disarray.

Sleeping in the mail room didn't agree with her, and having left all their things behind, it wasn't as if Violet could simply change out of her dress or even don one of the many hats she had stolen from Matron O'Neill.

"And what are you going to do?" Hinnah asked, wishing that she had spent a little more time trying to talk Violet out of all of this.

"I'm going to find August and get as much information out of him as I can. Just because we're fugitives on this ship doesn't mean we're going to let our plans get thrown off course." Violet stuck out her chin in a show of confidence, but really it made her look younger than her years. Like a stubborn child acting out.

"Violet, if we get caught—"

"I'm not going to let us get caught," Violet said. "Josefa isn't the only one capable of putting together airtight plans." Violet sounded like she believed in what she was saying, but Hinnah was having a hard time believing her. It wasn't that Violet wasn't clever—Hinnah knew she was. But Josefa had spent weeks, if not months, putting together their mission on the *Titanic*. Violet was trying to put things together in the space of hours—maybe even minutes. And she wasn't fueled by determination. Nor by her desire to reunite with Marko. She was determined because of her anger, because of the fact that Josefa had betrayed her. Anybody could see that in the way Violet had been carrying herself. The way she had been acting—brash and impulsive, so unlike herself.

"And if August recognizes you?" Hinnah asked.

"He still thinks I'm a waitress on the ship," Violet said with a reassuring smile. "I know how to handle him." With that, Violet turned around and began to make her way down the corridor. Hinnah watched for a moment, feeling her throat dry up with fear. She didn't know who was on the lookout for them. She didn't know how many people Wallis would send on the hunt for a few girls who had purportedly stolen a hair clip, but she did know that their mission was on the verge of falling apart.

As much as Violet didn't want to admit it, Hinnah knew the truth. They *needed* Josefa.

THIRTY-SIX

7:00 A.M.

---

19 HOURS, 20 MINUTES
JOSEFA

JOSEFA KNEW SOMETHING was wrong as soon as she woke up. There was a feeling in her gut—one that she did not like at all. And sure enough, when she glanced around the mail room, she noted how sparse it seemed. Other than a stirring Emilie by her side, there was nobody else here. No Violet, and no Hinnah.

Josefa scrambled to a stand, just as Emilie must have realized what had happened while they slept.

"Where are they?" she asked, glancing around them, and Josefa shook her head.

"Gone. They must have . . . I don't know, left through the vents? Hinnah knows this ship better than any of us. They could be anywhere."

"Your plan won't work without them . . . ," Emilie said.

"But they wouldn't abandon the mission . . . ," Josefa said. The gears in her mind were turning quickly, and she was piecing together what must have happened. "Violet wouldn't let anyone get in the way of her reunion with her brother."

"She certainly told me that enough times," Emilie mused.

Josefa bit down a smile, if only because now was certainly not the time. But she couldn't help the flash of memory from last night—what had transpired between her and Emilie. It almost felt like a dream, especially in the light of the morning with the pressing reality of their situation.

"So, that means . . . they wouldn't have simply left to go into hiding. They would have left to . . ."

"Carry out their own plans," Emilie finished off for Josefa, their eyes meeting as realization sank in. "Would Violet and Hinnah do that?"

"Violet had to survive on her own far before we met. She was fending for herself her whole life. She can make the best out of any situation. She wouldn't give up so easily. And she also doesn't forgive so easily," Josefa said.

"What should we do?" Emilie asked.

Josefa took a deep breath, trying to focus on the problem at hand, even though she knew all her carefully constructed plans were quickly falling apart. But for once, Josefa was less concerned about the mission she had spent months planning and more concerned about her friends. She knew both Violet and Hinnah had a right to be angry. She *had* lied to them both, and she needed to fix things.

"If Hinnah and Violet are out there . . . they could very well get caught by Wallis," Josefa said. "So, first we need to find them . . . and then we'll figure out the rest. The problem is getting around without Hinnah."

"I think I can help out with that," Emilie said. From the pocket of her dress, Emilie pulled out a sheet that looked suspiciously like a map of the ship.

"It's not as detailed as Hinnah's, I'm sure. And she has basicallly committed everything to memory, including the vents. But . . . we can use this." It was the blueprints of the ship. It would be enough for the two of them to get by.

"Why do you have this?" Josefa's curiosity was piqued.

Emilie shrugged. "I've been trying to paint. I guess . . . I've been inspired by this ship. And our mission."

Josefa suppressed another smile. "And the thrill of it all?"

Emilie *did* smile, and Josefa tried to ignore the flutter in her chest at the sight of it. Josefa and Emilie couldn't afford to get distracted by their feelings right now—not when there was a crisis at hand.

"This will be very useful," Josefa said, clearing her throat and glancing away from Emilie and toward the opening to the vents. "Let's go find our friends."

Josefa had never been a fugitive before. And as much as it troubled her and Emilie to have to look around every corner for the possibility of Wallis or to duck into corners and open cabins at a moment's notice—she would be lying if she said she didn't enjoy it at least a little. She would also be lying if she said her enjoyment wasn't dulled by that gnawing in her stomach—by this separation of their group that Josefa hadn't anticipated.

"Where do you think they'll be?" Emilie asked, as they slipped past another corridor unnoticed and onto the second floor.

"Wherever August and Lake are," Josefa said. "But . . . I don't know where that is. If I know August, he's doing whatever he can to draw attention away from the fact that the book is destroyed."

"But Lake won't even want to look at it until later tonight," Emilie pointed out. That was the information Violet had gathered on their first day on the ship.

"And August will be trying to figure out how to keep him away even then," Josefa said. The problem was there were far too many places on this ship. But Josefa knew August—or at least she had known a version of him. "When he was troubled, coming up with his schemes, he preferred his solitude. He liked to plan things out on paper, just as I do."

"So, we just need to find his cabin," Emilie suggested.

"Or we can find him in the reading and writing room," Josefa said. "August told me that's where he sometimes slips away to in the morning." She didn't wait for Emilie to approve; Josefa was already on the move, leading Emilie through the corridors as they rushed forward.

Unfortunately, it seemed their luck had run out, because just as they approached the staircase that would lead them up to their destination, Wallis's voice echoed down the hall toward them.

"They have to be somewhere on the ship still. They won't

hide out for the rest of the journey; that's not the feeling I got from them," Wallis said, her voice carrying through the secluded corridor.

"Come on, over here," Josefa said, grabbing hold of Emilie's hand—ignoring the goose bumps erupting on her skin at the touch of Emilie's warm fingers threaded through hers—and pulling her into a hidden corner just behind the stairs.

"Perhaps we should check the cabins and alert all the crew on the ship, but . . . I don't want to unnecessarily alarm passengers," Wallis continued. There was hesitancy in her voice, unlike the authoritative air that she usually carried around with her.

"Since no passengers have been affected as yet . . . I think the best solution is to alert some crew to keep an eye out. They'll come out of hiding sooner or later, and when they do, we'll get them," a man's voice said firmly.

"Probably best to keep it away from the first class," Wallis added. "But we should send some guards around to patrol. I can give them descriptions of the girls."

"That would be very helpful, Ms. Wallis," the man said. Their voices were already getting distant, until Josefa could hear nothing but a low hum.

"Well, at least we know as long as we keep from being spotted by Wallis or the guards, we should be okay," Emilie said, the optimist for once. Josefa, though, couldn't find it in her to be hopeful. Not when the four of them were separated, their plan was in tatters, and Wallis was getting more people aboard the ship involved in looking for them.

"The sooner we find Hinnah and Violet, the sooner we can deal with all of this," Josefa said firmly.

"What are you doing here?" Hinnah's voice startled Josefa even before she could step into the reading and writing room.

"I thought I'd find August here . . . and maybe Violet," Josefa said. She wasn't sure what Hinnah thought of her—she must think pretty badly if she had decided to leave the mail room in the middle of the night with Violet.

But to her surprise, Hinnah looked relieved to see the two of them. "I'm so glad you're here," she said. "Violet has decided to go rogue. She's in there right now, determined to speak to August. To get information out of him. Though . . . what, I'm not sure."

"Information about the *Rubaiyat*?" Josefa asked. Because she wondered if there wasn't more to Violet's desire to seek August out. What if she was simply trying to corroborate Josefa's story? She wouldn't blame Violet for wanting to hear another perspective after Josefa had spent so long lying to her about August.

Hinnah shook her head. "Apparently she has a plan, but . . ."

"I'll take care of it," Josefa said with a confidence in her voice that she didn't quite feel. With that, she turned away from Hinnah and Emilie and pushed open the double doors to the reading and writing room.

The room was not what Josefa had expected. The first thing Josefa noted was the light streaming in through massive windows on either side of the room. Bigger windows than

Josefa had seen anywhere else on this ship and beautifully decorated with soft pink silk curtains. It gave the room a certain glow—as if even though it was early in the morning, the light streaming in illuminated the room like the blush of the mid-afternoon sun.

On one end of the room rested a white marble fireplace, and beaded crystal chandeliers hung from the ceiling. What really impressed Josefa, however, was the furniture. Yellow-and-blue chairs and settees were placed around the room, surrounding tables and writing desks. The floral upholstery of the seats looked as beautiful as they did comfortable.

Josefa glanced around carefully, and the only person here was—in fact—August. He looked deep in thought with a notebook in his hand. Violet was nowhere to be seen. Josefa wouldn't be surprised if she had ducked into hiding when she heard approaching footsteps. She hoped she wasn't too late.

"Maybe we just need to find Violet and draw her away from August before—" Emilie began.

"I'm going to speak to him," Josefa said, squaring her shoulders.

"Josefa, I don't think that's a—"

But Josefa was already striding forward. She took a deep breath, hoping that would give her the confidence to do what she had to do.

"August," Josefa said, coming to a stop in front of him. He glanced up, a flash of anger in his eyes as soon as he recognized Josefa.

"What are you doing here?" he asked. "You've already cost me a night's sleep, and I'm sitting here trying to figure out the solution to the problem that *you* caused. I should have known wherever you go, problems follow."

Josefa tried not to let the anger simmering in her blood out. She wanted to tell August that he was the one who problems followed—that he had been the one to start their rivalry. The one who betrayed Josefa and left her unmoored. But she wasn't here to fight with August.

Instead, she pulled out his journal, the one she kept on her person at all times. A reminder of the revenge she was seeking out at all times.

"I wanted to return this to you," Josefa said. August eyed it for a moment with suspicion before reaching out to hold it. Josefa could tell he recognized it from the way his face flushed pink. He should be embarrassed of it.

"Why do you still have this?" he asked.

"I'm not sure," Josefa lied, and from the flicker in August's eyes maybe he knew Josefa was lying. "But I think it's time I returned this and we stopped our rivalry. I didn't mean to destroy your book last night—it was an accident. And I thought maybe you'd realize that if I gave this back to you."

He opened it up to its first page, and Josefa noted the way his gaze traveled back and forth along the words of the poems he had written. She wondered if he was remembering their friendship too. If he regretted what he'd done. How he'd ruined everything.

He closed the book with a snap and turned to Josefa with a frown. "Am I really supposed to believe that you've forgiven and forgotten, simply because you gave this back to me?"

Josefa shrugged. "I don't know what you're supposed to believe, I just know that *I've* done my part."

With that, Josefa turned around and walked out of the reading and writing room. And straight into Violet.

THIRTY-SEVEN

7:20 A.M.

19 HOURS, 0 MINUTES
VIOLET

"VIOLETTA!" JOSEFA EXCLAIMED as soon as she spotted her. But Violet wasn't so keen on seeing Josefa, or hearing that familiar nickname that only she ever used.

"What did you just do?" she whispered, her eyes tracing back to where August sat with the leather-bound journal in his hand.

"I returned his journal to him," Josefa said, and Violet shook her head.

"But why? You had plans for that!" Violet couldn't understand how Josefa could let go of it so soon, as if it were worth nothing. She would never part with her own anger so easily. She would hold on to her father's pocket watch until her dying breath and remember what it had meant to him. And what it meant to her to have taken it from him.

"I'm sorry," Josefa surprised her by saying. And for a moment, all of Josefa's walls seemed to come down in a way that

Violet had never witnessed before. There was a strange vulner-ability to her as she looked at Violet, even in the way she carried herself. Her air of confidence, the easy grin she often wore—they were all gone. "I know I was wrong to lie to you all. To prioritize what I wanted above everything else."

"So you just gave it up?" Violet asked, baffled.

Josefa simply shrugged as if it were an easy thing that she had just done. "I would rather give up August and my revenge than you or Hinnah." And if Josefa had said this to anyone else, Violet would have believed it was one of her cons. That it was another part of Josefa's charms—another trick to get what she wanted in the end. But Violet knew that Josefa was being utterly sincere. And she couldn't begrudge her that.

"While I'm glad that you're finally being honest with me, the last thing I wanted was for you to give up your revenge," Violet said with an air of frustration in her voice. But from the hint of a smile on Josefa's face, she knew Josefa realized she had been forgiven.

"I also had to find a way to stop you from jeopardizing our mission," Josefa added. "August knows who you are. He knows you're not just a waitress at the Café Parisien. He's seen you with me."

Violet smiled wryly. "Well, then, it's a good thing he never got a look at me today." Josefa had a feeling there had been more to Violet's plans than just a meeting with August to goad infor-mation out, but she didn't push for more. Violet would tell her everything she needed to know in her own time.

The two of them turned down the corridor and toward Hinnah and Emilie, who had been patiently waiting—both as lookouts in case any crew members or Wallis came this way, and as a means of giving Josefa and Violet their privacy.

They both grinned as Josefa and Violet walked down side by side. The bad blood between them had seemingly vanished.

Josefa paused in front of Hinnah and took a breath. "I owe you an apology too, Hinnah," she said, meeting Hinnah's gaze hesitantly. "I'm—"

"We should get back to the mail room before Wallis and her guards catch any whiff of us," Hinnah interrupted. Violet knew Hinnah had never been one to hold a grudge, which was lucky for Josefa.

"We do need to figure out how we're going to pull off our plans when we're fugitives on this ship," Violet agreed with a nod.

The four of them shared a smile, and Violet finally felt like things were back on track—even if her own plans had not panned out how she would have liked.

THIRTY-EIGHT

17 HOURS, 20 MINUTES

JOSEFA

WITH THE FOUR of them finally on the same page again, it was like the energy among them had completely shifted. Instead of hesitance and doubt, it was like all four of them were energized by the possibilities now in front of them. They were back in the mail room and ready to get things back on track.

"August is definitely trying to concoct some plan to keep Lake from the book for as long as possible," Josefa said.

"I think we should let him look like a fool and wait for Matron Wallis to forget about us before we continue with our plans," Violet suggested. "Then . . . before the ship docks in New York, we can slip in and take the book."

But Josefa shook her head slowly.

"What if Matron Wallis figures everything out before then?" Josefa asked. "She confiscated all of our things, all of our plans. We know everything we need to already. It made sense to wait before Matron Wallis was on our tails. But it doesn't make sense anymore."

"We didn't exactly leave a letter detailing everything we were planning to do," Violet scoffed.

"But Matron Wallis is clever," Emilie added.

"I think there's enough in what we left behind in our cabins for her to figure *something* out," Josefa said. "And if she even has an inkling that we want the *Rubaiyat*, how difficult do you think she'll make it to get it?"

Violet's eyebrows threaded together. "But what if this makes it worse? After we get the book, where do we go? There are still three days until we make it to New York, and there's no way off this ship. We'll have to hide out here for all this time, with the *Rubaiyat*, knowing the matron, and Lake, and August are all out there looking for us."

"This ship is gigantic. Hiding will be the easy part," Josefa said with a shrug. "Nobody knows this place like Hinnah does anyway. With her help, we can hide out for as long as we need to."

Violet glanced at Hinnah, her eyebrow raised, like she was issuing a question. "Hinnah, do you think this is the best plan? Do you really think we'll be able to disappear in the ship until we dock in New York?"

Hinnah shifted from one foot to the other. "I'm not . . . I think . . ." She stumbled over her words, like she wasn't really sure about whose side she wanted to be on.

"Hinnah," Josefa said, in the steadiest voice she could muster. "You know if we don't get to the *Rubaiyat* now, we might miss our chance. You know your way through the vents, and who knows how many other places there are on the *Titanic* that the matron doesn't even know about?" Josefa held Hinnah's gaze steadily, and after a moment, she nodded.

"I think . . . it's possible," she mumbled in agreement. Josefa grinned, turning to Violet once more.

"I know it would be better if we had days to plan out every little step, but if we don't act now, no amount of planning will get us what we want," Josefa said.

"You're right," Violet said with a nod of her head. "With this, we get the *Rubaiyat* . . . but Josefa, you're going to get your revenge too."

Josefa blinked at Violet for a moment, unsure if she had heard her words correctly. "I already gave him back his journal. That was all I had that I could frame him with."

Violet rolled her eyes. "Did you really think Hinnah and I got nothing from our escapades this morning?" Violet unfurled a piece of paper—a letter—in a familiar scrawl: August's. "He's not as clever as he thinks himself."

And he wasn't, Josefa realized as she skimmed over his letter detailing what had gone awry with the *Rubaiyat*, and how he still planned to lift it off of Lake when he inevitably got the chance in New York.

"When Lake sees this letter alongside the missing *Rubaiyat*, he'll *have* to believe that it was August who took it. That's who he'll be searching for once the book goes missing. If all goes to plan, he'll never even suspect us." Violet grinned.

Josefa tried not to smile too wide at Violet's conviction.

After last night—after worrying that she had lost her trust forever, it felt good to be working together to pull this off. Not just for her, but for all of them.

"Hinnah . . . do you still think you can get in and out of Lake's room undetected?" Josefa asked.

"I know the exact path through the vents to his room," she said. "You just have to tell me what to do."

"If Hinnah gets caught . . . ," Violet said, letting her voice trail off, like a threat hanging between them.

"Hinnah won't get caught," Josefa said, casting a smile toward Hinnah. "She got us away from Wallis yesterday. Nobody is as perfect for this job as Hinnah."

Hinnah sent a flickering smile back at Josefa.

"If all goes to plan, in just a few hours, the *Rubaiyat* will be ours." Josefa felt a surge of exhilaration at simply uttering those words.

In just a few hours, *she* would have the *Rubaiyat* in her hands.

And out of August's.

THIRTY-NINE

4 HOURS, 30 MINUTES

HINNAH

HINNAH HAD ESSENTIALLY committed the map of the vents to memory by now. She knew how to get anywhere on this ship, be it first class or third class. She just had to be careful and discreet.

There was nothing easy about traveling through the vents, and the cold metal was uncomfortable on her skin. But she pushed herself through slowly, using her elbows to move as fast as she possibly could.

Passing through cabin after cabin, Hinnah finally found herself positioned where she wanted to be. Below her, she could see a lavishly decorated room. It was one of the largest rooms she had seen on this ship yet—and considering she had been traveling by vent, Hinnah had seen many rooms. Oak paneling covered the walls, and from up above Hinnah could make out the intricately designed carpet pattern that adorned the room. A large double bed rested to one side, pushed against the wall. A lush lounge chair to its side. The mirror next to it had beautiful gilded edges. And while Hinnah admired everything about this room, from its lavish decor to its ornate furniture, it was the simple fireplace at the edge of the room that she was drawn to. Because on top of it was the safe she had come here for.

Hinnah felt an uncomfortable gnawing in her stomach as she observed the empty room. She had told Josefa, Violet, and Emilie that she was on board with this plan. She *had* to be. Josefa seemed so confident, so sure.

But now that she was here, Hinnah's doubts were burrowing themselves in her mind. Their plan before had seemed so thoroughly plotted. That was what working with Josefa and Violet had always been like. Weeks and months of preparation amalgamating in a few hours of work, executed flawlessly, or close to. Hinnah always felt anxious, but never this sense of wrongness.

Still, she shrugged it off. Everything would be okay. And if she told herself that enough times, Hinnah was sure she would believe it.

She waited out of sight, watching the door to the room while the minutes ticked by. According to Violet's information, it was around this time at night that Lake checked the *Rubaiyat* to read one of Omar Khayyam's poems, and unless August was a much more skilled talker than Josefa gave him credit for, tonight would be no different.

Hinnah didn't have to wait long until she heard the distant sound of familiar voices. Lake and August must be just around the corner. That feeling of wrongness tightened around her chest. But she didn't have time to rethink anything now.

Hinnah watched from above as a moment later the door swung open. Lake entered first, with August following close behind. August spoke nervously, stumbling over his words in a rush to get them out, but Lake seemed distracted. He was focused on the safe, rather than August's words.

"And he—he really wanted to see you to talk about the *Rubaiyat*, so I think we should probably go there right now," August said.

"August, you know this is my reading time," Lake said. He moved closer to the fireplace with the safe on it. The two of them were almost below Hinnah now. She could make out the top of Lake's balding head and August's thick head of curls.

"But Mr. Lake, he could be an important buyer." There was a hint of panic in August's voice. Hinnah thought August was supposed to be an expert con artist. At least that's what Josefa had said. Maybe working for a man like Lake had softened him, because he was certainly no Violet.

"August." Lake didn't sound impressed. He leaned forward even closer to the safe now.

This was Hinnah's moment to act. She had only a small window of opportunity. Hinnah pulled Josefa's pocket mirror out of her petticoat and flicked it open. She slowly lowered herself out of the vent, just enough so the top of her torso was visible. If Lake or August were to look up now, they would be able to see the girl seemingly hanging from the ceiling, but they were far too focused on the safe to pay attention to anything else.

Hinnah angled her mirror just so she could see the mirror on the other side of the room. Lake's hands worked quickly, like opening the safe was an instinct. But Hinnah was fast too—she caught the numbers as quickly as they came: 35-10-81.

Just as Lake settled on the last number, the click of the safe being opened sounded. And before either of them had the chance to look up and see Hinnah, she used the lower half of her body to pull herself back up into the vents.

"He showed me pictures of some of this estate," August said. Hinnah heard rustling papers before Lake and August shuffled a little to the side. Hinnah watched as they bent their heads together. They were looking over some pamphlets, pictures of various items covering them. From one quick look, Hinnah could already note priceless antiques and jewelry that would probably cost anyone a pretty penny. She glimpsed pocket watches, gold-embossed boxes, emerald pendants, and a headdress of gold and gemstones.

Lake sighed. "I suppose it's not every day we are invited to join someone of his caliber in the smoking room."

There was a hint of relief in August's voice as he said, "Yes, Mr. Lake. And it was difficult enough to catch his attention. I promise this will be worth it."

"Well, let's not keep him waiting, then." Lake clapped August once on the back.

Hinnah heard the click of the safe shutting, and then August and Lake slipped outside. The door closed behind them.

Hinnah quickly began her descent from the ceiling. She

had to be careful as she dropped into the room. Grabbing hold of the space where the vent met the ceiling, Hinnah slowly lowered her body down. Her shoes softly thudded as they made contact with the floor. She rushed to the safe, the combination still repeating in her mind. She turned once to 35, then 10, and finally 81. The safe opened with a satisfying click. Hinnah didn't have the time to revel in the success, as she normally might have done.

She could make out the book sleeve that held the *Rubaiyat*. She slipped the book out with no issue. It was cold and heavy in her hands. Its jewels glimmered brightly and enticingly. The peacock feathers that adorned the cover reminded Hinnah of India, when her ammi and abbu had taken her on a trip to Kashmir, where she had spotted a beautiful peacock roaming around freely. It was one of her fondest memories of her family. She felt a twinge of sadness mixed with a shiver of excitement. She tried to ignore it. She had a job to finish first.

Without sparing the book another glance, Hinnah reached into the pocket of her petticoat, extracting the letter Violet had given her. She slipped it inside the safe with the book sleeve, just as Violet and Josefa had instructed her. When Lake opened it and discovered the *Rubaiyat* had been replaced with this letter August wrote, he would immediately suspect him. Even if he could talk his way out of the missing book, he couldn't convince Lake that he hadn't been at least planning on stealing the *Rubaiyat*.

Hinnah closed the safe once more, feeling some of that

gnawing in her stomach lessen. She had the book in her hands, and Lake and August were probably still in their meeting. She had succeeded—*they* had succeeded. Hinnah could almost see the pride in her friends' eyes as she went back to them with the *Rubaiyat*. She could already imagine their celebration as she approached the door. She turned the handle, but it wouldn't budge. It was locked tight. It must have locked automatically when Lake and August left. Unlike in Andrews's cabin, where the small transom had allowed Hinnah to climb in toward the beginning of their journey, there was nothing here.

"No, no, no," Hinnah whispered to herself. She had hoped that her escape from here would be the easy part, once Lake and August left the room.

Hinnah had never been the best at lock picking, but she had a few tools at her disposal. She slipped out the hook she kept on her person for emergencies like this. Sliding it into the lock, Hinnah moved it slowly, trying to find the exact pressure point that would open this lock. But no matter how many times she tried, it wouldn't budge.

Hinnah took a few steps back and stared at the door. If she couldn't pick the lock, surely there was some other way out? But she came up with no solutions. It was a heavy door—obviously Lake had spent money to get the most secured room to protect the *Rubaiyat*.

Hinnah turned back around the way she'd come. She glanced up at the vent that she had jumped down from. But it was far too high for her to reach now.

Hinnah searched around the room, desperate for something. There *had* to be a way for her to escape. But there was nothing she could climb up on. Even the fireplace was too far away from the vent in the ceiling. It wouldn't be long before Lake and August returned. She couldn't get caught. Not like this. Not *now*.

FORTY

3 HOURS, 5 MINUTES
JOSEFA

JOSEFA GLANCED AT Violet's pocket watch for the ump-teenth time. She thought looking at the hands slowly moving from one number to the next might calm her anxiety, but it didn't.

A tense silence cloaked the entire room. Thankfully, they hadn't had any run-ins with guards yet, but Josefa wasn't sure how much longer they would be able to hide out here.

"She should have been back by now, right?" Emilie broke the silence with her quiet question. "What if something went wrong?"

"Hinnah knows what she's doing," Violet countered, but even she didn't seem particularly confident.

"I'm not saying she doesn't," Emilie said. "Just that . . . something might have happened. What if she needs our help?"

"If we go out there and the guards catch us, we'll be in even more trouble," Violet said.

"But what if Hinnah *does* need us?" When Josefa posed the

question, the other two fell silent. She looked at Violet's pocket watch again. It was well past eleven. Hinnah should have been back ages ago, and they couldn't just sit here and wait.

Making a split-second decision, Josefa stood up and handed the pocket watch back to Violet. "I'm going to go and find her."

Violet and Emilie shared a look before jumping to their feet too.

"We're not letting you go on your own," Emilie said.

"It's better if it's just one person rather than all three of us. I don't know who all is looking for us, but we have to be careful." Josefa would rather she took the brunt of everything than the rest of them. She was, after all, the person who had gotten them in trouble in the first place. She was the one who had been careless. She took too big a risk, though she couldn't say she regretted it.

"You're going to need us." Violet was already walking toward the door, not waiting for Josefa's permission. "We're coming, whether you want us or not."

"You did pick us for this mission," Emilie reminded Josefa as she followed behind Violet.

Josefa sighed and conceded defeat. It wasn't like they had left her with any other choice. They were right anyway. The four of them were in this together.

Getting past the mail room and into the first-class cabins was no problem. They just had to make sure nobody spotted them. Considering the time of night, most people were already tucked away in their rooms, sound asleep. A few crew members and guards were roaming around, but it wasn't too difficult to sneak past them. Josefa knew that Wallis hadn't put the entire ship on alert anyhow, so if they were discreet their chances of getting caught were low.

Finally, they reached Lake's cabin. The problem was immediately obvious.

"It's locked." Josefa tried to open the door, but it wouldn't budge. She even tried to pick it, but it was unlike any lock that Josefa had encountered before. She definitely didn't have the right tools to break in.

"Hinnah." Violet knocked on the door of the room, calling out softly. "Are you still in there?"

Hinnah's voice came almost immediately. "I can't get out," she whispered through the door. "The vent I came in through is too high; I can't climb up. And the door's locked; I haven't been able to pick it."

"Where is Lake? He didn't see you, did he?" Josefa asked.

"He and August went to meet with someone. But they're going to come back soon. He didn't get a chance to look at the book before they left."

"Shit," Josefa murmured under her breath. There had to be a way for them to get in.

Josefa turned to face Violet and Emilie, hoping that one of them would have the answer. But Emilie's face was frozen with panic, while Violet's eyebrows furrowed, as if she were deep in thought.

"Do you think we can get someone from the crew to unlock the door for us?" Violet finally asked.

"How?" Josefa asked. "Violet, we're fugitives, in case you've forgotten."

Violet rolled her eyes. "Do you not trust me?"

Josefa and Emilie exchanged a look. Of course Josefa trusted Violet, but drawing attention to themselves didn't seem like the best idea at this moment.

"Just follow my lead." Violet turned around and began to rush down the corridor, her hands up in the air and a panicked look on her face.

She was emitting a low wail, a sound frail and heartbreaking.

A crew member turned the corner, obviously looking for whoever was in distress, and Josefa and Emilie ducked behind a pillar and out of sight.

Violet was still wailing, but it seemed there were a jumble of words coming out of her lips at the same time. "P-please." The rest of her words came out garbled with tears—absolutely incomprehensible.

The crewman looked around him for a moment, as if he were searching for someone to help him deal with Violet. "Ma'am?" he asked slowly. "Are you . . . is everything okay?"

In response, Violet simply continued her sobbing. It was so loud that Josefa was afraid for a moment that she might actually draw the attention of others.

"Stay here," Josefa whispered to Emilie. From the corner

where they were tucked away, Josefa could make out the master key in the crewman's belt buckle. If Violet could keep him occupied for just a few more moments, Josefa would be able to take it without much difficulty at all.

"Where are you going?" Emilie's eyes were wide as she looked from Josefa crawling out of their hiding space to Violet and the crewman.

"Just look out for anyone else approaching?" Josefa asked. "I'll be right back."

Violet was in the midst of tearfully explaining to the crewman about how she couldn't seem to find a precious pocket watch that her father had given her. The crewman was doing his best to comfort her, though he looked overwhelmed at suddenly being accosted by a tearful girl.

"If it's somewhere on this ship, we'll find it," he mumbled softly.

Josefa slowly approached the pair. With the crewman's back to her, the only way he would see her was if he turned. He was so occupied with Violet, though, that he didn't even sense Josefa's fingers slipping the key off of him.

As swiftly as she had grabbed the keys, she rushed back to Emilie's hiding spot. She looked at Josefa appraisingly, and Josefa felt a strange glow of pride. She had forgotten that Emilie had never really seen her at work.

Josefa turned and caught Violet's gaze as soon as she was tucked away, the key safely in her hands.

Violet sniffled and wiped at her tears with one hand. But

with the other, she slipped her father's pocket watch out, dropping it just by the crewman's feet. She kept the tears going for a few more minutes, until the crewman noticed the pocket watch right below them.

He picked it up gently, holding it up to the light. Like he wasn't sure how it had gotten there.

"Well, this wouldn't be it, would it?" he asked.

"You found it!" Violet exclaimed, her smile so bright that it could put the sun to shame.

The crewman looked at Violet with a weak smile too. Like he couldn't believe he had solved her problem so easily—but also enthralled by Violet's smile. Josefa had seen that smile charm many a man.

"Thank you, thank you!" Violet almost threw her arms around the man, though she withdrew at the last moment. A blush rose to her cheeks, like she couldn't quite believe she had almost embraced a near stranger. This seemed to endear her to the crewman even more.

"Don't mention it." He handed the pocket watch to Violet, who slipped it away into the folds of her dress.

"I should be getting back to my cabin; I can't thank you enough for your help. I won't keep you any longer," she said, brushing back a strand of her hair and wiping away the remnants of her fake tears.

"Of course." The man gave a nod of his head before turning around and walking back the way he had come. Josefa let out a breath of relief.

But no sooner had the breath escaped her than August's voice floated from around the corner.

"I think we definitely made a sale there, sir," August said, his voice full of the boastful pride that Josefa hated with all her being.

Josefa and Emilie slipped out of their hiding place and moved toward Violet. "Lake and August are on their way," Josefa explained to Violet in a rush as she slipped the key into the door and pushed it open.

The three of them managed to burst in just as August turned the corner and came into view. Josefa closed the door behind them, hoping that he hadn't spotted them.

"Hinnah!" Josefa exclaimed in a whisper. She was in a corner of the room, with the *Rubaiyat* cradled in her hands as if it were a child rather than a book.

"You did it!" she cried when her eyes landed on them. "Let's get out of here."

"We can't . . . Lake and August are coming!" Emilie exclaimed in a panic-stricken voice.

Josefa took a deep breath to calm her racing heart. "We have to find another way out of this room. Now."

FORTY-ONE

2 HOURS, 55 MINUTES

HINNAH

HINNAH HAD BEEN trapped in this room for what felt like hours. She had racked her brain, trying to figure out a way to escape. While Josefa jammed the lock with some leftover twine to keep Lake and August out for as long as possible, Hinnah turned away from the door, and her eyes settled on the porthole.

Hinnah's stomach flipped uncomfortably at the thought of it. Of course, she had considered climbing out using the porthole before, but she had hoped there was some other solution that didn't involve risking her life.

"There's only one other way out of here," Hinnah said, approaching the porthole. She glanced out at the dark depths of the water underneath the ship. Just one mistake, one slip, would mean certain death.

When Hinnah turned back to the others, they were staring at her as if she had lost her mind. But she felt like she was finally thinking clearly. Listening to her own instincts instead of what her friends considered the right solution.

"How are we going to get out through that tiny space?" Violet asked at the same time that Emilie mumbled, "Impossible." Even Josefa seemed at a loss for once.

"It's our only option," Hinnah insisted. No matter how much she wished it *wasn't* their only option, Hinnah knew that they had minutes before Lake and August would burst through this door.

"We squeeze through the porthole," Violet said. "And then what?" Her eyes flashed dangerously as she glanced at Josefa—not Hinnah. "This could get us killed."

"It's definitely not my first choice," Josefa said, and even her voice seemed to be wavering for once—as if she really hadn't thought through all these possibilities. Hinnah should have—she knew that now. She should have never agreed to rush in here simply because Josefa was so insistent she knew what she was doing. But now wasn't the time to talk about it.

"We *have* to do this," Hinnah cut in, stepping in between her two friends. "I can get us all out of here; I promise."

Josefa was the only silent one. Her shoulders tensed and her expression seemed somber, as if she were deep in thought. After a moment, she glanced up to meet Hinnah's eyes. "Do you really think we can get out through there?"

But Violet was still shaking her head. "I could distract them. Keep them occupied while the three of you slip away."

"He'll recognize you," Emilie said. "He's seen you before . . . and we're already fugitives." Emilie didn't seem happy as she turned to Josefa. "We have to, don't we?"

Hinnah was only half listening to the conversation as she gathered together bedsheets, pillowcases, clothes—anything she could find for a makeshift rope. After all, nothing mattered if they spent so long discussing their options that they didn't even have the opportunity to carry out their escape. She pulled the glass of the porthole open and peered out at the midnight-black water. It stretched as far as she could see—which wasn't very far in the darkness.

A pulse of fear rose through her chest, and her fingers trembled on the makeshift rope she had tied together. Hinnah knew she didn't have time for fear. She barely had enough time to get the four of them out of there.

Hinnah closed her eyes for a moment and took a deep breath, dulling her terror to nothing but a low hum.

"Wait for my cue." She glanced back at her three friends with a small smile that she hoped was encouraging. "And . . . try not to get caught."

Without waiting for their responses, Hinnah slowly pulled herself out of the porthole. She had to search for only a moment before her eyes landed on what she was looking for.

"One . . . two . . . ," she mumbled under her breath, and on three, Hinnah jumped up to grab hold of the brass window casings above the porthole. With her free hand, she tied an end of the rope to the casings, knotting it as tightly as she could.

"God, I hope this holds," Hinnah mumbled to herself. She had to try to ignore the rush of cold air all around her, the knot in her stomach, and the little voice in her head asking her what she thought she was doing here.

In the circus, things were easy. Hinnah practiced one trick a hundred times before she ever had to perform in front of people. She got the chance to fall, and get hurt, and try again and again and again. Better yet, Hinnah knew that if she made a mistake, the worst that would happen was a ruined trick. Maybe a bruise or two.

But all four of their lives depended on Hinnah being able to carry out the task at hand.

Hinnah swung the loose end of the rope forward only for it to swing back a moment later. The second time, it found its target through an open window farther down the ship. The distance stretched longer than Hinnah was comfortable with.

Gulping down her worries, Hinnah glanced below to call to her friends. "Come on, climb up. I'll hoist you up to the rope." Hinnah surprised herself with her steady voice, but if she gave way to her fear, she knew her friends would never make the crossing.

"Hinnah . . ." Violet stood by the porthole, her eyes cast down toward the water. There was a tremble in her voice. This was the first time Hinnah had seen her fearful. She knew, maybe better than anyone else, what Violet had at stake, and somehow that bolstered Hinnah's strength.

Outside the door, they could now make out the commotion of Lake and August struggling with the lock. They had to hurry.

"Violet, you can do this," Hinnah insisted, her voice firm. Confident. The kind of voice Hinnah's ammi used to use with her all the time. The kind of voice that projected strength.

"Okay." Violet took a deep breath and reached up to Hinnah. She ignored the pain of keeping her grip steadily on the window casings and focused on balancing herself as she pulled Violet up with her other hand.

"Grab the rope and go down into the window. I'll get everyone else."

"Are you sure this is going to hold us?" Violet examined the rope with a sharp eye.

"It's going to be fine." Hinnah tried to make her voice as soothing as possible. She had done the best she could with what she had, but she could not say with utter confidence the rope would hold them all. She could only hope.

Violet nodded once before she grabbed on to the rope and began her climb. Hinnah watched her for a moment before ducking down the porthole.

She had to do the same twice more—first Emilie, then Josefa. Once they were both safely on the rope, slowly making their way to the second cabin, Hinnah watched them. Her stomach was in knots, and her arms ached. But she had gotten them this far. They were *so* close.

Just as Hinnah was about to shift herself onto the rope, she heard the sound of the door to Lake's room click open. She didn't have a moment to waste. It would take Lake and August a minute to realize the *Rubaiyat* was missing—to figure out that someone had broken into their room.

Grabbing hold of the rope, Hinnah climbed as fast as she could while holding on to the book. She kept her eyes trained ahead of her the entire time, trying to ignore the sound of the water, the sharp smell of the sea, the air whooshing all around her and whipping her hair every which way. She tried to ignore the pull of her muscles with every single movement, and the way her arms had begun to stiffen and throb. Trying to shut all of that out, Hinnah concentrated on the unsteady climb and on Josefa's fierce gaze waiting on the other side.

As soon as she landed on the floor of the room with a soft thud, Josefa, Emilie, and Violet pushed the rope out the window. It swung out into the darkness and disappeared from sight.

Hinnah pulled the window closed. For a moment, the four of them could only stare at each other. They were all breathing fast.

Finally, it dawned on Hinnah: they had made it.

FORTY-TWO

2 HOURS, 45 MINUTES

JOSEFA

"**LOOK AT THIS** place," Josefa breathed, stepping away from the window and into the room they had broken into. Hinnah couldn't have picked a better spot for them to find refuge. The room was empty but massive. It was decadent, dripping with the kind of opulence that Josefa couldn't imagine in her wildest dreams. The place was draped with magnificent carpeting, the walls lined with rich oak paneling. The bed in the middle had figurines carved in wood, and it was bigger than any bed Josefa had seen in her whole life.

A plush lounge chair rested by the window they had climbed through, with beautiful red upholstery. In the middle of the room, two floral-patterned armchairs surrounded a marble table.

"The rich live different lives, don't they?" Violet asked, taking the room in with an impressed smirk.

Violet pushed open a small door near the window that led into a bathroom that certainly didn't look like it belonged on a ship. Even in second class, the four of them shared a small bathroom with other passengers. And their shared bathroom was nothing like the one Josefa had just stepped into. This bathroom housed the largest bathtub Josefa had ever seen. Its marble exterior seemed to glitter under the glow of the dim lamplight.

"Imagine bathing in *this*," Violet mumbled, trailing her fingers along the marble.

"Soon . . . we won't have to imagine any of this, will we?" Josefa asked, grinning. She ushered Violet out of the bathroom, and the four of them gathered together. They had finally caught their breath; some of the adrenaline from the past few minutes had dissipated. Josefa, though, was still buzzing with excitement. She could barely contain herself.

"Do you have it?" she asked.

Hinnah pulled the book out from her dress and passed it to Josefa. All of them moved closer together, until they were standing in a circle. Their gazes focused on the book in Josefa's hands.

The *Rubaiyat*. The reason they were all here.

In the light of this room, the cover glinted gold. Josefa brushed a hand over it, feeling the cold seep from the book into her hands. It sent an excited tingle down her spine. The jewels encrusted in the book sparkled in the light—blue and red and green. And there was one magnificent jewel that was bigger than all the rest—the one that seemed to glint the brightest. This would be the jewel that changed all their lives.

Josefa flipped the book open gently. The pages of the *Rubaiyat* were thick but soft as she turned them slowly. Page after perfect page. The four of them took in the words of Omar Khayyam. And though they were all silent, it felt to Josefa that there was something binding them together. It wasn't Omar Khayyam or his poetry, as beautiful as his words were.

"It's perfectly intact," Josefa said as she closed the book gently. "You managed to get it out unscathed." She gazed admiringly at Hinnah, who was grinning from ear to ear now.

"It was easy to grab it once I got the safe combination."

Josefa could just imagine what was going on in Lake's cabin at this moment. August was probably finally getting what he deserved.

"You've finally got your revenge," Violet said, and there was no anger in her voice now. She was smiling—like this wasn't just Josefa's victory. It was all of theirs.

"The cost of it was almost too high. We almost got caught," Josefa said.

"Isn't that your favorite type of con?" Violet asked.

"No . . ." There was something different about the almost getting caught this time. There was something different about putting her friends at risk—it didn't bring her that familiar feeling of thrill, but instead cold anxiety. She glanced at Emilie, who was still admiring the *Rubaiyat*, and she knew why it was so different. Because this wasn't about August, or even the *Rubaiyat*, really. This was about the people who she trusted. People who she would give anything to protect. To keep in her life.

"Emilie," she said, reaching forward and entwining their fingers. From the corner of her eye, she could make out Violet and

Hinnah exchanging a glance, like they knew what was going on between them. "Come to America with me. I know you want to travel to Haiti, but in America . . . we could be together."

Emilie seemed to consider her proposition for a moment.

"It's not that easy," she said finally. "My mother's family still lives in Haiti. I want to find them; I want to know them. And I want to know about the place I was born. About where my mother came from."

For all that she knew about Emilie, Josefa had never realized *this* was why she wanted to go to Haiti. While Josefa was running away from her family, Emilie was desperate to find hers.

"I'll come with you," she said. "To Haiti."

"I can't ask you to do that."

"I want to," Josefa said. "This is what I wanted, Emilie. Freedom. To go where I want to go, be with whoever I choose to be with. Will you let me come with you?"

Emilie parted her lips to answer, but before she could say anything, Josefa felt a jolt under her feet. It tipped them all off balance. The floor of the ship vibrated, the sound of grinding echoing around them.

Josefa had only a moment to catch Emilie's worried gaze before all four of them rushed to the window. In the glint of the moonlight, Josefa could only make out a huge black mass gliding past the ship.

"What is that?" Hinnah asked at the same time that Emilie mumbled, "What just happened?"

Josefa shook her head. "I have no idea."

FORTY-THREE

11:41 P.M.

2 HOURS, 39 MINUTES
JOSEFA

JOSEFA LEANED BACK from the window, her eyebrows scrunched together. It had been nothing, she was sure of it, even if there was a small, niggling worry in the back of her mind.

"It sounded bad," Violet said, still looking out at the water. For once, her cool confidence seemed to have dissipated.

"I don't think there's anything to worry about," Josefa said, hoping she sounded reassuring. But she couldn't help the feeling of dread plunging in her stomach after everything that had happened. So much had gone wrong with their plans. But they had the *Rubaiyat* in their hands now. They were all together.

They were successful. They could leave their worries behind. That's what Josefa tried to tell herself.

But the next moment, the doorknob to the stateroom rattled, as if someone was trying to open it from the other side.

"I thought this room was unoccupied," Hinnah whispered. Josefa had thought so too—everything about the room suggested that it was. There was nothing in the room that seemed to belong to a person: no luggage or clothes, hairbrushes or toiletries. Not to mention that it was almost midnight. If someone was staying in this room, Josefa assumed they would already be here.

"I'm sure it's no one," Josefa said, stepping forward slightly. "They probably have the wrong—" The door burst open before Josefa could finish her sentence.

August stood in the doorway, and there was a wildness in his eyes. In all the time Josefa had known August, there had always been something cold and calculating about him. It was what made him good at what he did. But this wildness in his expression—it was completely unlike him.

His brown hair, which was usually neatly combed and parted to one side, was now in disarray. The clothes he wore these days were meant to make him presentable, to fit in with Mr. Lake's peers. But there was nothing about August now that was presentable. His shirt hung loose from his trousers, rumpled up and disheveled. His coat was half off and half on. A sneer turned his handsome face into something vile and horrid.

Josefa's heart plummeted at the sight of him, but she had dealt with August before. She was sure she could handle him.

"August," she said. "What are you—"

She was cut off by August lunging at her. A knife glinted in his hands, shining bright against the glow of the moonlight. And in all her time breaking into people's homes, pickpocketing, stealing, getting chased, running from the law, Josefa hadn't felt fear like she did right then. For a moment, all she could see was that glint of the knife and the blur of movement as August came for her.

But before Josefa could wrap her head around what was happening, August hit the ground with a resounding thud. Hinnah stood over him, her hair loose and anger blazing in her eyes. In the time it took Josefa to blink her eyes and adjust to what had just happened, August was up on his feet once more. As if he was completely unfazed by being tackled.

But Hinnah was ready, arms in front of her, teeth gritted together. Josefa had never witnessed a fight like this before. August—all rage and limbs, moving heavily toward Hinnah. He was taller than her, bulkier than her. Josefa wanted to move forward and tug Hinnah out of the way. But Hinnah didn't need Josefa.

Hinnah pulled him over her shoulder and slammed him on the ground. The sound reverberated around the room, heavy and ugly. It settled in Josefa's stomach with a lurch, along with the groan of pain that escaped from August's lips.

Hinnah, though, wasn't even out of breath. Her lips curled up in a grin as she turned to the other three. "I've been doing judo for a long time," she explained. "You have to learn how to protect yourself when you're on your own."

"Are you okay?" Emilie asked Josefa. She was clutching the *Rubaiyat* to her chest as if it were a lifeline. Worry creased her forehead.

"I'm fine," Josefa mumbled, even though she was still trying to process what had just happened. August had tried to stab her.

Sure, he had gotten her in trouble with the police all those years ago. She had held that anger toward him for years, waiting for the chance to get back at him. But she would never dream of hurting him. Not like that.

To think that just a few years back, Josefa had considered August a friend. Even a mentor. She had believed him to be the only person who would look out for her, who would be willing to help her. The only person who understood her.

"Josefa . . ." Emilie stepped toward her, but there was a rush of sound that interrupted her.

August had recovered faster than any of them could have predicted. Perhaps it was his fury that fueled him. With his knife gripped in his hand, August ducked past Hinnah and toward Josefa.

Before Josefa could move out of the way, an indecipherable shout pierced the air. August's knife met the heavy book Emilie had thrust in front of Josefa like a protective shield. And with its jewel-encrusted cover, it had basically worked as one.

August just blinked at the book, like he couldn't register what had happened.

"You little bitch," he whispered under his breath. The wildness in his eyes changed into something else. Lust? Desire? Hunger? It sent a chill down Josefa's spine.

"You're not getting this back, August." Josefa expected her voice to shake with fear, but there was no tremble in it.

August lunged for the book this time, the knife clattering to the floor, forgotten. But he was too late. Emilie was faster than him. She flung the book across the room and toward Violet. It landed in her hands firmly, and Josefa rushed toward her. The door to the stateroom was in front of her. They just had to get out of here. They would lose August soon, and they could go back into hiding. They were going to win. She could almost taste their success.

The thrill of it all was returning to Josefa's chest the closer she got to Violet. But then she saw Violet's wide eyes. She followed Violet's gaze to the other side of the room, where Emilie lay on the ground, struggling against August. He had his arms around her in a tight grip.

"Go!" Emilie cried. "Take the *Rubaiyat* and go. I'll be fine." Somehow, Emilie sounded like she really believed it, even though August had grabbed hold of his knife again, and it glinted dangerously in the moonlight, too close to Emilie.

"You're not going to kill someone, August," Josefa said. She hoped that the conviction in her voice would get through to him. "I know you wouldn't do that."

But August just shook his head. "If you give me the book, I'll let her go. You don't even understand what you've cost me, Josefa, do you?" he said, hatred shining in his eyes. "All of these years . . . everything I've built for myself . . ." He shook his head again.

"August," Josefa said. "You don't have to do this. We can figure something out. You're not a murderer." But Josefa wasn't so sure about that as August's eyes flashed dangerously at her words.

"Lake fired me," August spat out. "You made me lose everything." He paused to glance at the *Rubaiyat*, still clasped in Violet's hands. "Well, I'm not going to let you ruin me, Josefa. If I'm going down for this, so are you."

"August, just let Emilie go, and we can talk," Josefa tried again, her voice appeasing and low. But she wasn't even sure if August heard her words.

Instead, his grip on Emilie tightened. "I don't want to hurt anyone. I just need *that*." He nodded to the book.

Hinnah, who was closest to August, analyzed him quietly. When he caught her gaze, August inched farther back. He pressed the knife to Emilie's neck so tightly that a bead of blood formed on her skin. Josefa could see Emilie biting back a cry of pain.

"If you give me the book, I'll let her go," August repeated.

Emilie caught Josefa's gaze, and there was a fierceness to her eyes.

"He won't hurt me," she said, her voice firm. "But he *will* hurt you."

Josefa hesitated, even though Emilie's words rang true. August hadn't come for the book, not really. He had come here hell-bent on revenge.

"August, just let her go," Josefa said, hoping he would listen to reason, even though all reason suddenly seemed completely lost on him.

"The book . . . or her," August said, something dangerous in his voice. Something that told Josefa that giving up the book wouldn't make him stop. But didn't she owe Emilie that? She glanced at the book in Violet's hands. And as if she could read her mind, Emilie said in a pleading voice, "Josefa, please." She was shaking her head, a minuscule movement with August's grip still tight.

Josefa took a breath and tried to keep the waver out of her voice as she turned to the others and said, "Let's go."

Violet and Hinnah blinked at Josefa for a moment, astonishment in their wide eyes.

"But—"

Josefa cut them off before they could say any more. "She's right; we have to go."

As the three of them rushed out the door, leaving an angry August behind with Emilie, Josefa hoped that she hadn't made the wrong choice.

FORTY-FOUR

11:50 P.M.

2 HOURS, 30 MINUTES
EMILIE

EMILIE WATCHED JOSEFA, Hinnah, and Violet disappear out the door with a lump in her throat. She expected—hoped, really—that August would let her go when he saw that his plan wasn't working. He let out a growl of anger, but his hold on her was as strong as ever.

"Come on." His voice was grim as he pulled Emilie up to a stand and began to lead her out of the room.

"You won't be able to catch up with them," she said. "They know every room on this ship. They could be anywhere. You won't even know where to look. And they have a head start."

"I'm not looking to catch up with them" was all August said, his voice grim. It sent a chill down Emilie's spine.

She tried to pull free of August once more, but he just turned to shoot her a glare. He was much stronger than her. His fingers digging in her skin left a dull throb of pain. But she thought perhaps when he was distracted, she would be able to slip away from him. His anger, after all, had made him impulsive. Even a little unstable if Emilie was being honest.

Emilie couldn't imagine how Josefa had ever been friends with a boy like this. She deserved better, but maybe she hadn't known it until now.

"They can't even come back for me!" Emilie exclaimed after her attempts at freeing herself failed over and over again. It seemed that August was completely unbothered by her squirming against his grip. His hands were ironclad on her. "Where are you taking me?"

She looked back at the empty hall they had left behind them, surprised that nobody had stirred yet when they had made so much noise.

"Somewhere they can't look for you." The words made Emilie's stomach sink.

They wove past hallways, cabins, and the dining hall. They passed passengers and crew members, and though some glanced at them curiously, nobody seemed worried about a boy dragging a young girl behind him as if she were a plaything.

"Don't bother asking for their help," August spat out when he noticed Emilie watching the people they passed. "Lake already called the guards. He thinks I helped you, that I'm a criminal just like you. But once I have the book I'll clear my name, and Josefa will be the one answering for all her crimes."

Finally, they arrived at the second floor. August stopped in front of a cabin door that Emilie didn't recognize. But when he knocked, the face that peered out of the open door was too familiar.

"Matron Wallis," August said. "I heard you tell my boss that you were looking for this girl?"

Without another word, August all but shoved Emilie toward Wallis. She grabbed hold of Emilie roughly, examining her with a grim frown. As if she were displeased to see her.

"Where are the other three?" she asked August, before swiftly turning toward Emilie. "Where are your friends?"

"I don't know," Emilie said, shaking her head.

"They tried to escape. They stole a rare collectible book from Mr. Lake. It's priceless," August said.

"Tell any crew members you see to search for them. If they're on this ship, we'll root them out," Wallis said.

"They'll come for her. I bet they won't rest until they know she's safe." August directed a grin at Emilie that made the hairs on the back of her neck stand.

Emilie had to explain what had happened in the stateroom. How August had tried to attack them. "Matron Wallis. You don't know the full—"

But the matron cut her off, as if she weren't worth listening to.

"The four of you came onto this ship, under my watch," she mumbled, more to herself, Emilie thought, than to anyone else. She dragged Emilie inside her cabin as August watched gleefully. "I wanted to believe it was a one-time mistake. But you thought you could get away with stealing from these passengers over and over again. With taking their valuables. You should have thought again."

"But, Matron Wallis, you don't understand. We—"

Wallis slammed the door shut in Emilie's face. There was the sound of a click as she locked the door, leaving Emilie all alone in this solitary cabin.

Outside, she could hear Wallis ordering crew members to find Josefa, Hinnah, and Violet. She felt hopelessness rise in her chest with each passing moment. How long would Wallis keep her locked up in here? And what would happen if they found Violet, Hinnah, and Josefa?

Maybe if it was the crew members who found them, the worst that would happen was prison. But if August found Josefa . . .

Emilie tried not to think about it as she moved away from the door to the cabin. The place was small, with a bed squeezed to one side and a desk to the other. There was barely any space to move about.

But maybe Emilie could find a way. She was certainly no Hinnah or Josefa or Violet. She was sure if they were in this situation, they would figure out some escape. By picking the lock of the door or even climbing out the porthole once more.

Maybe Emilie could do it too.

She stepped toward the porthole and glanced down into the icy depths of the sea. The sight alone was enough to send her heart into her throat.

Emilie was no Josefa, or Hinnah, or Violet.

And she was all alone.

FORTY-FIVE

11:50 P.M.

2 HOURS, 30 MINUTES
VIOLET

VIOLET COULDN'T BELIEVE they had left Emilie behind. If August was willing to attack Josefa with a knife, who knew what else he was capable of? But in front of her, Josefa didn't seem fazed by their decision. She didn't even glance back once they had escaped from the stateroom.

The three of them turned away from the hallway and climbed up a staircase. Violet could hear the hum of music floating down, as if there were no sleep for the rich.

"We have to go back for Emilie," Violet said. She would have never imagined she would be the one advocating on Emilie's behalf.

"We'll find her." Josefa's voice was firm. "But . . . we can't help her if August finds us first."

"Josefa's right," Hinnah added softly. "We should find a place to hide. After that, we'll get to Emilie."

"August won't hurt her," Josefa said finally. There was confidence in her voice that Violet didn't think should be there.

She couldn't forget the wild look in August's eyes. If Hinnah hadn't tackled him, who knew where they would be right now? By Josefa's side, hoping she didn't bleed to death?

"You don't know that," Violet said. She couldn't help the feeling in her chest. There was something gravely wrong. Like the universe had been tipped off balance somehow. Violet couldn't figure out what it was. Just a feeling in her gut, telling her that she should be doing something different. That she should be somewhere different. Not maneuvering around the first-class cabins of this ship, holding a jewel-encrusted book in her hands.

"Look, he wants the book and he wants me," Josefa assured her. "If I thought he would really hurt Emilie, I would have never left her."

Violet had to believe that. It was too late to believe anything else.

They wove past hallways and cabins, but they had never been here before.

"I think if we climb through here, we might be able to—" Hinnah was cut short as a man in uniform turned the corner. His eyes flashed at the sight of them. He called behind him, "I found them, they're here!" There was no time to think about climbing or hiding, because behind him came another man in uniform, followed by Lake himself. His eyes immediately landed on the book in Violet's hand.

"Come on!" Josefa called, turning away from their pursuers and beginning to run once more. Violet instinctively clutched the *Rubaiyat* tighter and followed Josefa as fast as she could.

"We need to go down," Josefa said between gasped breaths. "Maybe we get into the boiler room again and sneak out through one of the vents like last time."

"Okay," Hinnah and Violet agreed immediately. It wasn't as if they had the time to sit down and think through plans. They turned a corner, only to come up to the end of the hallway. There was nothing but the painted-over wall.

The others following them hadn't turned the corner yet, but it wouldn't be long until they did. Violet could hear their footsteps just behind them.

"There has to be a way out of this." Josefa was looking around like a solution was going to jump out at her. Like this was a puzzle she had to solve.

"I don't think we can talk our way out of this one, Josefa." Violet's sigh felt heavy as it reverberated around her body.

"We might not be able to talk our way through, but we could fight?" Hinnah's words came out more like a question than anything else.

"We can't fight," Josefa said. "We're not trained in that."

"I can take them." Hinnah shrugged, like it was no big deal. "Enough to distract them anyway."

"We can all fight." Violet held the book up, remembering how Emilie had used it to shield Josefa from August's attack. "It's three against three. Those are good odds."

They didn't have time to agree, because the next moment, the three men came hurtling around the corner. The two crewmen stopped at the sight of the girls waiting for them. But Lake didn't even pause. He extended his hands and ran right toward Violet. His eyes focused only on the book.

Violet used that to her advantage. Sliding to the side at the last minute, she sent Lake stumbling behind her, nearly crashing into the wall. With Lake trying to regain his balance, Violet tossed the book to Josefa. As if they could read each other's minds, Josefa grabbed it easily, squeezing past the crewmen before they could process what was happening all the way.

Hinnah was quick on her feet too. She tackled one crewman, sending him crashing into the other. Then Violet and Hinnah chased after Josefa—back the way they had come. But one turn later, they were face-to-face with several more crewmen running toward them with determined expressions.

"How did Lake manage this?" Hinnah asked as the two of them backed out of the way and turned toward another corridor.

"Rich men have a way of getting everybody to do their bidding," Violet said. They had lost sight of Josefa completely now, but Violet had little time to think about her. The pounding of heavy feet behind them was too loud. The blood pulsing through Violet's ears was even louder.

She just hoped that Josefa managed to get the book to safety.

FORTY-SIX

2 HOURS, 20 MINUTES
EMILIE

EMILIE WASN'T SURE how long she had been locked inside this cabin, but with each passing moment the dread seemed to press in on her. There was no escape from here, and she had no idea where her friends were.

August had left Emilie here in the care of Wallis. What if that meant he had found the others? That he had found Josefa? Hurt her?

There was some kind of commotion going on in the ship. Emilie could hear the buzz of people. At this time of the night, the ship should be quiet, but it wasn't. This couldn't just be because of Emilie and her friends; she was sure of it.

Emilie rose from her place by the door, where she had been diligently trying to work away at the lock—as she had seen Josefa do—with no luck. She didn't have Josefa's skills, her experience, or her equipment. She wished she had spent a little more time with her when they were back in

Dublin. For more reasons than one.

She peered outside, hoping to catch a glimpse of *something*. But what she saw sent a cold pinprick through her. Emilie rubbed at her eyes, hoping that it was somehow an illusion brought on by all the events of the night. But she wasn't mistaken. It looked like the water was rising slowly up the ship.

She scrambled back from the window and toward the door. There was commotion outside. It wasn't just an illusion. Other people had noticed too.

Emilie remembered what she had figured out from studying the blueprints of the ship. It wasn't unsinkable. Only some of the compartments were watertight, and if water managed to rise above them, that would be disastrous.

Emilie closed her eyes, as if that would somehow rid her of this reality. She reached into the pocket of her petticoat where she had tucked away her blue hair clip. Now she slid it into place in her hair once more. It reminded her both of her past—her parents—and her present—Josefa.

It was a strange sort of comfort as she tried to wade through everything she knew about this ship. Everything she had learned from the newspapers before she even boarded. Everything she had learned since.

Was it possible that the ship was really sinking?

It was *supposed* to be unsinkable; that's what everyone had said.

Emilie thought back to the moments after the four of them

had obtained the book. *Something* had caused the ship to shake. She remembered seeing it in the water—unclear, indecipherable in the dark of the night.

She peered down once more, and—if Emilie wasn't mistaken—she was sure that the water was rising steadily. Did everybody know that the ship was sinking? Had they left her in here to drown while they got themselves to safety?

But that couldn't be right. Emilie wasn't fond of Wallis, but she didn't believe her to be cruel. She wouldn't leave Emilie locked in here if she knew the ship was sinking.

And that meant . . .

Emilie's stomach sank. That must mean she didn't know. Emilie had to tell her. She had to get out and find her friends. She had to get everyone to safety.

Turning away from the porthole, Emilie hurried to the door. Instead of trying fruitlessly to pick the lock, she banged against the metal. The sound reverberated around the cabin, but Emilie couldn't hear anything outside. Not Matron Wallis, nor anyone else. She tried again, only to be met with silence once more.

Emilie slid down to the ground, the cold sending a shiver through her. She wondered how long they all had.

FORTY-SEVEN

12:10 A.M.

---

2 HOURS, 10 MINUTES
JOSEFA

JOSEFA HAD RUN away from a lot of people in her life, but she had never felt this pounding in her chest before. It wasn't the thrill of almost getting caught. Of *getting* caught. This was something else entirely. Some sort of fear that made her legs feel heavy even as she pushed them to their limits. That made her chest ache and dread course through her veins.

She knew that there were still people behind her. She couldn't bring herself to turn and look. But she could hear the heavy fall of footsteps getting closer and closer with each passing minute.

Still, Josefa thought of only one thing—Emilie. She had to get to her before anything bad happened. So even as she wove through known and unknown halls, she was trying to map a way back to the room where Josefa had left her. Surely, August would be in pursuit of her. Surely, Emilie must be okay.

She had said as much to Violet and Hinnah. She had tried

her hardest to convince them. She thought she had even managed to convince herself.

But now, separated from her friends, Josefa's confidence and reassurances dissipated. She could think only of the worst possible outcome. After all, they were all stuck on this ship. Where could they go? Where would Emilie hide?

Josefa found herself getting lost in the weaving hallways of the *Titanic*. Every time she turned, she looked for a place where she could stow away and leave her pursuers behind. Finally, she slipped into an open cabin, hoping against hope that nobody was inside. It was pitch-black, and she slid behind the open door, holding her breath as she waited for the sound of footsteps to catch up to her.

The footsteps grew closer and closer. The hammering in Josefa's chest was so loud that she was sure anybody passing her would be able to hear it. That her heart would give her away this time.

But then the footsteps passed right by. She let out a sigh of relief before stepping out from behind the door. Peering out of the cabin, she saw some of the navy blue uniforms of the crewmen disappear around another corner.

Josefa was still trying to catch her breath as she turned back the way she had come. They had left Emilie in a first-class cabin. That meant retracing her steps. That was also where she had lost Violet and Hinnah. But would any of them still be there?

Josefa didn't have time to spare. For all she knew, at any moment the crewmen who were on the hunt for her would realize she wasn't ahead of them and turn around. Or—worse—she would run into August. She still had no idea where he could be. How had August managed to persuade the crew to come after them?

That's when it hit her. August didn't have the power to tell the crewmen to come after them, but she knew someone who did. Someone who was already determined to catch them. Someone who had driven them to be fugitives even before they'd stolen the *Rubaiyat*: Matron Wallis.

Downstairs it was.

Instead of going back toward the corridors she had already passed and down a set of stairs that might leave her exposed, Josefa decided she would take a page from Hinnah's book. She found a nearby vent and, managing to open it after some effort, pulled herself through the opening.

The problem, of course, was that unlike Hinnah, Josefa had no idea where she was going. As she crawled along, she noticed that there was some commotion going on in the cabins that she passed.

She couldn't help the feeling of dread that settled in her stomach. This surely couldn't be all because of them, could it? The *Rubaiyat* was a priceless artifact . . . but surely it couldn't be precious enough to put the whole ship on alert.

Still, she pushed ahead, peering through every space she could find in the hopes of spotting Emilie or Violet or Hinnah. Instead, the farther down the ship she went, the more worried she became. There was something happening. She spotted a few passengers out of bed, their hair disheveled and their clothes rumpled. There was one man who rushed past with no shoes on—as if he hadn't had the time to put them on. Even the few crew members she spotted looked grim, with their lips pressed into thin lines.

She tried not to dwell on the growing discomfort in her stomach. She hoped that the others were okay.

Finally, Josefa found an opening in the vents and pushed herself through to an empty room. She landed gently on her feet and cast a quick look around the cabin to ensure that nobody was waiting to pounce on her.

Josefa pushed the cabin door open slightly, peering outside. She had climbed down to one of the lower decks but still wasn't sure where she was.

There was an eerie quiet about the ship as Josefa crept down the corridor. It didn't feel like Josefa had been running from the guards just a few minutes ago. She slipped the *Rubaiyat* out from underneath her dress for a moment, running her fingers along its spine. Like a reminder of what they were here to do.

Once Josefa found Emilie and reunited with her friends, everything would be okay. They had the book. The difficult part was over. They could hide out until they reached New York.

This is what Josefa told herself as she continued her search.

FORTY-EIGHT

2 HOURS, 0 MINUTES
EMILIE

EMILIE HAD BEEN banging against the door of the cabin for what felt like hours. Outside, she could hear commotion. Maybe—she hoped—people had realized what was happening. She knew that the sound they had heard earlier couldn't have been nothing. It was too loud. She had felt the vibrations as if they were in her very bones.

But no matter how long or loud she banged against the door and called out for Matron Wallis, there was nothing to suggest that she was even nearby. Maybe this would be it for Emilie.

She went back to the porthole, peering at the way the bottom windows of the ship were already underwater. How did the matron not notice? Or perhaps she had and decided to leave Emilie there? Perhaps—

The familiar click of the lock sounded. When Emilie turned back from the porthole, Wallis was standing in the doorway. Emilie didn't think she had known true joy until this moment. Wallis had come to free her.

But the look of disbelief on her face said something else. When Emilie tried to rush toward her, the matron held up a hand to stop her.

"Just because you've been banging on the door and screaming doesn't mean I'll let you go." Emilie felt her stomach twist. She didn't think stealing the *Rubaiyat* should mean death by drowning. Surely, nobody deserved that fate.

"The ship is sinking," Emilie said. "You can't just leave me in here. And you have to go too."

The edges of her lips curled up, but there was nothing pleasant in the matron's expression. "The *Titanic* is not going to sink." The confidence in her voice baffled Emilie.

"There are watertight compartments on the ship. It might look like it's sinking, but it isn't. You don't know what you're talking about." She turned to leave once more, and Emilie felt her chest compress.

How could she convince Wallis of the truth that she already knew?

Then an idea hit her. She fished into the pockets of her dress, where she had tucked away the blueprints of the ship. She had kept them close while she was working on her painting of the *Titanic*. She couldn't be happier for them now.

"Wait!" She ran up to the matron, opening up the folds of the plan and laying it on the floor of the cabin. "Look at this," Emilie said. "Yes, there are watertight compartments." She pointed to them on the map. The matron's eyes followed her fingers, though the frown still held tight. "But these bulkheads don't go to the ceiling. The water is going to rise above the watertight compartments. The ship is going to sink."

Emilie looked at Matron Wallis, hoping that this information would change something in her expression. Something in her mind.

"I'm supposed to believe you over the engineers of this ship? The ones who obviously know better?" Wallis shook her head. Emilie felt frustration itching up her skin, but she couldn't let it overwhelm her. She had to stay calm and collected—maybe then she would have a chance at convincing Matron Wallis.

"These maps are from the designer who helped build the *Titanic*," Emilie tried. "I made a copy of his floor plan. Don't believe me. Believe him."

But it seemed no matter what she did or said, Matron Wallis wasn't budging from her position. She turned and closed the door of the cabin once more. Emilie felt dread rise up her body. Dread like she had never experienced before. Because she was sure this was the end.

As she slid the floor plan back into her pocket and hoped against hope that her three friends would somehow find her in this cabin, Emilie saw the first hint of what she knew would be their demise: water rising up through the floorboards.

FORTY-NINE

12:25 A.M.

---

1 HOUR, 55 MINUTES

HINNAH

HINNAH WAS CERTAIN they had finally lost their pursuers as they turned into a massive room populated with dining tables and chairs. The sound of footsteps had faded away to nothing, and it was just Hinnah and Violet.

Violet was breathing hard as she leaned against the wall, trying to catch her breath. Hinnah tried not to think about her aching arms and legs. She was sure she had never been this tired in her entire life. Her time in Clayton Lake's cabin already felt like it had happened an eternity ago.

"We need to find the others," Violet said finally, when her breathing had returned to a normal speed.

Hinnah nodded her agreement, but she wasn't sure where they would even start. She crept up to the door leading out of the room, opening it up a crack to glance outside. There was nobody waiting for them. There were no thundering footsteps of pursuers, no shouts for them to be caught.

"Maybe they finally realized we don't have the book anymore," Hinnah said.

"It's worse if they go after Josefa," Violet said. "If August finds her . . ." She let the words hang there for a moment, because the both of them knew what that meant.

"We should get out of here," Violet pressed. "The longer we stay in one place, the higher the chances of us being caught."

Hinnah knew she was right, but she couldn't help the fear that plunged into her stomach at the thought of leaving the relative safety of this place. Something about the lack of pursuers, about the silence outside, unsettled Hinnah. But she shrugged it off, pushing the door open and stepping outside, with Violet at her heels.

"Which way should we go?" she asked, glancing around, trying to get a sense of where they were.

If Hinnah was right—and since she had memorized the floor plan of the ship, she was pretty sure she *was*—they were in the second-class dining room, though it looked different without anybody here. They probably weren't far from the cabins they had been staying in for most of their journey. They had to get out of second class fast.

"We could go up to the first class. . . ." Violet trailed off. "But we'll stick out more." When Hinnah cast a cursory glance at Violet, she had to agree with her conclusion. Both of them looked out of sorts, with their disheveled hair and dresses. Tonight they certainly would not be able to pass for first-class passengers, even with Violet's acting skills.

"So, we should go down," Hinnah said, leading the way. "Hopefully they won't be searching for us there."

But the deeper the two of them traveled through the ship, the more it dawned on Hinnah that nobody seemed to be searching for them now. There was some kind of commotion on the ship, getting more and more panicked the farther down they traveled.

"Maybe we should go back to the mail room," Violet suggested, though she didn't seem particularly confident for once in her life. Hinnah suspected she could feel the shift in the air too. Something was going on, but neither of them could put their finger on what.

"Maybe . . . Josefa and Emilie would know to find us there, right?" Hinnah asked.

"Well . . . unless . . . Josefa got caught," Violet said.

"And Emilie couldn't get away from August," Hinnah added. They exchanged a worried glance between them. This ship was massive, and Emilie and Josefa could be anywhere. So could August and Lake.

Hinnah and Violet's luck must have run out, though, because as they turned the corner, they nearly crashed into a stricken August. His eyes widened at the sight of them. He leaped forward, like he had been waiting for this opportunity.

"Where's Josefa? Where's the book?" he growled.

Hinnah and Violet jumped out of the way, sending him crashing into the wall behind them. Hinnah could still see the knife glinting in his hands. She didn't understand how someone hadn't confiscated it from him yet. How could they be so concerned about four thieves but not bat an eyelash at a young boy carrying a knife around the ship?

"We have to go!" Violet tugged at Hinnah's arm, and the two of them fled down the corridor before August could gain his balance once more. Still, when Hinnah glanced back, she spotted August sprinting behind them, that wild look flashing in his eyes. She wondered how long they could outrun him.

They cut around a corner and nearly tumbled down a set of stairs—managing to keep their balance only at the last minute. Violet was breathing so hard that Hinnah worried for her. They ducked through corridors, taking every turn they possibly could, weaving in and out of open doors. Finally, when even Hinnah was running out of breath, the two of them paused, leaning against the white walls of the corridor and gasping for air.

"I think we lost him," Hinnah whispered, when she couldn't make out the sound of August's footsteps. In fact, she couldn't make out anything. There was too much silence down here. It seemed to press in on them.

"Where are we?" Violet asked, looking around the corridor. It was narrow, the walls white with no paneling, and the floors were a linoleum pink.

"We must be in the lower decks," Hinnah mumbled. She had lost track of any direction once she had caught sight of August. Even though she had managed to fight him off before, men like August always sent a jolt of panic through Hinnah.

There was something unpredictable about him, and that scared Hinnah to death.

She peered around the empty corridor in front of them. All the cabins seemed to be empty—or abandoned.

"I think something's wrong," Hinnah whispered.

"I think so too," Violet said. "Did you notice the crewmen didn't care about us? They weren't chasing us anymore."

Hinnah exchanged a glance with Violet, a feeling of dread rising up through her.

"We should find Josefa and Emilie," she said.

"We can't go up," Violet said, striding ahead of Hinnah. "What if August is there, waiting for us?"

"Right . . . so we keep going down."

The two of them weren't running anymore, but there was a quickness to their gait as they strode past empty cabins. The few people who they spotted seemed panic-stricken. They were going the opposite way than the girls were—up the stairs to the upper decks.

Hinnah spotted a woman with kind eyes going past her up the stairs.

"Excuse me," she said, even while Violet shot her a glare. Maybe it wasn't a good idea, but Hinnah felt like they were traveling somewhere they weren't supposed to. She wanted to know what was happening. "What's going on? Where is everyone going?"

The woman shook her head, barely registering Hinnah and Violet in front of her.

"The ship is sinking," she mumbled. "There's water everywhere." With that, the woman turned on her heel and fled up the stairs.

"Do you really think . . ." Violet trailed off, letting the question hang between them.

"I'm not sure," Hinnah said, shaking her head. And she wasn't sure if it was that she didn't believe the woman or that she didn't *want* to believe her. "Let's keep going."

They couldn't afford to stop, not when August was still on their heels. Still there was that sinking feeling in Hinnah's stomach.

The two of them finally spotted another set of staircases. Hinnah quickened her pace, eager to put even more distance between her and August. She was finally starting to piece together where she and Violet were on the ship. And if she wasn't mistaken, they shouldn't be too far away from the safety of the mail room. She hoped that Josefa had already made her way there. She hoped that Josefa and Emilie were already safe.

But when she came to the top of the stairs, Hinnah stopped in her tracks. Because the deck below them was full of water.

And if Hinnah wasn't mistaken, the water was steadily rising.

FIFTY

1 HOUR, 45 MINUTES

JOSEFA

JOSEFA WAS SURE now that there was something she had missed. She noticed too many passengers outside their cabins. People with panicked looks in their eyes.

"Excuse me, you need to go to the decks," a crew member said, passing her by. He didn't seem to care much if Josefa heard his request. Now that she thought about it, passengers seemed to be steadily moving toward the deck.

Josefa kept her eyes peeled for her friends. Even if August still had Emilie, surely Violet and Hinnah would be following the rest of the passengers toward the deck? But she couldn't see any sign of them.

Of course, she realized, they could already be out there. Or it was possible that they weren't on this deck at all. Josefa slipped by the passengers to the opposite side of the deck. Whatever was going on didn't matter. She needed to find Violet and Hinnah. More important, she needed to rescue Emilie.

Josefa tried not to think too much about the wild look in

August's eyes when he had entered the stateroom. The knife gripped in his hands, and the way he pressed it to Emilie. He would never use it, Josefa kept telling herself. Like a mantra to calm her anxious thoughts.

Finally, Josefa spotted Hinnah and Violet approaching from the distance. She couldn't help her smile at the sight of them. She felt like it had been an eternity since she had broken off from them. Josefa kept waiting for Emilie to appear behind them, but she never did.

"You're here!" Violet said, stopping in front of Josefa. She blinked at her with wide eyes. "Where have you been? We've been searching for you everywhere."

"I've been looking for you," Josefa said. "There's something going on. People are going toward the deck for some reason. Where's Emilie?"

Hinnah and Violet exchanged a look.

"I don't think what we felt back in the stateroom was nothing," Violet finally said. "Hinnah and I saw water rising in the decks below."

"I think the ship is sinking . . . ," Hinnah mumbled.

"Sinking?" A knot tightened in Josefa's stomach. The *Titanic* was supposed to be unsinkable. "There's no way the ship is sinking."

"We need to get out of here," Violet said, ignoring Josefa's last words. "We ran into Lake, but I think he gave up the chase once he realized what was happening."

"The ship . . . can't be sinking," Josefa repeated, like if she said it enough times it would simply come true. There was no evidence of it, she thought to herself. But . . . wasn't there?

Josefa had noticed that something was odd about the ship tonight. Passengers out of bed. Crewmen abandoning their search for the four fugitives on board. Barely paying attention to her as they urged passengers onto the deck.

The ship was sinking. The thought sent a chill through her. Josefa could have never imagined this as the worst-case scenario for their plans.

"If we get to the deck . . . they'll have lifeboats. We can get away," Josefa said, urgency finally seeping into her voice. She glanced at the passengers still making their way toward the deck. She was sure they would be saved. Help must be coming, if the crewmen knew what was happening. "We need to find Emilie."

"Do you still have the book?" Hinnah asked.

Josefa nodded, slipping it out from under her dress.

"Do you think we can climb through the vents to find Emilie?" Josefa asked Hinnah. She thought it might be the easiest way to find her. They would be able to see through into various cabins.

But Hinnah simply shook her head. "If the water rises, we could get trapped in there in a matter of seconds. We won't have any time to get out."

She knew Hinnah was right. The vents would be too dangerous. But searching for Emilie through all of these people trying to get onto the deck would be even more difficult. Emilie could be *anywhere*, and Josefa didn't want to think about how long they had before the ship went underwater completely.

"You two should get to safety," Josefa finally said. "Get onto the deck and find a lifeboat. Get out of here. I'm going to find Emilie."

But before Josefa could move a muscle, Violet stepped forward, pressing her hands onto Josefa's shoulders in an attempt to stop her.

"You don't even know where Emilie is," Violet said. "She could already be off the ship."

"The water is rising fast," Hinnah added. "You don't know what could happen if you go down farther."

"Who knows how long this ship is going to stay afloat?" Violet's words sent a lurch through Josefa's stomach. Violet and Hinnah were right. Of course they were right. But Josefa couldn't just leave Emilie.

"I'm the reason why Emilie isn't here. I decided to leave her behind, to . . . to let August take her," Josefa said, feeling a lump climb up her throat. She could feel the pinprick of tears against the back of her eyes. She had never been an emotional person, much to her mother's disdain, but now she felt a wave of emotions in her chest. Regret and fear, and something that seemed a little too much like love. "I can't leave her. I have to go back."

"Whether you go deeper into the ship to find her or you come with us to try and get out, there is no guarantee you'll be able to help Emilie. But in one case you might not make it out alive," Violet said.

"We're not going to let you risk your life," Hinnah said, stepping forward too. Between the two of them, Josefa's path was blocked. And somehow, she didn't think her friends were joking about not letting her go any farther.

"But, Emilie . . . ," Josefa said, blinking back her tears. "We *left* her down there. *I* left her. With August. It's my responsibility to—"

"Hopefully she's gotten away," Violet interrupted. "She wouldn't want you to go searching for her. You know she wouldn't."

Josefa knew this was true, but she was having a hard time convincing herself. The longer the three of them spent here, debating whether Josefa was to go find Emilie, the more dangerous it was for all of them. She wasn't going to let her friends put themselves in harm's way for her sake. Even if it meant abandoning Emilie to her fate.

"Okay," Josefa said, trying to keep the waver out of her voice. The lump was crawling up her throat, but she tried to push all her feelings down as far as they would go.

Right now, Josefa had to make sure Violet and Hinnah could make it to safety. Josefa couldn't lose everyone.

"Let's go," she said, turning toward the deck. But she was already making plans for how she could go back into the sinking ship to save Emilie.

FIFTY-ONE

1 HOUR, 30 MINUTES
EMILIE

THE WATER HAD risen past Emilie's ankles. It was rising faster and faster now. She could hear the commotion of people outside. She hoped that they were rushing to safety. She hoped that there was safety to rush to.

She pushed against the door once more, but it wouldn't budge. She really wished now she had spent more time with Josefa when she'd had the chance back in Dublin. If nothing else, maybe Emilie would have learned some lockpicking skills. That was apparently the difference between life and death now. But she was trying not to think about Josefa or Hinnah or Violet. There was a part of her that hoped they would come for her—that they were still looking. But another part of her— maybe a bigger part—hoped that they had managed to find a way off this ship.

Emilie was going to try one more time to push against the door, though she was tired now. Her dress was wet and heavy from the water.

But as Emilie readied herself for one last push, the door clicked open as if on its own accord. There was Wallis in front of her once more. This time, her expression was not one of grim disbelief but of something else entirely.

"You were right." She was looking more at the rising water than at Emilie.

"I'm sorry." Emilie wished that she hadn't been right. She wished the *Titanic* really was unsinkable as they had all been promised.

"You can go," Matron Wallis surprised Emilie by saying. She pulled the door open as far as it would go with the water pushing against it and stood out of the way. "Find your friends and get to safety."

"Come with me." Emilie stepped out of the oppressive room, already feeling some of her fear and anxiety slipping away. She wasn't out of danger yet, but at least she wasn't hopeless and trapped in that room any longer. She didn't dare hope, though.

"I have to make sure everybody is safe." Wallis was already turning around, not toward the staircase that would lead her out to the deck, but the other way completely.

"Matron Wallis," Emilie called. She turned only halfway, the ghost of a smile on her lips.

"You remind me of my own daughter," she said. "Doing mischievous things when you should probably know better. But she has a good heart, and I know you do too. You just have to think a little more before jumping to action."

Emilie knew that she definitely would. If there ever was a

next time. She didn't get a chance to voice any of this, because the matron was wading through the other side of the hallway, where the water was even deeper. She knocked on a passing cabin. "Anybody in there?" she called, her voice trembling slightly. When there was no answer, she moved along to the next door.

Emilie hesitated for a moment. She wondered if there was a way she could persuade Wallis to come with her. But she seemed determined to check all the cabins. Emilie had already wasted so much time locked away. She couldn't waste any more.

She began to run as fast as her legs could carry her. But with her clothes weighed down by water, it was difficult to run at all. The water pushed against her, making it even harder to pick up any pace. Emilie grabbed the bottom of her soaking dress and lifted it up as far as she could. Carrying it with her hands, she slowly made her way up the stairs, nearly tripping on the rising water, or the end of her dress, multiple times. She was losing precious time, but Emilie couldn't go any faster.

She passed by people who barely gave her a second glance as they traipsed past her in their panic.

"Excuse me, can you—" She tried to call out to one of the passengers—a woman who was herding two children up the steps. She gave Emilie a sympathetic glance.

"The cabins are all empty," she said, ushering her children to run faster. "You'll have to get out of those clothes if you want to have any chance of making it." With that, the woman rushed after her kids, disappearing from sight.

Emilie could feel the water seeping through the fabric of her dress into her very bones, sending shivers through her entire body. The woman was right. If she didn't manage to get out of these clothes and get dry soon, Emilie would have no hope of surviving.

On the next floor, she stumbled into the first empty room she found. The water hadn't risen up to here yet, but who knew how long she had until that happened? Emilie began to rifle through the drawers in the chest by the bed. Surely there must be something here that she could use. Finally, she found a dress that seemed a little too big for her. But it would have to do.

FIFTY-TWO

1 HOUR, 10 MINUTES

JOSEFA

THE WATER MUST have been rising fast because there were people everywhere, clambering to get to the deck of the ship. It seemed that the entire ship had awoken. There was a man to the side with the buttons of his shirt askew and disheveled hair helping to guide passengers to safety. On his other side, a girl who couldn't have been much older than Josefa was gently trying to calm down a distraught mother and baby. When Josefa spotted a few crewmen, her stomach gave a lurch of fear. But they didn't notice the girls. Or—Josefa thought—they didn't care. With the ship on its way down, it wasn't like finding four thieves was at the top of their list of priorities. They must have been more concerned with the hundreds of people whose lives were at stake.

Josefa, Hinnah, and Violet managed to push through to the deck. There were already people boarding lifeboats. There were so many people. Josefa scanned the area, searching for Emilie, but she couldn't see her, though it was difficult to pick out a face in the midst of the crowd.

"Maybe she already boarded a lifeboat." Violet had never been the optimistic type, and Josefa wasn't sure if she liked or hated that she had decided to try in this case.

"Maybe." Josefa didn't believe the words out of her mouth, but there wasn't much she could do about it. They pushed forward through the people. Josefa spotted a lifeboat with enough space for the three of them.

"This way." She led the other two over to it. When Josefa glanced back again through the throngs of people, there was still no Emilie. She glanced down instead, at how the water had already taken so much of the *Titanic*. To think, Josefa had been down there just hours ago. The lower decks were almost completely submerged.

"We have to go," Violet urged Josefa. "We just have to hope that Emilie is okay."

"She'll be okay." But there was no reassurance in Hinnah's words. Josefa could only nod. With one last longing look back, Josefa moved toward the almost full lifeboat.

"The three of you?" the crewman helping everyone board asked, with a nod at Josefa.

"Yes," she answered for all three of them. She felt no relief as the crewman stepped back to allow them to board. She had concocted her plan—she would let Violet and Hinnah board the lifeboat and slip away once she was sure they were safe. Then she would find Emilie and save them both. Somewhere in the back of her mind, Josefa knew this probably wasn't the best plan she had ever come up with. But she also knew that she had no choice—she couldn't leave this ship without Emilie.

"Josefa!" the familiar sound of Emilie's voice called out. Josefa whipped her head around, her eyes searching for her. Finally, she spotted Emilie rushing toward them, a smile lighting up her face. She must have been here all along, but Josefa hadn't noticed her among the crowd of people.

"Violet! Hinnah!" The relief in Emilie's voice was almost palpable as she stumbled toward them.

Josefa's stomach finally unclenched—though she hadn't known she was holding so much tension there. Almost instinctively, she reached toward Emilie.

"You're okay," she said.

Emilie nodded. "And you're all okay."

Josefa's fingers found their way to Emilie's. Warmth enveloped her for a moment, and even in the chaos of the night, in the panic of everything that had happened to them, Josefa felt a sense of peace. Not just because they had all found each other, because they were all safe, but because something about Emilie made everything seem calmer, stiller. This was how Emilie always made her feel, and Josefa had never been more grateful for that.

"We should go," Violet—ever the voice of reason—said.

Josefa nodded, but the panic that had been shooting through her just moments ago had dissipated now. For the first time this night she felt a sense of relief. True relief. They had the *Rubaiyat*. They were all together.

Before she could turn back to the lifeboat, Josefa spotted someone on the other side of the deck who made her go cold.

August.

His eyes narrowed, his face scrunched up with hatred and anger the likes of which Josefa had never seen in her life. Without any hesitation, August rushed straight toward them.

Josefa glanced at her three friends—three people who had boarded this ship under her leadership. Three people who had put all their trust in her.

She had to protect them.

Without a second thought, Josefa leaned forward and pressed her lips to Emilie's. It wasn't like the kiss they had shared before. That one had contained joy and relief. It had felt like possibility. This one felt like a goodbye.

When they pulled away from each other, Josefa nudged Emilie until she was inside the lifeboat. "You need to get on," she said, turning to Violet and Hinnah. Her eyes flickered toward August, edging closer. She couldn't let him stop her friends from getting to safety.

"Josefa, hurry!" From the lifeboat, Emilie held out her hands, ready to help the others climb in after her.

Josefa shook her head, stepping back.

"The three of you need to go," she said.

Violet's eyes flicked back to August, nearly upon them.

Something flashed in her eyes—like in that moment she knew Josefa's plans.

"We're not leaving you behind," she said.

"If I go with you, August is going to find a way to keep coming after us," she said. She could imagine it—him jumping after their lifeboat, his knife at the ready. She was the one he wanted. And she knew the time had come for them to face each other.

"Josefa—" Violet was cut off by Emilie's cries from the lifeboat.

"Wait! Stop!" she called out. Her lifeboat was being lowered already. It had filled up with people, and Josefa could make out only the top of her head and the glint of her blue hairclip.

"You have to find another lifeboat," Josefa said. "You and Hinnah have to find safety." She didn't wait to hear Violet's protests before she whipped her head around. For a moment, she looked straight at August. Holding his gaze in hers. Like a challenge.

Then she ran. As far away from her friends as possible.

FIFTY-THREE

1:30 A.M.

---

50 MINUTES
VIOLET

VIOLET COULD ONLY watch as Josefa dashed away from the two of them and disappeared into the growing crowd of people. That gnawing feeling of wrongness that had weighed on her since they left Emilie behind clawed its way to the surface once more. At least now she didn't have to wonder why she was feeling it: everything was going wrong in ways that Violet could have never imagined.

But she knew that none of them had the time to ponder their fate, or even the fact that Josefa and Emilie were now separated from them. And they might not be reunited again.

"Should we go after her?" Hinnah asked. She was a lot more composed than Violet would have thought of her.

"No, we have to go," Violet said. "Josefa is right. Follow me."

The lifeboats all around them were filling up, but she knew the two of them had no chance of pushing through the throngs of people to the front. There was a woman helping her three children climb aboard at the very front—all four of them with tears streaming down their faces. Violet hoped she and Hinnah would find space soon. Surely, there would be enough lifeboats for all of them. Or at least someone would send help.

She pumped her legs faster, nearly running into panicked passersby. It seemed that with each passing minute, the deck was getting more and more crowded. Violet couldn't even hear the rush of blood in her ears, or the sound of her own thoughts, because they were surrounded by people screaming, crying, pleading for their lives. In front of them was a couple Violet had seen at their first-class dinner. And despite their decadent outfits and first-class status, they looked panic-stricken about the possibility they might not make it off this ship after all.

None of them had enough time.

"Violet, wait!" Hinnah called out. When Violet glanced back, she saw what Hinnah was pointing to. There was a lifeboat to one side that still had empty spaces. They were close enough to climb on.

"Come on!" Hinnah waved at her to hurry before rushing toward the lifeboat. There were people darting on board, and a crew member was directing people to their seats. It was almost completely full already, but they would make it.

Hinnah reached back to grab Violet's hand as she pushed past the people in front of them. They were going to survive this. Because Hinnah and Violet were survivors—they had survived much worse than this.

They were almost there when Violet spotted . . . Marko. She halted in her tracks.

"What's going on?" Hinnah asked, tugging at Violet's arm. But she pulled away, blinking at the boy in front of her.

It wasn't Marko—of course it wasn't. He was oceans away, awaiting Violet's return. But there was a young boy standing right beside the lifeboat. Inches away. Silent tears leaked from his eyes, and he rubbed at his tearstained cheeks. His watery eyes were trained on the lifeboat, though he made no attempt to step closer. No attempt to climb aboard.

Violet could not separate her memories of Marko and this boy in front of her. She remembered when Marko had wept as a child, the way he rubbed at his tearstained cheeks in the same way. But when her father had dragged Violet away to Zagreb, torn her away from Marko, she was the one who had wept with her face pressed up against the cold window. Silent tears that her father ignored, and that it pained her to remember now. She should have put up a fight then. She should have returned to Marko the first chance she'd gotten.

Now Violet slowly approached the boy. "Shouldn't you be on that boat?" she asked, bending down to her knees until she was almost level with the boy.

He turned to her with fresh tears shining in his eyes. With pink fingers he wiped away tears on his cheek.

"The man won't let me get on," he mumbled.

Violet glanced at the crewman out of the corner of her eye.

"Why not?" she asked, turning her gaze back to the boy.

"He says only women can go on the lifeboats."

Violet frowned. How could anyone look at a cherub-cheeked boy like this and tell him that he wasn't allowed to save his own life? She glanced at Hinnah, then at the lifeboat. There was only one spot left—she couldn't take that away from Hinnah. She had an idea that she hoped would work.

"I can get him on the lifeboat," she said. "And maybe the two of you could fit in. I could try and—"

"I'm not leaving you," Hinnah said. "If there's only one spot left, I think it should be him. . . ." Her eyes rested on the boy. Violet wanted to protest. After everything Hinnah had been through, she deserved to survive this too. But they didn't have time to argue, and Hinnah was right.

Standing up to her full height, Violet began unraveling her shawl. The boy just watched with wide eyes, tears still slowly sliding off his cheeks.

"Take this." She bent down and wrapped the shawl up tightly around him, covering his head and shoulders. "I'll get you on the lifeboat." She stood and extended her hands to the boy. He looked at them for a moment with hesitation, before grabbing hold. His hands felt soft and warm in hers. It almost felt familiar. Violet had to gulp down the lump in her throat as she led him toward the officer.

"Excuse me," Violet began in her most broken voice. It wasn't difficult, all things considered. The officer turned to her with a frown. "My little sister, you have to find her a space on the lifeboat." She rested a hand on the shoulder of the little boy. "She's so small, she'll barely even take up any space."

"It's at full capacity," the officer said, though his expression shifted with discomfort as he glanced down at the boy.

"P-please, Officer." Violet's voice trembled. "She's only a child."

The officer looked once more at the lifeboat. It was slowly being lowered already. She could see the faces of all the people on it, peering down into the depths of the water.

"She's my only family." Violet's voice caught in her throat. "You have to save her. Please." She blinked back tears.

The officer nodded. "Come on, this way."

When the boy's hand left hers, it was like a piece of her was being snatched away. Violet watched as the officer led the boy toward the lifeboat and guided him in. She looked over the railing of the deck at the boat being lowered, at all the people below. The boy looked up at her, bright blue eyes so reminiscent of Marko's that Violet had to remind herself that it wasn't him.

He mouthed a thank-you. Violet could only smile as she turned away.

"I think that was our last chance off the ship," Hinnah mumbled once the boy was out of sight. And when Violet scanned the deck, she realized Hinnah was right. There were no more lifeboats, but plenty more people.

"What do you think we should do?" Violet asked, though

328

it seemed like a fruitless question. How long could the two of them survive this—really?

"Survive for as long as we can?" Hinnah asked.

Violet nodded her head and reached out her hand to Hinnah. She took it, and the two of them walked away from the edge of the deck. Toward the more crowded areas. She didn't know what they were looking for, but she knew that they weren't going to find it.

She wasn't sure how long the two of them walked around for, shivering in the cold of the night. But somehow, having Hinnah by her side made the hopelessness in her chest easier to ignore.

Finally Violet spotted a crewman waving toward the front of the ship. She followed his gaze.

"What's that?" Hinnah asked.

There was a light in the distance.

"Maybe someone is coming to help us. . . ." For a moment, Violet felt her heart soar. They would all be saved.

But it wasn't another ship. It was the brightest of starlight, or maybe something else entirely. She and Hinnah exchanged a glance, both knowing that this was the end. Violet could only hope that Josefa and Emilie had made it to safety. It was really all she had left now.

FIFTY-FOUR

1:30 A.M.

50 MINUTES
JOSEFA

JOSEFA COULDN'T SEE her friends anymore when she turned around, but August was still on her tail. From the lifeboats around her rapidly filling up, she knew she didn't have much time left. It wouldn't be long until this ship went down.

She came to an abrupt halt near the edge of the deck. Taking a deep gulp of air, Josefa turned around. Facing August was her closest way to getting out of here alive—and even that was a close call.

"You want the book?" Josefa called out, holding it out in front of her. August stopped a few feet away, his eyes flicking to the *Rubaiyat*.

"You won't ever give it to me," August said after a moment, his gaze meeting Josefa's. "I know you don't give up on what you want that easy."

Josefa laughed. "You don't know me at all, August, if you really believe that. In fact, I'm not sure you ever knew me at all," she said. "I wasn't the one who got so caught up in what I

330

wanted that I betrayed my closest friend."

"What was all this, then?" August asked, waving his arms around them. "It was no coincidence that we were on this ship together. No coincidence that you wanted the *one* thing I was supposed to be protecting, the *one* thing I wanted most in the world."

Josefa shook her head. Maybe he was right—maybe she didn't give up on what she wanted so easily. But she was beginning to realize that the *Rubaiyat* and every jewel on this rare book wasn't worth her life. And definitely wasn't worth her friends' lives.

"This ship is sinking, August," she said finally. "You can lunge at me with a knife if that'll make you happy. You can take this book if that's what you want. I'm not going to fight you. I just want to survive."

She held the book up farther, not sure what she expected August to do. They didn't know each other anymore. They hadn't known each other for years. And he had always been unpredictable. It was what Josefa had liked about him—how he taught her to make the best of her skills.

But she didn't need him. And she didn't need to get revenge to put their past behind her.

August eyed the book for what felt like a long time. Then he plucked the knife out from his pocket. It glinted silver under the lights of the ship. Josefa gulped down her fear. Not sure if she should make a run for it now. Not sure if it would make a difference anyway.

"Did you read the journal?" Josefa asked, her voice coming out a little choked from her fear and panic.

"Why would I?" He caught Josefa's gaze, like he was genuinely confused why she was asking him this. "You obviously only gave it to me to ridicule me and how I felt about you."

"I didn't . . . I wouldn't do that. We were friends, August. You were the only person I trusted. I gave the journal back to you because . . . you should have it. It meant something to you to write in it. It meant something to you to give it to me. Just because I didn't—don't—feel the same way doesn't change that."

"That was a long time ago," August said.

"I know," Josefa agreed. "But it doesn't change that I trusted you, considered you my only friend when I had no one. That's why I held on to it for so long. The betrayal hurt that much more because of everything you meant to me once. I know it's the same for you . . . otherwise you wouldn't be here, still wanting your revenge when your life is at stake. If our friendship meant anything to you, if I meant anything to you, you'd let me go. End this here and let us go our separate ways once and for all."

He considered her words for a moment, still gripping the knife as if his life depended on it. Josefa knew neither of them had time. The *Titanic* wasn't going to wait for them to finish their conversation, to find a way beyond their past, their hurt, their betrayals.

But then the knife dropped from August's hands and clattered loudly against the deck. He glanced up one last time, his eyes boring into Josefa's, before turning around and disappearing into the crowd.

Josefa wasn't sure why, but she felt her knees buckle underneath her as soon as August disappeared. She leaned back against the railing for just a moment, closing her eyes and holding the *Rubaiyat* to her chest.

But Josefa couldn't stop now. She blinked open her eyes to the disaster in front of her. There were no more lifeboats, but she could see so many people trying to find a way off this boat. To safety.

Josefa realized she was one of them.

But she couldn't stay on this ship, among a mass of panic, waiting to die.

She couldn't give up so easily even if the exhaustion in her screamed at her to stop. She had to keep going.

Josefa approached the edge of the deck.

She watched the water stretching out in front of her for a few moments. In the dark depths, she could make out something jutting out of it, not too far in the distance. Leaning closer, she narrowed her eyes, trying to make out the shape in the darkness in front of her.

If Josefa wasn't mistaken, there was an overturned lifeboat at some distance. From the shape that Josefa could make out, she was sure that was all it could be. Clutching the *Rubaiyat* close with one hand, Josefa climbed up the railing and to the other side. She balanced herself there for a moment, trying to ignore the quickening thrum of her heart. She took one last glance at the *Titanic* and its people before jumping.

Josefa hit the water with a splash. The cold rushing up to her all at once. It crept through the layers of her clothes to her skin, and her teeth chattered. She tried not to pay it any mind—as hard as it was. Instead, she began to swim.

Her eyes focused on the overturned boat in the distance. It was like a shining beacon in the dark, though it was nothing but floating wood in a treacherous sea.

Suddenly, everything went pitch-black. Like someone had snuffed out the very stars in the sky itself. Josefa realized what must have happened with a sense of dread in her stomach—the ship had gone dark. There was no light to speak of. Josefa could see only blackness now. She couldn't make out the boat in the distance anymore.

But she could see shapes in the water—and from the cries surrounding her, Josefa knew they were people trying to survive just like her.

She tried to swim farther—hoping that somehow she would be able to find something to cling on to. But the more she swam, the harder it seemed. There was water everywhere, and Josefa kept being pulled down below the surface.

Around her, others swam forward too. Josefa could hear the splashing of water, the cries of people. But there were unmoving shapes too, and Josefa didn't want to think about what, or who, those shapes were. She feared what she would see if she stopped moving forward. She couldn't bear to think about the death and devastation.

She coughed up a lungful of water, feeling it burn down her throat. But she pushed on.

She was growing increasingly aware of the heaviness of her own clothes. She could feel them dragging her down. More than that, the hand clutching the *Rubaiyat* was making it harder for her to swim. The *Rubaiyat*, too, was heavy in her hand. It seemed to grow heavier with every passing moment. She was pulled underwater once more. And though Josefa struggled to swim up, she could hardly break the surface of the water this time. Josefa wondered for a moment if it would be better to just give up.

Did she even have a hope of making it out alive?

But her mind flashed with an image of Emilie on that lifeboat, reaching out for her. Of her friends' stricken faces as she ran away from them.

Josefa couldn't give up. Not now. Not when there was still a chance she could survive.

Josefa held the *Rubaiyat* in front of her, staring at it. It was beautiful, really. She understood why Emilie had been so hesitant to take it apart for the sake of a few jewels.

Josefa ran her hands over the book, feeling some of the jewels give way. When August had hit the book with his knife, it must have loosened something in the cover.

She grabbed as many of the jewels from the cover as she could, clutching them tightly in her fist. This was all she could do, before she finally let the book go, feeling it loosen from her grip and plunge into the ocean. For a moment, she watched it disappear into the depths of the sea. Then she began to swim, struggling for air and strength. Her arms and legs were weak with everything that had happened this night. The running, the chaos, confronting August, jumping off the sinking ship, swimming for who knew how long.

Gasping for air, she swam forward. She would swim forward until she couldn't anymore, she decided. She wouldn't have one more moment of weakness. Not tonight. She didn't know if she could afford it.

She swam and swam until she was sure her arms couldn't carry her anymore. Until she was sure she had reached the end of her rope. Then she saw a shape in the dark. The lifeboat. She swam faster, suddenly feeling a surge of adrenaline. Her body struggled with her. Her arms were heavy by her side. Still, she swam on.

Finally, her hands found something hard to the touch. The boat. Though her arms were weaker than they had ever been, Josefa managed to pull herself up onto its surface. She was breathing hard. Blood rushed in her ears. The world was a blur as she climbed. She had barely made it onto the wooden boat before she collapsed onto its surface. She closed her eyes, her breath coming hard and fast.

She couldn't really feel anything anymore, except the cold.

When Josefa finally blinked her eyes open, she could feel the darkness all around her pressing in.

FIFTY-FIVE

2:05 A.M.

15 MINUTES

HINNAH

HINNAH COULD FEEL the ship tilt underneath her, as it slowly sank farther and farther into the ocean. She knew that it wouldn't be slow for much longer.

"We have to stay on board for as long as we can," Hinnah instructed Violet, though it seemed futile.

"Okay," Violet said with a nod, gripping Hinnah's hands tighter.

There were cries of panic as the ship tilted even more. Hinnah and Violet gripped on to the railing, trying to keep their balance. Trying to stay on the ship. Hinnah knew that once they hit the water, they wouldn't have long left—if they had any time at all.

She searched for something to keep them above the water. Anything that she could hold on to.

Finally, she spotted what she was looking for.

"We have to make it over there," Hinnah said, nodding to the flag post on the stern.

Violet didn't seem to understand Hinnah's logic, but she simply nodded. She followed as Hinnah led the way toward the flag post, almost skidding and falling as the ground gave way underneath them. When Hinnah looked below, she could see the scattering of people, of objects. There were so many people in the ocean by now. She wasn't sure how many of them were alive and how many of them had already died.

Still, she used one hand to pull herself up to the flag post. With the other, she kept hold of Violet.

"Hinnah," Violet mumbled from below her. "You can't carry my weight like this for long."

"Don't worry, I can handle it," Hinnah said. She glanced at Violet reassuringly, even though her fingers ached. They were blistered from climbing through the vents and helping her friends out of the porthole earlier that night. The pain of it all was catching up to her now. The tighter she held on, the more painful it became.

"Do you think Emilie made it?" Violet asked.

"She must have," Hinnah replied. Only because the idea that she didn't would be too much in this moment. At least one of them had to have made it out alive. "And Josefa too."

"Really?" Violet didn't sound like she believed that.

Hinnah laughed, and it seemed to pierce the air all around them sharply. Like it didn't quite belong here.

"I just think . . . Josefa is a fighter, through and through," Hinnah said. "And if she's not here, we have to believe she's okay, right?"

"Right," Violet agreed easily. "She and the *Rubaiyat* are somewhere safe and sound."

Hinnah glanced down at her friend once more, trying to ignore how everything felt heavy. How below them, the ship was fast disappearing underwater.

Hinnah closed her eyes and took a deep breath, but it did nothing to calm her.

"Maybe if we hit the water, we can swim to safety," Violet said. Hinnah had never taken her for an optimist, but now Violet looked below them with a strange kind of hope in her eyes. She was in denial.

And even though Hinnah's heart felt like it was going to beat out of her chest, her whole body ached from all the efforts of the day, and she could feel her limbs shake from the fear and the cold, she wanted to make this moment easier for the both of them. She knew it might be the last moment that they had.

"Violet," she said, though it was some effort to get the words out. "Marko knows that you love him, even if you couldn't go back to him."

Below her, Violet let out a choked sob—like she was trying very hard not to cry. "Hinnah," she managed through her tears. "You know that you're my family too. Not just Marko."

"I know," Hinnah said, feeling the pressure of tears behind her own eyes. When she had left Dublin a few days ago, Hinnah felt like there was nobody in the world who cared for her. But here, on the brink of death, holding on for dear life, Hinnah knew that there were at least three people who loved her. Not for the person they wanted her to be, but for the person who she was.

"You . . . have to let go, Hinnah," Violet said through her tears. Hinnah knew she was right. There was no point delaying the inevitable.

Hinnah looked at the darkness in front of her. She could still make out the shape of the lifeboats in the darkness. Somewhere in one of those lifeboats was Emilie. Hinnah and Violet might not have made it out, but at least one of them had.

That thought filled Hinnah with a calmness she hadn't expected. After all, she had spent too much time living life the way others had wanted her to. Listening to her parents' whims and trying to live up to their expectations. Or boxed away in an awful boardinghouse in Dublin, ashamed of all of the ways that she didn't fit in. Josefa, Violet, and Emilie had given her something like the freedom she sought, the feeling of belonging she had always craved—even if it was only for a few days.

Holding on to the flag post was getting more and more difficult with each passing moment. But the thought of letting go no longer filled her with the kind of dread and fear she expected. There was something peaceful in the knowledge that everything she had done wasn't for nothing. There was something calming in knowing that she had made peace with everything that had happened in the past. That she had made peace with her future.

"If you could say one last thing to Marko, what would you say?" Hinnah asked.

Violet was looking ahead at the dark waters too. Like she was already far away from here. "I would tell him . . . sorry," she whispered. "I would tell him that I love him."

Hinnah nodded, and under her breath, she mumbled, "One, two, three . . . ," though she could hardly hear the count herself against the sound of the cries of the people around her and the blood thumping in her own ears. It didn't matter. At three, she finally let go of the post. And the two of them rushed into the icy cold water below.

FIFTY-SIX

10 MINUTES

EMILIE

EMILIE KEPT THINKING about her last moments on the *Titanic*. She watched the ship sinking deeper and deeper into the water, barely registering all that had happened in the past few hours.

If she could have, Emilie would have leaped from the lifeboat onto the sinking ship. She almost regretted not finding a way to do that earlier on, when she was being lowered down, when Josefa had chosen to save her instead of herself.

But Emilie couldn't go back. She could only watch from where she was, safe as guilt gnawed its way through her body. Because she had survived again, and maybe her friends hadn't.

On the *Carpathia*, she felt only a sliver of relief at her own safety. Mostly, she just felt numb, like all her feelings had washed away with the cold. Like the sinking of the *Titanic* had sunk everything in her too.

Emilie watched as more and more survivors climbed aboard, people with ice clinging to them, passengers who looked like they had narrowly escaped death. She wanted to feel a surge of hope in her chest; she could almost envision what that would feel like. But she couldn't. She could only think of her last moments with her friends. The moments when they thought they had made it—that they would survive.

Wrapped up in a blanket that barely did anything to assuage the cold, Emilie kept watch of every face that boarded the ship. She was looking for the familiar traces of her friends: Violet's terse frown, Josefa's easy grin, Hinnah's mass of black hair. But none of them were here.

She knew she was supposed to be grateful. She had survived where so many hadn't, but she couldn't bring herself to feel that. Instead, her mind reeled back to a year ago in Paris. How for weeks, she had watched her father wither away from illness. How she had sat with the knowledge that he would die and there was nothing she could do about it. She hadn't cried. Not because she didn't want to, but because she didn't want her father's last memory of her to be of seeing her so weak and vulnerable. So incapable of holding herself together.

But in the aftermath, after he had been buried and all of his things sold, Emilie had felt an emptiness inside of her. Like a black hole that had sucked her dry of everything.

And since Josefa, since boarding the *Titanic*, since everything, she had felt that hole get smaller and smaller. She had felt herself soften into the person she used to be before: someone who could have hopes and dreams, who could love.

Now that was withering away again. The black hole inside

her was growing wider and wider, taking all her hopes and dreams away. And maybe Emilie deserved that—because she was the one who had made it out alive.

So many people must have been lost in the last few hours. She had seen bodies in the water. When the ship sank, Emilie had seen the people still on it. She had heard their screams as they plunged to their death. They echoed over and over again in her head, like a nightmare she couldn't wake up from. The *Carpathia* had come hours too late to save them.

Emilie closed her eyes, though her mind still replayed flashes of last night that she wanted to relegate to the back of her mind. It was all too vivid, and in her mind she could see her friends on the ship too. Running from August, exactly as she had left them.

She had left them.

But when Emilie opened her eyes again, she spotted a familiar face. She blinked—afraid that it was just a figment of her imagination. That she would simply fade away, a remnant of her memories.

Except she was coming closer. Her bright blue eyes wandering through the crowds of reuniting friends and families, like she—too—was searching. Finally, her eyes landed on Emilie.

For a moment, Emilie and Josefa only took each other in, a gaping distance between them. Josefa looked the same—of course she did—but she also looked completely different. She was still wet from the water, and her face had lost its color, taking on a pallid blue complexion. But the starkest difference was the hollow expression that seemed to weigh her down.

Emilie felt all the emotions she had kept bottled up rise to the surface: fear and relief and happiness and sadness, mingling together into an overwhelming rush that came crashing down onto her.

Before she could take a step forward, Josefa was rushing toward her. In that moment, it was as if everything else disappeared. Josefa threw her arms around Emilie, drawing the two of them together. Josefa pressed her lips to Emilie's, and it was a kiss completely unlike their first. It was slow and soft, like Emilie was refamiliarizing herself with someone she had long lost. It felt as if she and Josefa had been separated for years, not hours. And Emilie felt a kind of warmth in Josefa's embrace that she could have never imagined feeling again.

When they pulled apart, Emilie realized there were tears on her cheeks. She didn't know when she had begun crying, but now the tears were flowing steadily down her face and her voice wavered as she spoke. "What happened to Hinnah and Violet?"

Josefa was crying too, though her sobs were soundless. She shook her head through her tears. "I lost them on the ship. I told them to find a lifeboat, to get to safety. I was leading August away from them but . . ." She glanced around, as if Violet and Hinnah were hiding among the crowds of people and would appear at any moment.

But really the both of them knew. And Emilie wished they didn't.

Emilie felt more tears fighting their way up her body. She

leaned forward, resting her forehead against Josefa's. If she could help it, she would never let there be distance between them again. Now that the two of them were reunited, she never wanted to let Josefa go. She never wanted to be away from her warmth, her beauty, that certain way she smelled that Emilie wanted to press into her very skin.

"It's not your fault," Emilie said.

"It's not yours either." Josefa pulled away from Emilie and looked at her sharply. Like she was afraid because Emilie had been the one on the lifeboat, she would blame herself. She was right. The guilt had been eating away at Emilie, but Josefa's words seemed to thaw some of that. Maybe she was right. It wasn't her fault for being one of the survivors.

Emilie leaned in once more, pulling Josefa close to her. Even though they were both still freezing from the water, there was comfort just in the knowledge that she was there. She was safe. They were together.

Even if the others weren't.

"I have to show you something," Josefa whispered into Emilie's shoulder. She raised her arm slowly. The skin of her hand had turned pale and blue from the water; Emilie could make out a blossom of ice covering her skin. Josefa's hand was clenched tightly into a fist. Slowly, through gritted teeth, she began to open her palms.

"What are you doing?" Emilie reached out her own hand to cover Josefa's. Like she could somehow help the fact that it was nearly frozen. It was ice-cold to the touch.

But Josefa ignored her, opening her palm enough until Emilie could see what she held there. Embedded in Josefa's hand were glittering jewels. "How . . ." The question died on Emilie's lips. She didn't know how to ask it. She didn't really want an answer anyway.

It didn't matter how Josefa had managed to keep this. None of that really mattered anymore.

Emilie covered Josefa's hand with her own. Knowing that no matter what happened from here on out, the two of them would have each other.

That was the only thing that mattered.

FIFTY-SEVEN

JOSEFA

"**THAT WILL BE** three dollars and fifteen cents."

Josefa heaved a hefty sigh as she dug into her purse and pulled the coins out. They clinked a little too loudly, and when she nestled them in her hands, they felt cold to the touch. She almost didn't want to part ways with them, but she handed the money over swiftly.

The man over the counter examined the coins with a keen eye for a moment, obviously counting them up. Like he thought Josefa would cheat him. She supposed she couldn't blame him for that. She did have a look about her, even if that wasn't quite her life anymore.

"It's all there," she said impatiently, hoping he would hurry up. "I haven't got all day, you know."

"Shouldn't your husband be the one doing this?" the man asked with a frown. So maybe it wasn't that she had a look about her, but because he simply assumed someone like Josefa wasn't capable of making a simple purchase without a man by her side.

"No," she said. "Now, do you want the money, or should I just go elsewhere?"

The man didn't look happy, but he nodded his head. He ducked below the counter, and for a moment all Josefa could hear was the rustle of his search. Then he appeared once more, holding something in the palm of his hand.

"Here you are," he said, handing it over a little too roughly for Josefa's liking. She cradled it in her hands, bringing it close to inspect. The ticking of it was like a heartbeat against her hands; the rusted metal was cool to the touch. And there, on the back, Josefa read the words *Doći će i naše vrijeme. Our time will come.* It looked almost completely like the pocket watch that Violet had carried around with her in all the time Josefa had known her. *That*, sadly, had been lost to the sea, never to be found. Like Violet and Hinnah. And though Josefa couldn't recover her friends from the sea, this, at least, was something she could re-create.

"Thanks," she mumbled, tucking the pocket watch away and clearing her throat to get rid of the lump rising in her throat. Even though it had been a year since the *Titanic* sank, thoughts of it still tugged at her in a way nothing else ever had. She didn't want this shopkeeper to see her near tears, though, so she swiftly turned on her heel and headed out the door.

It wasn't a long walk back to their little apartment, and as soon as she walked in through the front door, Emilie nearly pounced on her.

"Did you get it?" she asked.

"Of course I got it," Josefa scoffed, pulling the pocket watch out and waving it in front of her face.

"Perfect," Emilie breathed. She took hold of it, running her fingers along it and examining it a little too closely.

"It's not an exact replica, you know," Josefa said.

"I know that, but it's close enough. I don't think it matters. This is the important part," Emilie said, running her hands along the inscription. Violet hadn't told her about it, but in the year since the *Titanic*'s sinking, Josefa had told Emilie everything. She had rehashed every memory she had of Violet. From their first meeting to the last words she spoke to her as they had parted ways. It was the only way she had to honor her memory.

As if he knew that Josefa had arrived, a fresh-faced Marko peeked out of the kitchen door and into the hallway. For a moment, Josefa was struck again by how similar this boy looked to her friend. He had the same striking eyes, the same blond hair, the same shape to his face. Even the way he spoke, with a slightly clipped accent at times, reminded her of Violet.

"Good afternoon," he said—in a decidedly non-Violet way. It had been only a few months since he had arrived in New York, after many months of exchanged letters. Still, he hadn't quite gotten used to them. Josefa couldn't blame him. He had spent most of his life knowing only the walls of an orphanage in Croatia, and with vague memories of his parents and sister. And now he suddenly found himself here, uprooted from everything he knew to something quite different.

"We have something for you," Josefa said in a rush. She

plucked the watch out of Emilie's hand and held it open in her palm so Marko could see. "It's not the watch, exactly. But it's like . . . a replica. And the words inscribed in the back are as they were on Violet's." She explained quickly, all the while watching for Marko's reaction. He simply blinked at the watch, like he wasn't sure how real it was.

"I know it's not the same as having something of Violet's . . . ," Emilie added, appearing by Josefa's side and linking their arms together. "But we thought you'd like to have it. She carried it with her. She liked that saying . . ."

"Our time will come," Marko finished off with a nod of his head. He didn't look either Josefa or Emilie in the eye, but he took the pocket watch into his hands, turning it over and over like he was having a hard time believing it was real. "Our father used to say it all the time, and . . . Violet was never fond of that."

"I think it just reminded her to be different from him," Josefa added in agreement. "Maybe it'll help remind you of her, though."

Marko nodded once more, and he did look up this time, his gaze flickering between Josefa and Emilie. An appreciative smile lit up his face, and in that moment, Josefa was reminded of Violet too. Because Marko's smile—from the small, timid one that barely changed his expression to the beaming one that made him look completely different—it was all too similar to Violet's.

"And Emilie had something to show us too," she said, turning to Emilie with a smile of her own. This, even she did not know about. But Emilie had insisted that today was the day she was to show them.

"Yes, follow me," she said, pulling away from Josefa and waving them both toward the little room in the corner of the flat she had converted into an art studio. Josefa and Marko were seldom allowed in there, especially since she had started working on this project she was about to unveil. She opened up the door and led them both in, and with the three of them inside, there was barely any space to move around. It was the size of a closet at best.

"I've been working on these for a few months," Emilie said slowly. "And I'm not sure if I got them quite right. . . ." She leaned forward and removed the cloth covering the easel. Two paintings stared up at them. Two paintings of familiar faces: Violet and Hinnah.

Somehow, Emilie had managed to capture them just as Josefa remembered them. Not just in the shapes of their faces, in the colors of their eyes or hair. But in all the small ways that Josefa had never thought about before that she had to dig into her memories to remember. Like the glint in Violet's eyes that some might mistake for anger but Josefa knew was confidence. Or the kindness and vulnerability of Hinnah's face.

"Wow." It was Marko who spoke, blinking at the paintings with his bright blue eyes. "When I knew my sister, she was . . . so much younger. Much . . . more different."

Emilie's shoulders fell. "I was working from memory, and so it might not be exactly how—"

"No, it's perfect," Marko interrupted. "It's just as I remember her, but . . . different too."

Josefa nodded in agreement. "It's like the essence of her," she said. "And you even managed to include the pocket watch."

Emilie brightened at that. "I thought . . . others who lost people on the *Titanic* have graves or memorials etched with their names. Some even have their names printed in the newspapers. But . . . we're the only ones who really knew that Violet and Hinnah were there too. And this way we'll be honoring them." She stared at the paintings, and Josefa knew she was thinking back to her last moments on the ship—her last moments with them.

"Are these the paintings you'll showcase in that new gallery you've been invited to?" Josefa asked.

Emilie turned back to them with a grin. She had been working as an apprentice for a local painter in New York for the past few months, and he had gotten her the opportunity to showcase some work in a new gallery opening next month. "I thought . . . this way, everybody could see them. Even if they don't know their whole stories," Emilie said. "What do you think?"

Josefa couldn't help but smile back. She couldn't think of better stories to share than those of Violet and Hinnah, two of the best friends she would ever have. And no better way to share them than through paintings that seemed to capture who they were. "I think this may be the best idea you've ever had."

FIFTY-EIGHT

APRIL 15, 1913, 6:00 P.M.

JOSEFA

JOSEFA HAD NOT been back to the sea since the *Carpathia* had docked in New York. Now, as she stared at the Atlantic Ocean stretching out in front of them, a shiver ran down her spine. She wasn't sure if it was from the cool ocean breeze, or her fears, or memories come to haunt her. She wasn't even sure if the shiver was unpleasant.

"We don't have to do this," Emilie said. She reached out and linked her fingers with Josefa's, immediately dissipating all of Josefa's worries. Like she possessed some sort of magic touch. "I know it's not easy being back here."

"No, I think it's good to come back here. To . . . remember what happened one year ago," Josefa said.

"We could instead go to one of the memorial services that—"

"This is better," Josefa interrupted. And she believed that. There were several memorial services held at different churches. There were a few fancy ones that had invited only survivors of the sinking, or the families of survivors. Josefa and Emilie did not qualify for that, since they were never technically supposed to be on the ship. And they had never been churchgoing people either. This—coming to the sea—to the place where they had lost Violet and Hinnah—felt better. More personal.

Hand in hand, the two of them walked to the pier, to the very edge of the water, looking out into the horizon. Josefa imagined they were each lost to their own memories but tethered together too.

"I spent the last of our money from the *Rubaiyat* on the pocket watch and its inscription," Josefa confessed after a moment. They had made enough after selling the jewels she had recovered to support themselves for a little while. Enough to send for Marko to come join them. Enough to even send money to Matron Wallis—at Emilie's insistence—and a small donation to the Titanic Relief Fund, built to help the survivors who had lost everything.

"Well, we knew it wasn't going to last much longer than a year," Emilie said.

"It lasted us one year," Josefa pointed out. "But my question is . . . what now?" She had spent the past year avoiding that question. Emilie had found her spark and began painting again. It was different from what she'd envisioned her work to be once upon a time, but Josefa could tell that she loved it. Emilie had even gotten her grandparents' address from her father's friend in Haiti and wrote to them often. But Josefa wasn't sure where she fit in here yet.

"I know you've never been one for settling down," Emilie said slowly. "And . . . I know Marko won't be here with us long. So, if you wanted to go somewhere else, if you wanted to do something else . . ."

"I'm not going back to pulling cons," Josefa said. *That* was the last thing she wanted to do.

"What about the thrill of it all?" Emilie teased her with the words Josefa had used. She couldn't have imagined a different life for herself back then. But even here, in the hustle and bustle of New York, Josefa hadn't been drawn back into her old life. She was far too content with the thrill of something else: of Emilie, and their life together. A life that she would have never strived for, but one that had fallen into her lap regardless.

"I think I'll look for a proper job," Josefa mused.

Emilie chuckled, like she couldn't imagine Josefa at a "proper" job. Josefa wasn't sure if she could imagine it, either, but she was willing to try it. She was willing to try anything to hold on to the life the two of them had built together here.

"'Make the most of what we yet may spend, Before we too into the Dust descend,'" Josefa quoted from the *Rubaiyat*. Omar Khayyam had always been another means of communication between them. His poetry linking them together. But today, as Josefa gazed at Emilie, and at the ocean beyond her, it didn't seem enough.

"It doesn't matter where we go or what we do, as long as we're together," she said finally, squeezing Emilie's hand in hers. "That is all the thrill I've ever needed."

AUTHOR'S NOTE

When I started writing *A Million to One*, one of the first things I learned was that much of the world has no idea about the Irish connection to the *Titanic*, even though James Cameron's blockbuster movie *Titanic* sees heroes Jack and Rose set off from Cork, Ireland (as the real *Titanic* did).

As I grew up in Ireland, the *Titanic* was a part of passing history. This meant family trips to the *Titanic* museum in Belfast, visiting the *Titanic* Experience in Cork, and even teaching the third conditional to my students through the story of the *Titanic*!

But, of course, stories are fictional, and that meant I had to take a few liberties with history as I wrote down the story of these four marvellous girls, an unsinkable ship, and a book worth risking everything for.

THE *RUBAIYAT*

At the risk of sounding a little ignorant, I had very little idea about the *Rubaiyat*, or in fact, any of the wonderful artifacts that were lost when the *Titanic* sank in 1912. But the *Rubaiyat* was real. Written by the Persian poet Omar Khayyam, the edition of the book on the ship was not an ordinary one. It was commissioned by a bookshop in London, and it took two months to design the book and two years to complete! Made of leather and gold-leaf paper, it was inlaid with thousands of emeralds, rubies, amethysts, and topazes, and the cover was adorned with peacock feathers, as a symbol of Persia. While Josefa is concerned with attaining one rare gem from the book's binding that is worth more than the rest, this wasn't actually true of the real *Rubaiyat*.

The *Rubaiyat* was far from the only rare or expensive item to be lost with the sinking of the *Titanic*. A few others include expensive jewelry belonging to first-class passengers, a handwritten manuscript by Joseph Conrad, and rare, expensive artworks such as a painting called *La Circassienne Au Bain*, by Merry-Joseph Blondel.

THE *TITANIC*

The history of the *Titanic* is well-documented, and there are so many wonderful books that have been written about this ship and the history surrounding it. But again, there are certain creative liberties I had to take while creating this story.

For instance, there were no female waitstaff present on the *Titanic*. There were only two female staff members who worked in the restaurants at all, and of the *Titanic*'s crew of approximately nine hundred people, only twenty-three were women. So, Violet dressing up as a waitress in order to spy on those dining at the Café Parisien may have turned a few more eyes in a completely historically accurate version of the story.

It's also been suggested that there was only one Black family on board the *Titanic*, and probably not a lot of people of color in general on the ship. Of course, the term "person of color" didn't exist in the early 1900s as we know it now, and many people on the ship (like the Irish) would have faced a lot of prejudice in places like Britain and America at the time. Still, the *Titanic did* have on board those who would be considered people of color today: alongside its one Black family, there were also a number of Syrian (who would now be known as Lebanese) and Chinese passengers, in addition to a Japanese passenger and a Mexican passenger on the ship. So Hinnah and Emilie may not have fit right in on a very, very white ship, but that doesn't mean they would have been completely out of place either.

There's also a common misconception (which sadly I have added to here) that when the *Titanic* set off on its maiden voyage to New York, it was from Heartbreak Pier at Queenstown (now known as Cobh). In reality, the *Titanic* moored off Roche's Point Lighthouse in Cork Harbour. The 123 people who boarded the *Titanic* from Ireland (and our four girls would be among these people) departed from Heartbreak Pier on small boats, called tenders, which took them to the *Titanic*. These tenders were named PS *Ireland* and PS *America*.

Wireless operators on the *Titanic* received reports of ice before it struck the iceberg. There is a very real message included in *A Million to One*, which contains the longitude and latitude of heavy ice and icebergs. In reality, this message was received on April 14 at 9:40 p.m., a few hours before the ship struck the iceberg. But for the sake of storytelling, I took the liberty of moving this up to April 13 when Violet is in the wireless operator's cabin to see her message from her brother. In both reality and in the story the message did not make it up to the ship's bridge and no action was taken to avoid icebergs as a result of receiving it.

THE REAL PEOPLE

Of course, a few very real people show up in *A Million to One*, from passing glances at John Jacob Astor and Lady Duff-Gordon, to those much more engaged in the story, like Matron Wallis, Jack Phillips, and Francis Davis Millet. I took a lot of liberties here, because, of course, I have no idea what Matron Wallis, Jack Phillips, and Francis Davis Millet were actually like. Sadly, all three died during the sinking of the *Titanic*.

While Josefa, Violet, Emilie, and Hinnah's story is fictionalized, there were obviously thousands of real people on the *Titanic*. It is estimated that more than 1,500 people died when the *Titanic* sank. I hope that all of us can take a moment to pay our respects to all those who lost their lives during this awful disaster.

ACKNOWLEDGMENTS

Like Josefa, Violet, Emilie, and Hinnah had each other, I'm very lucky to have some amazing people alongside me in my writing and publishing journey.

Thank you first of all to my brilliant agent, Uwe Stender, without whom this book definitely wouldn't exist. Thank you for always being my biggest and best advocate. A big thank-you as well to everyone at Triada US, especially Brent Taylor, for all your hard work.

Thank you to Claudia Gabel for helping to shape this book into something very special and not letting me feel daunted at the idea of writing my very first historical. And thank you to Catherine Wallace for all your early editorial guidance.

Thank you to the entire team at HarperCollins for all your hard work on this book, especially Sabrina Abballe, Louisa Currigan, Sophie Schmidt, Kristen Eckhardt, Laura Harshberger, Alison Klapthor, Corina Lupp, James Neel, Mark Rifkin, and Mitchell Thorpe. A massive thank-you to Jack Hughes for such a stunning cover. I couldn't have dreamed of a cover so beautiful!

Thank you to all of my friends for your endless support. Thank you to Faridah for always threatening me with a knife emoji when I need it and for all the writing sprints and phone calls. Thank you to Alyssa for being one of my oldest and best friends and consistently being one of the best people I know. Thank you to Gavin for always being there for me and for showing up to almost every single virtual event I've ever had. Nobody else would do that but you.

Thank you to my Bengali squad, Tammi and Priyanka, for all the help, support, and cheerleading throughout the years. I'm not sure where I or my books would be without you guys.

Thank you to Lia and Ramona for all your support and for the Umi falafel dates. An especially big thank-you to Ramona for all the invaluable insights about Croatia.

A huge thank-you to Gayatri, for not only being a wonderful person and friend, but for being one of the biggest advocates for South Asian authors in kid lit. You are such a light in this community, and we are all lucky to have you.

Thank you to everyone who has continually supported me and my work, especially to Alechia Dow, Lucas Rocha, Arvin Ahmadi, and Pintip Dunn. And thank you to Chloe Gong, Olivie Blake, and Jordyn Taylor for taking the time to read and blurb this book.

A massive thank-you to all my readers. I wouldn't be writing the books that I do if it weren't for your support. It's impossible to list every reader who has supported me, but I want to say a very special thank-you to Sami (@samisbookshelf), Taz (@tazisbooked), and Jananie (@thisstoryaintover).

Finally, thank you to you, the reader, for picking up this book and giving it a chance.